DAAIMAH S.
POOLE

Kensington Publishing Corp.
http://www.kensingtonbooks.com

To the extent that the image or images on the cover of this book depict a person or persons, such person or persons are merely models, and are not intended to portray any character or characters featured in the book.

DAFINA BOOKS are published by

Kensington Publishing Corp.
119 West 40th Street
New York, NY 10018

ISBN-13: 978-0-7582-4626-4
ISBN-10: 0-7582-4626-9
First Trade Paperback Printing: February 2014
First Kensington Mass Market Edition: September 2016

eISBN-13: 978-1-61773-028-3
eISBN-10: 1-61773-028-9

10 9 8 7 6 5 4 3 2 1

Printed in the United States of America

wanted my daughter to have a two-parent home, and I wanted a nice life for myself, too. I fell short on that one.

My ex-husband, if you want to call him that, had our marriage annulled after a few months. He married me because I faked a pregnancy and got him to take me to Vegas and make me an honest woman. I said let's stay together, but he wanted to break up.

To get rid of me quietly, he agreed to pay me five hundred thousand dollars. I was reluctant to accept his offer; I wanted a million to walk away. However, my lawyer advised me to take what I could get. I followed her legal advice, and a month later he signed another contract with the Atlanta Falcons. If I would have waited a little longer, I would probably be two million dollars richer.

If someone was to give you five hundred thousand dollars, you would probably be pretty happy and think you're halfway rich, right? Hmph. A half a mil is not all it seems. When I first saw all those zeros deposited in my account, I wanted to scream, "Balling!" I had so many plans of what I thought I could do with it. Pay off my student loans, my house, take a vacation, go on a few shopping sprees. Now, flash-forward a year and a half, and I have spent a good amount of my small fortune. I've made so many impulsive decisions that I'm not proud of. There were a few really nice dresses, a must-have bag, and well, if you think about it, if you buy ten pairs of designer shoes, that's ten stacks right there. I honestly don't know what happened to my money. I just know that between giving my mom some money, shopping for myself and my daughter,

Malaysia, upgrading my vehicle, taking a trip or two, making a down payment on my condo in Miami, I spent a lot of money. Too much money!

My condo actually is what I spent the most on, but it was a great investment. When I purchased it, it was selling for a hundred thousand dollars cheaper than other condos in the area. I just couldn't pass it up. And I'm glad I didn't. I love living in Miami and being close to the beach. I run on the beach in the morning, and I love the nightlife. There is always something to do and somewhere to go. Miami is almost like New York City, but with warm weather all year round. Being from up north I appreciate the serenity, but I also know the flash and glitz are right here in South Beach if I want it.

So I got my wish. My daughter has the two-parent household; I'm just not one of the parents in it. Her father, DeCarious Simmons, is engaged now, and Malaysia goes back and forth to Atlanta with him. I hate her father and his fiancée, Cherise. I wish they both were out of my life for good, but I have about fifteen more years to be bothered with them.

That's why I'm glad I gave up baller/athlete chasing. I don't have to worry about all of that anymore. I am with an intellectual now, and very much in like.

My new man, Ian, is earthy and intelligent. He has golden sand-colored skin, shoulder-length dreads, and a goatee that is a few shades darker brown with flecks of blond natural highlights. His eyes are a mesmerizing shade of brown, and to say it plainly, my man is almost as gorgeous as I am. He cares about saving the world, is a vegetarian, recycles, and eats healthy. He would never wear a chain or place a big-ass diamond in his ear, like a lot of my exes.

I'm his complete opposite: I like steaks, fabulous things, and pampering myself. The only cause I fight for is me, and there is nothing natural about me, not even my nails. Though my man isn't rich, he makes good money as an independent film maker and producer. He's in the process of getting his first film bought.

Ian is the first man in years whose salary didn't matter to me. I think it is because: one, I have my own money, and two, he treats me like a queen. And he definitely is my king.

I met my king, Ian, at the black film festival in Miami. I noticed the love of my life a year ago. I was in the lobby of the Ritz-Carlton, checking into the hotel. He came up to me and handed me a flyer to his movie screening. I was in Miami to relax, and the African American Film Festival was coincidentally the same weekend.

His screening of *Loving Aisha* was a short film about a man quitting his job and taking care of his sick wife until she dies. I cried and thought it was amazing and wanted to know why his movie wasn't everywhere. Maybe I was emotional from going through my own issues with the annulment and custody dispute with my daughter's father, but after the screening I walked over to him and told him how wonderful I thought his movie was.

I gave him my number, and he invited me to breakfast the next day. He took me out of the tourist district and to a local eatery. By Sunday I was meeting his father and stepmother, who raised him. The following weekend I flew back down, and a month into our relationship I started looking for places, bought my condo, and we moved in together. Ian grew up in Washington, D.C., and holds a degree in African American Studies and Film from Howard University. He is brilliant and so kind and giving. Ian came into my life at the right time, because although I had a lot of money, I wasn't happy.

My daughter was being divided between Philly and Atlanta. I had failed at marriage, and so many other things that I felt responsible for.

His kindness has changed me some. However, we can't develop fully until I see how his film career takes off. I'm never going to be married to a starving artist.

Exhausted, I came in from my run and showered. I opened the curtains and let in the bright Miami skyline. Ian came out to the balcony with my breakfast. My plate was filled with egg whites, half a bagel, and blueberry yogurt with granola. Ian unlaced my sneakers and then fed me breakfast. It is the little things that you can't pay for that make him so special. I know it is love because that's the only reason I look the other way when my thirty-two-year-old boyfriend dresses like a lost college kid. This morning he was wearing tan shorts, a black tee, a vest over the tee, with a straw trilby hat sitting snugly over his dreads.

"Why are you up and dressed so early?"

"I'm going location scouting for this music video. Then from there I'm going to meet up with this producer, who knows DJ Ramir, and he is telling me he can get me a meeting with him. What do you have going on today?"

"I'm not sure yet. Maybe pick up a few things at the mall or sit by the pool. I don't know."

"Well, whatever you decide to do, make it memorable. I wish I had the luxury of shopping and stretching out in the sun, but I must go out and make a living." He kissed my cheek. "Enjoy your day, beautiful."

"I will."

I love it when Ian calls me beautiful, because I know he means it. His compliment traveled down my spine and right to my heart. Still, as much as I enjoy the life of a semi-house wife, I have to find something to do with my life and fast. I need a new career or a business to invest in. My thirtieth birthday is at the end of the year, and I only have a couple hundred thousand dollars in the bank that somehow has to turn into millions. I want a new career, because I never want to put back on my scrubs and work as a nurse again. It pays well, but it is too much backbreaking work. I don't have enough money to live a comfortable life forever. I guess that's the downside of being in a relationship for love and not for money.

Before I started contemplating my future, I tried to call my friend Tanisha. I hadn't spoken with her in a while and she had been trying to call me. It's actually hard for me to talk to her because of our history. Long story short, I told her to go on the run for something she didn't do. Her boyfriend's ex was stalking her. She tried to kill Tanisha, but instead Tanisha killed her—or at least we thought she was dead, but it turned out the stalker was alive and in jail, and I told Tanisha to go on the run for nothing. She and I had been through a lot, enough to fill a few books. But then she survived, and life is now going well for her. She's living in Greece with her husband, Kevin, and her kids. Kevin's a coach over there. Her daughter is in the military, and her son is in college. Her life is back together, and I feel so much better because I felt like I'd almost destroyed it. Once Tanisha's mess was cleaned up, I met up with my ex-nanny, Zakiya, and turned her on to her NBA rookie boo. I thought I had done a good thing. Who wouldn't want to be nineteen and dating a millionaire? But she couldn't handle all that came with being a basketball player's girlfriend. She was battling groupies and random people on the Internet. She lost her baby and almost succeeded in killing herself. When her suicide attempt failed, I was so happy I made a pact with God that I would try to live a different life. The key word is *try*, which means to attempt.

Chapter 2

Shanice Whitaker

"Shani, you want to go out tonight, don't you?"

"Yeah, I want to."

"Well, you know what you got to do if you want to go."

I'd already tried the shoes on, and picked out a dress and modeled them both in the mirror. I asked the salesgirl to put them on hold for me. I knew what Courtney meant, but I wasn't in the mood to have no old pervert rub all on me. I still was hesitant about going inside the hotel room.

"Okay, okay, I'm going to do it." Right as I got the courage, a father walked down the airport hotel hall and stopped at the ice machine with his young daughter and smiled at me. I smiled back. They were probably about to do something nice like eat pizza and watch a movie, and I was about to do something dirty. I took a deep breath.

"Shanice, just knock on the damn door. I'm right out here. All you have to do is close your eyes and think about how pretty you are going to look in that dress and them shoes. You know bitches going to be mad when they see us tonight."

My cousin was right. I needed to go out tonight and I had to look good. "As soon as we leave here, we are going straight to the mall and I'm picking up my stuff." I got hyped from her pep talk and knocked on the door. I like sex. I like sex a lot. I always have, but sometimes I don't feel like spreading it wide for old men. They smell, they want you to say kinky things to them, and they always try to stick their fingers in your ass, but I had done much worse and for less. Me and Courtney tried being strippers, but that didn't last because we kept seeing everyone from our neighborhood. Plus the bitches that worked there were all strung out on something, bisexuals, and the tips weren't that good.

I've tricked before, but usually it is with a regular dude that I kind of like and already know I'm going to fuck. The only difference is, I make him give me some money before anything happens. But this escort business was in a whole other lane. It was Courtney's idea to put an ad on this website. When she asked me was I with it last week, I said yeah. Then she got both of us "dates" for tonight.

The plan was for one of us to date, while the other collected the money and kept watch just in case 911 had to be dialed. Courtney had just finished up downstairs with her date, and now it was my turn.

"Okay, I'm ready, but get the money as soon as we open the door, Courtney."

"I'll get the money. You just go in there and make him cum real quick. He sounded really old, like he is only good for a few pumps anyway."

"Give me one more minute," I said, preparing myself.

"Look, if you not going to do it, I will," Courtney said as she moved toward the door.

"No, I'll do it. Okay, okay." I took a long, deep breath and knocked three times on the door. I heard a voice say, "Here I come." The gold door handle moved, and a few seconds later a man opened the door. He appeared just like I had imagined he would look: older, wrinkled, and perverted-looking. He was a middle-aged black man with black dyed hair with gray roots, and he was wearing a robe with water still beading on his thin legs. I knew at least he had taken a shower.

"Two ladies. Wow, I'm lucky, huh?"

"No, only one and we need to get paid first. I'm not here for you; she is." Courtney extended her hand toward him.

"Oh, come on in. Let me get my wallet."

We followed him, and I took a look around the room. There was a nice flat screen hung on the wall across from two neatly made double beds. He handed Courtney the money, and she let him know she would be right there if he tried anything.

"So, what's your name?" he asked me, looking my body over with lust in his eyes.

"My name's Simone, and I'm ready for you, Daddy." I opened my jacket, showing off my purple and black lingerie, and uncovered my butterfly-tattooed thigh.

He wanted to kiss me on my lips, but I turned his face and let him prick on my neck. Then I let him feel on my breasts and kiss them through my bra. His erect dick was standing up out of his white tight underwear. I rubbed him back and forth and felt wetness seeping through.

"So, how do you like it, Daddy?" I purred while posing for him. He looked up at me like he was in a trance and said, "Can you take your clothes off and can I feel them?" Instead of doing it, he kept asking for my permission every step of the way, and I had to keep hearing his voice. I unhooked my bra and let my big girls hang high. I placed his hands on them. *There,* I thought. He began salivating some.

"Nice and firm," he whispered after he squeezed my breasts and began to slurp on my nipples. I didn't like the way it was feeling, so I placed his hands on my bare lips. He grunted from the sensation of what his fingers were touching.

"Wow, you're frisky," he said, breathing hard. Yeah, I was frisky all right. I was trying my best to get this disgusting sex transaction done and over with, but he was slowing me down with all his stupid small talk. Oh my God, he was irritating. I couldn't take much more. I stood up and told him to take his clothes off then rolled a loose condom over him. I hopped on top of him and watched a panic-stricken look take over his face. A few twists and he released with an awful-sounding groan right into the tip of the condom. I thought he would be finished with me. Instead he sat up, patted my butt cheek, and requested that I spank him. He pulled out a wooden board. He bent over like a puppy and poked his ass out at me. I didn't know how many times he wanted me to swing, but I hit him ten good times as hard as I could. His flesh was welted and red. It was easy to whip his ass because I hated everything about what we were doing. But after I'd taken out my anger on him, I'd had enough. He was freaking me out, and I think he might have enjoyed the beating more than the intercourse. I threw on my clothes and rushed toward the door.

"What do I need to do if I want to see you again?"

"Just call us again." I was lying; he would never see me again. I walked out of the hotel room and saw Courtney sitting there texting. She jumped up and followed me down the hall.

"You weren't even paying attention! He could have been strangling me. You're all on your phone."

"No, I was watching out. I heard everything. That was easy, wasn't it? Let's go get what we are wearing to the club tonight." She pressed the elevator button to go down.

"Wasn't shit about that easy. That's the last time I'm fucking an old man. No more escorting."

We drove from the hotel in Courtney's off-black Grand Prix, heading for the Cherry Hill Mall. We entered the Ends Boutique, where the clerk had my dress and shoes on hold.

"Oh, so you are back? Here they are." The woman

brought the shoes out, and I was happy to try on my new items. Courtney was right; we were going to kill it at the club tonight. Bitches, beware!

I tried on everything again, and they still looked good. My brown skin was glowing, showing my tattoo. I had my tongue and eyebrow pierced. My piercings set off my curvaceous frame and a lot of guys told me they were sexy. Courtney and I are first cousins but were raised like sisters. We're both twenty-three and grew up in a three-bedroom apartment in North Philly, a section of Philadelphia. Our apartment was right down the street from where the Richard Allen projects used to be. They replaced the projects with nice town houses, but the same people were still living there, so it was still bad.

My mom is Courtney's mother's older sister. We lived together since we were younger. Me and my mom moved in with her and her mom one night after my mom's boyfriend Winton beat my mom so bad she needed thirty stitches in her head. Aunt Rhonda needed help with the bills and my mom needed to get away from her abuser, so it was a win-win for both of them. At first it was like a fun, never-ending sleepover, until my mom went back to Winton. Aunt Rhonda told my mom to let me stay, so I wouldn't have to be around all of the fighting. What seemed like a way to protect me was the thing that hurt me the worst.

A week after my mom went back to Winton, he beat her ass again and this time she fought back. She picked up a knife and stabbed him until he didn't move.

The neighbors told my aunt that my mom ran out of the house with blood all over her clothes, screaming, "Someone help me! Someone call the cops!" When the cops and paramedics arrived, she walked them in the apartment and they said they walked right back out, because there was nothing they could do to save him. He was already dead.

Ever since that tragic night, I wished I was home and not living with my aunt and cousin. I could have run into the room and saved my mom, like so many other times. If I had been there, I would have stopped my mom from killing Winton. I would have stopped Winton from hitting her in the first place. At least that's what I always told myself.

My mom was arrested and sentenced to twenty years in Muncy State Penitentiary. Since I've been grown I've tried to go visit and write her, but she always denies any visitors and when I write her she doesn't respond.

After she left, the only family I had left was Aunt Rhonda and Courtney. I don't know who my dad is, even though Aunt Rhonda says she thinks Winton was my dad. He probably was, because that's the only man I had ever seen my mom with, but who knows.

Courtney and I were home getting dressed and getting ready to hit up Luxe Lounge on Arch Street. Every city has the club that every six months or so has a new name and is under new management. That was Luxe Lounge, but it was always a guaranteed crowd. I couldn't wait to be seen tonight.

And hopefully, I'd find me a new friend with some money so I wouldn't have to go on any more pervert dates.

I was working my nude-colored dress and heels I bought at the mall. I was looking in the mirror, teasing my loose deep wave weave, waiting for Courtney to get out of the shower. She always took forever at the mirror doing her makeup and hair, although she didn't have that much hair. She had a brownish-blond, short curly cut. All she had to do was slap some mousse in her hair and it was done, but it still took her forever to get ready. She had long hair when we were growing up, but she always cut it because she didn't like dealing with it. The short cut fit her medium shade of brown skin and her slim body type. She had the perfect shape.

At Luxe Lounge we waited outside for the bouncer to start letting more people in again, but it didn't look like it was going to be happening anytime soon. If people didn't stop pushing and being hype, nobody else would get in the club. I wanted to get in and get my first drink and have fun. Somebody was going to be buying the drinks and then maybe take us to the after-hours club.

Guys knew we were about our change. Chicks knew, too. It was always, "Y'all so cute. Your shoes are so nice. Where did you get that dress from?" Aunt Rhonda had always kept us in the cutest, the latest, and the flyest, and when she didn't, me and Courtney learned how to get dudes to get it for us.

I don't have a boyfriend, because every guy I

meet thinks "sex" as soon as they see my body. They just want to fuck and that's it. Before I was even old enough, guys were sneaking a feel on my butt. If I could, I would slice some of my ass off and give it away. I really would, because it is hard to find jeans, and my butt always makes dresses and skirts rise a few inches in the back. It's like I can't hide it, even when I try, and that's all people ever focus on.

Courtney doesn't really have a man either. She kind of still messes with her daughter Ayana's father, Antwan. Antwan is thirty and comes around every now and then, but he proposed to his other baby mother that's like his age. He gives Courtney a little money and a little bit of his time. She claims it doesn't bother her that he has another family. But I know she wishes he was with her and Ayana instead of his ugly wife. I have a daughter, too; her name's Raven. Raven's five, a little older than Courtney's daughter, Ayana. My daughter lives with her grandmother and I try to go see her once a week.

We waited some more to get into the crowded club. The bouncer was still screaming at everyone to get in a straight line and threatening that no one else was getting in. His screaming was irking everyone, which made everyone sigh, get frustrated, and push even more.

"There go Raquel," I told Courtney. Raquel was Antwan's wife. Even though she was like thirty, she was petty. She did things like play on Courtney's phone and always started trouble. Like when they were getting married, she sent Courtney a wedding invitation just to fuck with her. Raquel was with all her friends and cousins. There was only two of us and about five of them. They walked past us, staring and mumbling something about bum bitches.

Courtney was quiet, but I wasn't about to let them talk shit. I turned to Courtney and said, "Girl, please, I'm not about to fight a group of bitches. I will cut someone's face up so quick and they will be leaking."

They looked over and took one look at my face, then they realized I was about that life and I was not the one they wanted it with. Instead of walking past us again, they walked the other way.

Once we were finally in the club, it was beyond crowded. I met a few dudes but every time I walked to the bar, no one offered to buy me a drink. *Damn, why all the broke dudes come to the club tonight?* I thought. I was not happy having to treat myself to Long Islands and shots of Patrón. Then the one dude I met who did buy me a drink wasn't really talking about spending, and I didn't have time to go to dinner. Fuck dinner; give me some money. What I didn't have time for was anyone who was not talking about money in the first conversation. Bye, boy.

Five drinks and ten songs later, the music was too loud and the club was closing and we needed to find someone to take us to breakfast. Everyone I had met was talking about taking me home. That wasn't going to happen. I was half-drunk and my cute shoes made my feet hurt and my head was spinning slightly. I followed Courtney out of the club. If Raquel and her friends wanted to fight us, they could get us now because I was too tore up to fight back. I stumbled behind Courtney, and my feet felt like they were being pinched each time they hit the ground.

"Courtney, wait up. Why you walking so fast?"

"Because I'm trying to get to the car. Why did you let me drink so much?" she asked.

"Bitch, I didn't know I was the drink police. I had my own drinks."

"You're not. Why you always got to get smart, Shani? Damn. I'm just saying I'm drunk as shit."

"What's up with the dude you was talking to? Is he taking us to the Diner or what?" I asked.

"I'm about to see," she said, drunkenly walking over to this skinny dude with a big beard to see if he was taking us to breakfast. I looked over at Courtney and just by the way her mouth was moving and how she was talking with her hands, I knew she was wasting her time. That bull wasn't doing anything, and she was doing too much. In a room full of niggas that's getting it, Courtney always ended up finding the corny dude with no dough and a long story.

Finally, she started heading back toward me.

"So, what he say?" I asked.

"Naw, he ain't doing nothing. Let's just stop at McDonald's." We got in the car and I realized Courtney was too drunk to drive.

"Move, drunk ass. I'll drive." She slid over and I

got in on the driver's side. I took off my shoes and tossed them in the back seat. Courtney was bent over, staring out the window, like at any moment she was going bring up the lining of her stomach and all her drinks.

I looked at her from the corner of my eyes. "Drunk girl, don't spit up and I hope you have some McDonald's money, because I spent all of mine."

"I spent all mine, too," Courtney slurred.

"Let me check. Maybe I have a few dollars left." I pulled over to the side of the road and dug around in my bag, but I only came up with a few dimes and pennies. I had one twenty-dollar bill left, but I had to take my daughter out with that.

"Naw, nothing. I spent my money on my dress, shoes, and our drinks," I lied to Courtney.

"Oh well, I think my mom went shopping. We'll get something to eat in the house."

We pulled up to the apartment, and we both had to clear our bladders. We raced to the door and I fumbled around to find my house keys and unlock the door, when I saw a white envelope drop to the ground. I opened the door and Courtney rushed past me and ran down the hall to the apartment. I picked up the envelope that had my Aunt Rhonda's name, my name, and Courtney's name on it. I ripped the envelope open.

I trailed behind Courtney and went into the bathroom. "Mr. Woods, the landlord, want his money," I said, reading the letter dated for today.

"Okay, but he be tripping. It is only the seventh."

"You know Mr. Woods always saying in that deep voice, 'Ay, uhm, now, ladies . . . rent is due on the first,'" I said, impersonating the landlord.

"You sound just like him. Whatever, Mr. Woods," Courtney said, rolling her eyes. "He'll get it when we get it. He need to come do some exterminating around here and maybe he'd get his money. Slumlord!" Courtney said, laughing.

"We will have to go out and make the money tomorrow." I had a frown on my face, imagining having to go out and hustle again.

"Yeah, I guess," Courtney said in a gloomy voice.

As soon as Courtney lifted up off the toilet and flushed, I sat down. All that liquor had me peeing for, like, forever. After I finished, I washed my hands and we walked into the kitchen to see what we could make to eat. All we had in the fridge was ketchup, eggs, spoiled lettuce, and flour. There was nothing I could make with that, so I shut the refrigerator door. We should have had some more food than that. I had given Aunt Rhonda money for the market, but she must have decided to do something else with the money, like get some beer.

I left Courtney in the kitchen trying to figure out what to eat. I walked down the hall to our room. I didn't even bother to take my clothes off or put sheets on my bed. I crawled into my twin bed and turned the light off. Courtney came into our room seconds later and turned the bedroom light on, started playing music, and then started talking to someone on the telephone.

"Bitch, I'm tired," I yelled. "Stop making all that noise and turn those lights off."

"Put the cover over your head. I'm not tired anymore."

It was times like this I hated sharing a room with Courtney and still living with them. It was time for me to get my own place.

CHAPTER 3

Zakiya Lee

I had twenty minutes before my Math 106 class began and I hadn't completed my take-home test. I was so busy with my other classes and work I forgot to do it. I don't know what I was thinking; it counted as a test grade. When I'd registered for classes this semester, I got this bright idea to take five classes to get most of my prerequisites out of the way. I'm already registered for summer courses, but if I don't step it up I'm not going to pass. Last semester I had three classes and had a 3.8 GPA. This semester I'll be lucky if I get a 2.5.

Somehow I had to get this test done. I walked over to the class to see if I could find anyone in my class who might let me copy their test. I saw a girl I recognized. She seemed like a nice person. She was wearing pink headphones on her head, black tights, and a light gray sweatshirt. I didn't want to interrupt her, but I needed to get a glimpse of her test. I tapped her shoulder, and she took off half of her headphones.

"Hey, are you in Professor Langer's class?"

"Yeah, why?" she asked.

"Oh, did you do the take-home test?"

"I did. Why?" she said, looking at me like I was bothering her.

"Oh, because I didn't get a chance to do it yet. I was just trying to see how difficult it was. I really need to pass this test or I might fail this class."

"Well, it wasn't that hard, so good luck." I could tell she wasn't going to help me. I wanted to kick her. I was trying to figure out a way to ask her to let me see her test. Maybe if I paid her, she might let me see it. While I was thinking about what I was going to say, I awkwardly stood in front of her. She looked up at me, took her headset completely off, and asked in an annoyed voice if there was anything else she could help me with.

"No, thanks. That's all," I said. She wasn't being that nice, so I left it alone. I would just act like I thought the test was due next class, instead of trying to write down a bunch of incorrect answers.

Everyone in class was prepared. They all turned in their tests. I saw Professor Langer take a head count and look at the test papers. It was obvious the numbers didn't match. I hoped he didn't decide to start calling out names. If he did I would be in trouble.

This was not how I thought college would be. My plan for college was to go straight through with no breaks and four to five classes a semester. If I could accomplish that, I'd be an RN in two years. Nursing wasn't something I really wanted to do, but I knew it paid well and I should be able to find a job. People will always get sick and hospitals will always be hiring.

I kind of always pictured myself attending a big university, living in a small dorm on campus and going to parties. But life doesn't always happen the way we imagine it. Sometimes our lives take detours and zigzag us in a completely other direction.

Last year I lived three lifetimes. My sister attempted suicide, I moved to L.A. with my aunt, moved back to Philly once my aunt said she was moving, became a nanny, and met my ex, who just happened to be a rookie guard for the Oklahoma Thunder in the NBA. We fell in love quickly, I lost my virginity and became pregnant within months, lost my baby, had a breakdown, broke up with him, moved back home, and started my life all over again. Now, here I am at community college, hoping my professor doesn't notice that I didn't turn in my test.

Sometimes, when I'm lying in bed, I think about everything that happened to me. I ask myself, why? Why did my mom kill herself and leave me and my sister, Lisa, to raise ourselves? Why did I fall in love with my ex and get pregnant? Why did my baby boy die before I got to meet him? When I'm not wrestling with my why's, I'm overwhelmed with the what if's. What if I had stayed with Jabril in Oklahoma City? What if our son had made it? I wonder what he would have grown up to look like. If he was still alive, he would be a little over a year old. What kind of mom would I have been? Would Jabril and I still be together, or would I be a single mom? I guess I'll never know.

I was devastated after losing my son, and so was Jabril. The only person I think was happy was his uncle Wendell. I don't think he liked me from the beginning. He thought I set up his nephew and was trying to have a million-dollar baby, but that was the furthest thing from the truth. I was a virgin when I met Jabril, and I still haven't had sex since we've been apart. I'm the one who told Jabril to put on a condom, even though he said we both were safe. And I was the one who used to wake up with him having sex with me. He trapped me, and I'm still upset with him, because it is still hard for me to see a baby and not cry. Seeing a baby is a reminder to me that I couldn't do something that millions of women do every day with no problem: have a baby. Everyone around me said it wasn't my fault, but I felt like it was. I felt worthless and miserable, and I didn't want Jabril to have to suffer with me through my crying spells and episodes of guilt, so I left him. I left the Mercedes-Benz he bought me, the mansion we lived in, all the diamond jewelry, and the money. I walked away from it all.

Jabril didn't want me to leave. He called and called and begged for me to return. He wanted to pay for me to go to school and get me my own place. I told him no and that I never wanted to be with him again.

* * *

Every few weeks, I'll receive a text from Jabril saying he still loves me, asking me to come and visit him, and my answer is always no.

Even though I have said no to Jabril over fifty times about rekindling our relationship, he still hasn't given up. I suppose that is the competitive athlete in him. He goes after what he wants with vigor, but he still can't have me and I'll never go back.

Plus, I'm sure he's met plenty of other women by now. Let one of them be his girlfriend and put up with all of his mess, because I don't want him or his lifestyle anymore!

It is a very different life being with a basketball player. When you are an NBA player, people know your name and are screaming for you just because you play good ball on a wooden court. And when you come off the court, you have women of all ages and nationalities throwing themselves at you.

The first thing everyone would always say to me when I was with Jabril was, "You're so lucky." I never understood that. I don't know what part about my old life was lucky. Was I lucky that Jabril was almost never home or lucky that groupies in every city wanted to sleep with him? Maybe I was lucky that every time I turned around he was on a blog and entertainment website, hugged up with different girls. Or better yet, I would find a picture of me with him and all the readers of the blogs would say how ugly I was and how I needed to be so honored that Jabril even looked at me because I was so hideous. Does any of that sound lucky to you? It doesn't to me, and that's why I'm proud of myself for being strong and leaving him and living for me.

* * *

When I returned home, I forgot about Jabril and that whole experience. The only thing I am focused on is my goal of graduating from college. I want to become a nurse, buy a house, and help my sister with my nephews. Miles and Kyle are twins and are eight years old and they are my everything. I want them to have the best in life. Right now they attend a charter school, but I want them to go to private school. They are getting older, and so many guys become lost to the streets right around middle school. I want better for them. My sister can't afford it on her own. So I am going to help her. Their father is around, but once she broke up with their dad, Mikey, he stopped coming around. He pays a little child support, but it doesn't really help. He was bad news anyway, and I'm glad Lisa left him.

I like my everyday anonymous living, no paparazzi flashing. I can wear whatever I want, and there is no pressure to be dressed in designer expensive clothes all the time. Yeah, my life isn't Hollywood. It is very normal, and I enjoy being home with the people who really care about me. My family, sister, nephews, and I don't need anything else.

I had a regular job at Pathmark market not too far from our house. I worked there before I met Jabril. It wasn't hard; it was pretty routine. Each day repeated itself.

A kid would run around the market and have a noisy tantrum, or someone would always drop

Hey, Bril, I was on my way to sleep. What's up?

He texted me in return.

I miss you, Zakiya, & I want to see you soon. I'm going to send you a ticket. When are you going to come? Why don't you ever answer your phone?

I typed in my phone.

I do answer my phone, but I be busy with my nephews and my classes. Maybe during spring break, I might be able to come see you.

He responded that he wanted to see me before that. I'm missing you. I still LOVE YOU.

I couldn't tell him I loved him, too, even though I thought I still did. I only ended our texting with a simple Good night, Jabril. I thought that was the end, but he texted back one more time. I looked at the screen to see I'm going to call you tomorrow after practice. Pick up your phone, Kiya.

Jabril still wanting me and telling me he loved me made me a little weak. The sad thing was that even though I'd separated myself from him, and started fresh, my heart still belonged to him. I knew it did, but our relationship would never work. So I wouldn't even entertain the idea. But then sometimes, I do wonder if I made the right decision by leaving him. I even think about going back and maybe trying to make it work, but then I remind myself how difficult it is to be me in his world.

Chapter 4

Adrienne

I checked my voice mail and my mom was on there asking when was Asia coming to visit her. I love my mom, but the minute I sent Asia to visit she would be a loving grandmom for one week and then she would start calling and harassing me and telling me she has had enough and that it was time to come pick Asia up. Even though I knew how our conversation would go, I still had to be a good daughter and return her call. My mother was fifty and white, but she still raised me as a proud black woman. I never really knew my dad's black family. They didn't accept me or my mother. And after my grandparents died, it was only me and her. I think she calls so much now because she is all alone, but she would never admit it. She has a boyfriend, but I know she wishes Asia and I were with her in Philly.

"Hey, Mom."

"Where's my baby, Adrienne?" She scowled from the other end of the phone. I could imagine her white skin tone turning red.

"She is with her father," I answered, preparing to hear why those people shouldn't be around her precious grandchild.

"I don't like Asia with them country people, Adrienne. His mother feeds her entirely too much, and they send her back home looking like a street walker with tight clothes and her stomach hanging out."

"Mom, when she gets back, let me have some time with her, and then if you really want her, you can come down here and pick her up."

"Adrienne, you can't drive her up here?"

"No, I'm not driving to Philly. I can buy you a plane ticket and you can come and pick her up."

"Adrienne, you act as if it's a bus ride."

"Mom, it only takes two hours. How else were you going to get her? Think about it and call me back." If I knew my mom, she would be down here by next week to come and get her only grandchild.

After debating with my mom, I opened my closet to try to find something to wear because my girl Angelique was coming in town and we were going to hang out. Every time she is around it's a paaaarty, and Miami has the best nightlife. We were going to party on another level.

Angelique was my girl. I met her at a Sixers basketball game back home years ago. She told me and my friend Tanisha about a party after the game. We went, and it was filled with wall-to-wall six-foot-something, rich, gorgeous men. I was in love with them all. We had a great time, and from then on she and I started hanging out together.

Angelique kept a baller on her team, literally. Since I've known her, she's always dated someone who has taken care of her. And I'm not talking about someone paying rent or buying an expensive purse. Angelique had her men buying her property and paying in full for her luxury vehicles. She lived a big, fabulous lifestyle without a job, and at the time I wanted that for myself, too! She led me to the dating-an-athlete path, and once I was on it, I navigated it for myself.

Hours later I knew what I was going to wear to the club, but I hadn't exactly told Ian I was going out. It wasn't like I had to ask for permission, but I did like to give a heads-up. Unfortunately, it was too late. Angelique arrived before I had an opportunity to tell Ian about our plans. I opened the door, and she sashayed into my condo. We hugged quickly and as soon as we separated I complimented her on her stylish, oversized Hermès bag.

"Oh, thank you. It is old."

"No, it is not. I think I was going to get it maybe a few months ago. I wanted to buy it, but I had to tell myself, *don't play yourself.*"

"Thank you. It was a gift from my boo. He likes to spoil me."

"All your men spoil you, girl."

"You're right, and if they didn't, they wouldn't be around." Angelique's appearance screamed high maintenance, and most men would be intimidated. Her arms, feet, and wrists were adorned by a year of college tuition, by way of her bag, shoes, and watch. She took her wide-frame sunglasses off and revealed her modelesque features. She immediately started giving herself an unauthorized tour of the condo.

"I like this place," she said, looking around, touching and feeling the textures of my furniture and walls.

"Thanks. I like it, too. It has a balcony and three bedrooms. And I still have my place in Philly."

"Yeah, it is nice. A little small, but nice. It has a lot of potential." She continued walking around so fast that she opened the door to Ian's office before I could tell her not to go in there. He turned around in his chair, very annoyed at us disturbing him. She closed it back fast, then started laughing. She made a face at the door and whispered, "My bad." I opened the door back up and introduced them. Ian came out, pushing his glasses up on his face. He said hello and Angelique gave him a nonchalant "hey." Then she went and flopped on the sofa, and Ian went back into his office, slamming the door behind him.

"Is he mad? Tell him I'm sorry."

"He'll be okay. He is in the process of editing and lost some valuable footage, so I'm trying not to bother him. He becomes very testy when it comes to his work. Plus, I didn't even get a chance to tell him you were coming or that we were going out."

"Oh, okay. So what are you wearing tonight?"

"I'm not sure. I think this little black dress I have."

"I'm sure it will look cute. Your legs are really toned. What are you doing?"

"That's from running in the sand every morning."

"Really? Ugh, I hate exercise. I hate sweating. I'd rather just starve. So, while I'm in town, I'm visiting with you today, and then tomorrow I'm going to see my other friend in Orlando."

"You're doing a little tour of Florida, huh?"

"Yeah, so let's go out tonight and have fun, and tomorrow before I leave I want to check out Bal Harbor."

"Shopping? I need to stay out of the mall. I've been spending so much money. Let me show you these shoes I just bought." I was walking toward the bedroom when Ian asked me to come into his office.

"Are you going out tonight?" he asked me. He was already frowning before I even gave him an answer. I could only assume he had been ear hustling on our conversation.

"I don't know. We may hit a few places. Why?"

"I don't know. Your friend seems like a real gold digger. What does she do?" Ian had read her correctly, but I had to convince him he hadn't.

"Um, she is a Realtor." I was somewhat lying. She had once taken a real estate course, but she quickly dropped it when her next sponsor came along. But Ian didn't know any of that.

"She is carrying a ten thousand-dollar bag. Business must be good."

"Why are you so concerned with her bag? Come on, Ian." The only reason he knew how much the bag cost was because I wanted one and he had convinced me not to buy it.

"She looks like a user with no ambitions. I hate chicks like that, who only judge a man by his wallet. And I don't like my lady being in that kind of company."

"How did you get all of that just from her busting into your office?"

I looked over at Ian. He was being petty and acting like a woman. That was the part of him I hated. At times I think he was afraid I might drop him for another athlete with money, but if he makes it at this film thing, he'll be just as rich. And he'll be making movies until his eighties, whereas most basketball players are broke three years after retiring. I always tell him this, but I don't think he believes me, and it doesn't do much to help his insecurities.

So, before I met Angelique at her hotel for our girl's night, I had to comfort an unconfident man by inviting him out with us. I probably shouldn't have looked so nice while I was doing it. I was dressed to the nines in a black and pink dress and matching YSL pumps. My hair and makeup were both gorge, and I knew it was going to be torture for him to let me walk out the door without him. I peeked in his office and said, "So, I think we are going to The 400 Club, Fountain Bleu, or maybe Saga if you want to meet us or just call me." Without looking up, Ian told me to have fun and that he wasn't going.

"Are you sure? Well, if you change your mind, just text me."

"I doubt it."

I didn't want him to go anyway. He could keep his grouchy ass in the house. I could see it was going to be hard meshing my old friends with my new man.

I picked up my keys and walked out of my place. I had just reached the elevator of my building when my conscience started kicking in. I wanted to go out and not care about how Ian felt, but I knew I had to take care of my man before I left. I went back to my condo, slid off my dress, walked back in his office, and then sat on Ian's lap. It took all of two minutes of sitting my almost naked body on Ian's lap, grinding on him, before he was thrusting toward me in a desperate way, trying to cease the foreplay. He wanted his thickening body inside mine, but I wouldn't allow it to happen just yet. I unzipped his pants and stuck the tip of him inside of my sultry, slippery walls, only allowing only the head of him pleasure. After a few moments of making him wait, I whispered in his ear, "You ready to get in all the way?"

"I'm ready," he moaned, trying to push farther inside me.

"Be patient," I said, teasing him. I then slid slowly down, maneuvering my hips like a slow, melodic belly dancer. Ian inhaled deeply, and his eyes were rolling back as he savored the warmth of my tender, juicy insides. I took control and tugged on his dreads. I slid my body up and down on him until right before I knew he couldn't take it anymore. He picked me up and carried me to our bedroom. He then slammed me onto our bed and forcefully entered my body again. After five minutes of thumping inside of me, he screamed, "Oh Adrienne. Shit . . ." And then he violently climaxed and fell to the other side of the bed.

Ian couldn't stay mad at me after what I'd just given him. He was quiet and hopefully not as angry that I was going out. I showered again, slipped my dress back on, and told him I wouldn't stay out that late and that I would see him later. This time he walked me to my car and even said he might join us.

Refreshed and feeling sexy, I pulled up in front of Saga and let the valet take my keys. He parked my car next to a fleet of imported luxury vehicles: Bentleys, Lamborghinis, and Aston Martins. The club regulars filed into the club, and Angelique and I were escorted to a table in the VIP section. Saga was more of a lounge where you could dance in one area or just sit and talk and have dinner in another. The club was just off the beach, and the breeze from the ocean caressed us as we sat and caught up.

Our pretty server promptly came over to us. She spoke with a Spanish accent and asked us what we were having to drink. I looked down at the menu and then over to Angelique.

"Do you want to order a bottle or just a round of drinks?" I asked her.

"We can start off with a few rounds of martinis, but let's also order a bottle." Angelique pulled out her credit card, but I let her know I had it. I handed the girl my credit card.

"Are you sure?" Angelique questioned me.

"Yes, you're visiting. You can pay when I come to visit you. Where are you at now?"

"I'm in Milwaukee."

"Well, I'm never coming there, but next time I have this." I laughed.

While waiting for our drinks, we began to people watch. Angelique spotted people she knew and she waved a few times.

"So your new boyfriend, he is a different choice for you. He looks like the natural type. He was really mad when I opened that door. I was like, oh I'm sorry."

I couldn't help but laugh because she was on point. I said, "This time around I needed a man who could teach me something and be there for me. He is such a sweet man. So, where are your two girls, Shavone and Nytika?"

"Those two are in the past. I had to drop both of them. Nytika still wants to party every weekend, and I tried to tell her you can't go that hard forever. If you do, you run out of new people to play the game with. I could not have all that mess around me any longer. It's time to have babies, be in the carpool line at the school, and park the Ranger in front of the mansion. You know what I'm saying. Not party nonstop. Plus, my boy don't know anything about anything, and I don't want one of his teammates to see Shavone and say, oh that's the girl such and such used to get with it. Um, no. Can you imagine all the people she slept with?"

"I can. DeCarious came to me once asking me

did I know this guy and that guy, and I had a straight face like, um, no, I have no idea what you are talking about." We laughed some more, then our server placed our drinks in front of us and we indulged in the perfectly made martinis and continued our conversation.

"So, who is your new man? Where did you meet him? " I asked.

"His name is Ronell Jones. He is the sixth man on the Milwaukee Bucks and he is putting up numbers. Look at his picture." She pulled up his picture on her phone.

"Oh, he looks real young, Angelique."

"I have nine years on him. He is only twenty one, but he does everything like a grown man. And his pockets are very mature." She laughed.

"Obviously, look at that ring." The oversized diamond was sparkling and weighing her hand down.

"Oh, this thing?" she said, giggling. "No, it was really fate meeting him. I caught him straight out of the locker room, literally. His team was playing the Knicks. I saw him and didn't let him out of my sight. We exchanged numbers, then we talked on the phone and was on Twitter for a few weeks. Then he flew me out and I've been with him ever since. I had to settle down with somebody. I was so tired of doing the city-to-city thing. He is from this small town in Indiana and is so clueless about this life." She laughed, pointing around the club. "He tells me all of his business, and gets my opinion on everything. My name is even on some of his bank accounts. I tell him what to do, what to wear, and he listens. I'm so in, his parents even love me. It's like I'm his best friend, big sister, girlfriend."

"Sounds like you got it made, so don't ever mess that up."

"That's why I'm having my last little bit of fun on my weekend trips. Because soon I'm going to marry him, have a baby, and be a basketball wife. And, of course, if anything goes wrong, I'm taking half, and I didn't have to be with you in the gym. Give me mines," Angelique said, gesturing her hands like she was counting money.

"You're silly. Just be careful, because I swore I would get half of DeCarious's dumb-ass income and I didn't."

"Well, you didn't make out so bad. He's still playing, right?"

"Yeah, I still get my child support, but it is half of what it used to be now, because he has her half of the time. I haven't seen my daughter in a month. And what makes it even worse is that his stupid fiancée sends me pictures of Asia having fun with them. I'm always near tears. I have to go meet them to get her back in a few days. Truthfully, I'd rather be with my child's father than pulling her all around sharing her."

"His fiancée probably sent you those pictures on purpose."

"Probably. Anyway, congrats on your new dude."

"Yes, let's open the bottle on that one."

We were dancing and enjoying our ladies' night out when this super-tall, I mean, really tall guy approached us. His gangly body hovered over us. I could tell he was nervous when he finally had enough courage to speak and said, "What's up, ladies? Can I buy y'all some drinks tonight?"

"Can you buy us a drink? We already have drinks and a bottle. What's up with you? You tall. You play ball or something?" Angelique questioned the nervous guy.

"Yeah, I do." He smiled happily.

"What's your name and where? How come you don't look familiar?"

"Texas and Lamont Johnston. I'll be right back." Moments later our server came over with the cheapest bottle of vodka on the menu. I thought it was a cute gesture, but Angelique began penning the giant a note. She had pulled up his stats and team, and she was not impressed. She sent the bottle back over to his table and we sent him a bottle of Moët. Angelique scribbled a note saying, *This is how you send a bottle. Cheers.* And with that she stole his pride. It was mean, but the funniest thing. I couldn't stop laughing and looking over at his table.

"Why are you so rude? You could have kept his little bottle." I laughed.

"Please. Anyway, if he was going to send something, he could have at least sent a bottle of champagne. That D League ass dude better get out of here. Six-eight ain't fun if you didn't make it to the majors. Big and tall for no reason." Between my laughter and her sending the bottle back to the tall guy, I noticed I missed a call from Ian. He was probably going to come out and meet us. The next time he called, I answered. "Where are you?" he asked.

"At Saga."

"I'll be there. I'm sorry for judging your friend." I muttered okay, letting him know all was forgiven, and ended the call.

"Is he coming?" Angelique asked.

"Yeah, he will be here in a little bit. He apologized for being a jerk."

"Well, you don't seem like you made out that bad," she said, looking around. "He's handsome and seems nice, but these women down here are thirstier than most. I wouldn't be able to have my man around all this. They don't believe in wearing clothes, do they? Ugh, too many naked bitches, looking for the next meal ticket. I really hate groupies. How do you deal with this shit every day?"

"I don't know. Ian is not into chicks without any ambition. Ass and tits is not his thing. He needs brains to go with it. That's one of the things I really love about him. I'm hoping his movie thing will take off. And if all else fails, I still have another fifteen years of child support. DeCarious's soon-to-be wife has a good job as a news lady, and she can help him out when all his money is gone."

"Right." Angelique laughed.

By the time Ian arrived at the club, I was so wasted that he had to drive me home and leave my car. I vaguely remember Angelique turning into the diva I said she wasn't. She and Ian were arguing, and I don't remember about what exactly.

The sun rose, and I opened my eyes to a serious headache. I had downed so many glasses of champagne that I stopped counting. Ian made me breakfast, and I couldn't even look at the food without feeling sick. I couldn't find my purse. My cell kept vibrating and beeping from messages and texts. When I finally found it, there were text messages from Angelique thanking me for such a good time and apologizing for arguing with Ian. I looked over at him as everything started to come back. We'd told him about the bottle the guy had sent us and how we'd laughed, and Ian called us immature and a bunch of other things. I know Angelique's mouth got a little slick and they were going back and forth before we left. Just as the details of last night floated in my head.

"Good morning."

"Yeah. Good morning," Ian mumbled.

"What's wrong with you?"

"Nothing, I just don't like the way you waste money, Adrienne. And your friend was so out of line last night."

"What are you talking about, Ian?"

"Angelique and your big bills. Last night when I commented on the bill being too high and that you two shouldn't be laughing at that guy, she told me that I needed to get used to dealing with a boss chick."

"Ian, she didn't mean it. I apologize for her. But you know, people talk reckless when they've been drinking."

"No, people say what they actually mean when they are drunk."

"And what was the problem with the bill?"

"This is the problem." Ian forcefully placed my receipt from the night before in front of me. I looked down at the receipt and said a quiet *wow* to myself. I knew bottle service was expensive, but not two-thousand-and-forty-six-dollar expensive. The pricey tab included a 20 percent gratuity that our server received for just opening our bottle and pouring our drinks.

"That's a mortgage payment, Adrienne. You know what you could buy with that kind of money? I guess it doesn't matter when you didn't have to work hard for it. But that's what happens when you hang out with your high-class friends." It was too early for him to be hitting below the belt.

"Ian, look, I already apologized for whatever Angelique said, but I do not need you to lecture me on my spending habits. I'll spend my money however I feel like it."

"You're right. Spend your money the way you see fit. I just hate to see people waste it."

I stood up. I was now very agitated and needed something to drink. I walked to the refrigerator and grabbed a bottle of water. I twisted the cap and poured the hydration down my throat. I needed a tactful response for Ian. Something that would reasonably explain why I'd spent thousands on drinks that I probably had already peed out. Ian was still staring at me, and the only thing I could think to say was, "I like to have a good time when I go out. I like to treat myself and whoever I'm with. I won't apologize for that."

"I'm not asking you to," Ian snapped back at me.

This was the other thing he did that I didn't like. Ian was sometimes bitchy and jealous like a woman and on occasion he would count my money. He always said that I shouldn't have hundreds of thousands just sitting in the bank and that I needed to find something to invest in.

I wasn't about to go back and forth with him. Instead I drank the remainder of my water and went to take a shower.

By the time I was out of the shower, he was gone and I was happy I didn't have to argue with him anymore. However, I did have to get to the bottom of everything. I dialed Angelique's phone.

"Angelique, did you know our drinks and bottles came to three thousand dollars last night?"

"Yeah, it didn't seem like a big deal last night. But that's a pair of shoes. I'll bring you my half before I leave."

"No, I'm not worried about that. I'm just thinking, like, a bottle in a liquor store is only seventy, eighty dollars for the big bottles. Two hundred at the max, and the club charged us five times that. I hope we had a good time because I can't remember shit."

"Yes, we had a great time. I'm not so sure about your boyfriend, though. I was arguing with him. I'm really sorry. He was going off about the bill, and I said something like the bill was nothing and asked him why he wasn't paying for it and just complaining about it."

"Oh, wow. Yeah, he is mad. Anyway, forget him. I want to know how you can legally cheat people out of their money like this and get away with it. I should open a damn club."

"You should!" Angelique laughed.

"No, I'm serious. I'll charge fifty to get in and thirty dollars a shot, five hundred a bottle, and only let certain people in."

"Sounds about right. Well, when you open this club, invite me, because I will be there."

Chapter 5

Zakiya

On Wednesdays Lisa didn't do overtime; she came home and took Miles and Kyle to karate and I didn't have to go to work. I was going to find a spot at this coffee shop on Spring Garden Street not far from school and open my textbook and study. I felt like a big cliché studying in the midst of people on their midday breaks; other students, and people just typing away on their computer. Cliché or not, I was able to complete so much of my schoolwork there.

My phone went off and I saw my sister's name. "Hey, Lisa."

"Can you watch the boys tonight?"

"Yeah, I'm not doing anything, just studying. Where are you going?"

"I'm going out for drinks with coworkers. If you

can't do it, I understand and I'll just tell them I can't."

"No, I can do it."

"Oh, and can you take the boys to their karate class, too?"

"Yeah, I will take them."

I took my rock heads to their karate class. Their class was held in the basement of a church. There were a bunch of children kicking into the air screaming martial arts terms. The boys hurried and changed into their karate gear, and I took a seat against the wall and planned to continue to study during the next hour.

One of the guest karate teachers came over and introduced himself. "Hey, I'm Brian." I brought my head up long enough to give a faint hello and returned to reading my textbook.

The instructor was cute. He had dark, wavy hair and an olive-colored complexion. He kept watching me and smiling and looking over in my direction. I knew he wanted to say something, but was trying to figure out what his approach was going to be. He was handsome and looked about my age. He came back over and said, "Your nephews, they are really good students. I never saw you bring them before."

"Yeah, because my sister usually brings them. I have classes and I work."

"What school do you go to? I'm in school, too. I'm at Drexel."

"I just began classes at community college," I said. In no way did it compare to Drexel.

"My dad went to community. It's cool."

"Yeah, it is. I'm going to stay there until I get my associate's degree."

"So, what are you doing later on? Maybe we can hang out or something."

"Maybe. I think we can do that." I gave him my number and he said he would call me around eight and then we would figure out where to meet up.

I was so excited about my date with Brian. The kids had no idea that their auntie had snagged a date during their lesson.

Lisa came in the house, and I couldn't wait to tell her my good news. I had texted a little bit with Brian and found out more information on him. He was twenty-two and about to graduate school in the fall. His major was political science with a minor in business.

"I took your kids to karate and I now I have a date."

"About time, Zakiya. I've been wishing for you to start acting like you are twenty and not seventy-two."

"Well, your wish has been granted tonight. I'm so excited. I don't know what I'm going to wear." I rocked from side to side around my room trying to figure out what I was going to put on.

I met Brian at the movies. So far he was extremely well mannered, and our date was going okay. We talked between the action scenes and he let me have the last of the Raisinets.

After the movie we were still talking and getting to know each other, so I agreed to go back to his house. We walked out of the theater and walked for several blocks when I finally asked him where his car was.

"I'm not driving. I don't have a car; I walk everywhere. If you want, we can walk to my place or catch the trolley. I live like another fifteen blocks." Another fifteen blocks was about two miles and way too far to walk. I opted for us to take the trolley. We waited on the corner of Baltimore Avenue for the trolley to come. We boarded the crowded and noisy 34. There weren't any seats left, so we stood and swayed each time the trolley came to a halt. At each stop, people pushed by us to get off and I was becoming a little irritated. I was happy when it was finally our turn to get off.

Brian's block was full of rows of big Victorian-type houses with huge trees and bushes in the University Penn section of west Philadelphia. He unlocked a big wooden door with paned glass. On the other side of the door, there was a young white guy on the sofa playing a PlayStation 3. Brian said hi to the guy, and then like six more people poured into the living room talking and shouting. It was like a fraternity house. The group was a mixture of white and black, late twentysomething guys, who all were wearing T-shirts with logos and phrases, and ripped jeans or khakis. Between their shouting he managed to introduced me to every single guy.

"How many people live here?" I asked. He had to count and then said he had five roommates and a few guys who stayed over every now and then.

"You live here with five other people?"

"Yeah, we all have our own rooms. If you are uncomfortable, we can go into my room."

I looked around at the loud strangers and decided his room might be better than the overcrowded living room. We walked down the hall into his crammed space. His room wasn't full of people; it was full of junk. He pushed things off the bed to make room for us, and then he turned on his television.

"So what do you want to watch?" I glanced around at the mess and decided I could watch television at home. His room was too junky and smelly. I stood up, gathered my bag, and very bluntly said, "No, I don't think I want to watch television. I'm going to go on home."

"You're not having any fun?"

"No, it's not that. I just have a lot of things I need to take care of." I'm sure he could tell I was lying and I didn't care. I needed to get out of there. Before he could say anything, I walked out to the living room past all of his friends and roommates. He caught up to me once I was halfway down his block and walked me to the bus stop. We talked a little more until the trolley came. I promised I would call him, but I had no intention of doing so.

Lisa heard me come in the door and ran downstairs to get tidbits about my date. She took a look at me and shook her head.

"Your date must have been awful?"

"It was horrible. He didn't have a car and we had to catch the trolley to his house. Then once we got to his house, he had a bunch of roommates and a filthy room. Lisa, you know I'm not hard to please, right? And I considered myself a pretty down-to-earth person, but don't you warn someone that you don't have a car and give them a heads-up that ten other people might be at your house?"

Lisa began laughing. "I'm sorry. I don't mean to laugh, but that's how most college kids live. It is just that you haven't dated a regular guy in so long. And then your last boyfriend was a millionaire, so not too many other guys are going to compare. There is going to be a major difference unless you date someone more established and older."

"I don't want an older guy. I won't date anymore, if all the guys my age live and act like this. And by the way, I never want to see him again, so I'm not taking the kids back to karate."

Lisa laughed some more, then patted my back and chuckled. "It will be okay. You'll find someone else."

"I hope so. I was so excited and thought I had someone to go out with again." I sighed and then the doorbell rang, and I opened the door to see Mikey, Lisa's ex-boyfriend. I looked over at Lisa, perplexed. It was a little late for him to be stopping by, since the boys were already in bed.

"What are you doing here? Is Lisa expecting you?"

"Yeah, Lisa knows I was coming. I just got off the phone with her." I left him at the door and Lisa came behind me, greeted him, then let him in. Mikey came in and had a seat on the sofa. I walked into the kitchen and she followed me.

"Why are you being all short with Mikey?"

"Lisa, I still don't like him. So, are you getting back together? It is a little late for him just to be stopping by."

"No, we've been talking, and he is going to be more helpful with Miles and Kyle. You know, picking them up after school."

"He is?"

"Yup. He's working now, and his job is right down the street from the school, and they need to start spending some time with him. That'll free up some of your time and help me out, too. He's just being a good dad, nothing more."

"Yeah, I guess." I hoped that now that he was reappearing in the boys' life that he would not try to make guest appearances in my sister's life, too. I didn't really feel comfortable with Mikey back in the house. Lisa could say whatever she wanted, but I knew for sure what his true motives were.

If she wanted to deal with him again, that was on her. I had to study for real for the third time today. I sat on my bed and turned on the computer, and it just started powering on and then back off again. I made sure it was plugged into the outlet, then I took the battery out and tried to turn the computer on again and nothing happened. I yelled downstairs.

"Lisa, who touched my computer? It won't turn on."

"I don't know. Let me wake the boys." Lisa stormed up the steps into the boys' room. I walked in as she turned the lights on. Kyle was still asleep. But Miles looked over at him and said, "I don't know who did it, but it wasn't me."

"Then who was it?" Lisa demanded. He couldn't dime his twin out, but he wasn't going down for him, either. "I don't know, ask Kyle."

Miles could see that I was upset, and he suddenly started blurting out the truth. "I didn't mean to do it, Aunt Kiya. I just wanted to look up a cheat code for the game, and it said do you want to download yes or no and so I clicked no, and then something popped on the screen, and I tried to get it off and the computer wouldn't work."

I was so angry I just went in my room and slammed the door. I always tell them not to get on my computer and not to download anything and they do it anyway.

CHAPTER 6

Shanice

"I have a doctor's appointment. My leg is bothering me again. Do you know where Courtney at?" Aunt Rhonda asked, sitting across from me applying lotion to her short hairy legs.

Something was always bothering Aunt Rhonda. She was only fifty-something, and she was falling apart. Her knee, her hip, her back. I planned on taking good care of myself to make sure I'd still be in shape when I reached her age.

"No, she went out last night and didn't come back yet," I told her. I was about to get dressed and go see my daughter later on. I knew she wanted me to watch Ayana, but I wasn't because she was bad as shit.

"What are you about to do?"

"I'm about to go pick up Raven."

"It would be nice if Ayana could see Raven. They haven't played together in a while."

"Yeah, I would, but you know how her grand-mom be tripping on me. So I can't."

"Then I guess I'm going to have to take her with me." Aunt Rhonda looked over at Ayana. "Ayana, get dressed," she hollered in an aggravated voice. "Your mother gets on my damn nerves. Hurry up before I leave you here by yourself," she yelled down the hall.

Aunt Rhonda returned her attention to me. "If you talk to Courtney, tell her to answer her phone. Oh yeah, I need y'all's bill money as soon as possible."

"Okay," I said but had no idea how I was going to get it.

Once I was dressed I left out to meet up with my daughter, Raven, and her grandmother Valerie. Valerie and her husband have been raising Raven for me since she was born. My daughter is in pre-K at a Montessori school and she's five years old. Her school is already teaching her how to speak different languages. I'm happy she is going to be smart and doesn't have to grow up in rough-ass Philly like I did. Courtney always says that my daughter talks like a little white girl, but I don't think she does. Raven talks like she is going to be somebody one day. I wished she lived with me, but I'm happy she's getting all the advantages I never had.

* * *

Ray's mom and dad are doing what I couldn't, because I wouldn't have been able to give her a nice life right now.

I met my daughter's father, Ray, when I was in the tenth grade. We were all walking on South Street. This guy came driving up in a BMW. He was young and cute. He had on a light blue polo shirt and his Nikes matched. I knew he wasn't like most of the guys I knew. He was cool but not a thug, and I liked his style. He asked one of my friends what was up with me. My friend said, "Ask her yourself," and then she introduced us. Me and Ray went to the movies that night.

From there I started going out with him a couple of times a week. Ray was four years older than me and was home on break from college. He took me out and gave me money for my hair, nails, and stuff. He would always bring me to his big house in Abington right outside of Philadelphia. Every time I would visit I was amazed because I'd never seen black people live like that. His father was a principal at a high school and his mother worked for the electric company. We would chill at his house and have sex all the time. When I got pregnant months later, he said he knew it was his, but he didn't want a kid because he was going back to school. I didn't want a baby, either. I told my aunt Rhonda, but she didn't have an opinion either way. She said if I wanted to keep the baby it was my choice. At first I didn't want Raven and I was confused. I'd already had two abortions, but then I decided I would just keep it.

Once I made the decision to keep Raven, Ray

stopped speaking to me. He actually drove past me a couple of times with his new girlfriend in the car. It didn't bother me, though. When people asked who my baby's father was, I just lied and made up a name.

By the time I was five months' pregnant, Courtney was pregnant, too, with Ayana. We planned to raise our kids together.

Then everything changed when Ray's parents called me when I was eight months along and asked me to come over for dinner.

I went over to their house and they sat me down at their dining room table. Valerie looked me in my eyes and said I was too young for a baby. It was too late to get rid of the baby, so I didn't know what she wanted me to do. Then she surprised me and said they would take care of the baby for me once I had it. I was so happy. It seemed like they were handing me a get-out-of-jail-free card. During my entire pregnancy, my aunt Rhonda kept telling me she wasn't going to be watching my baby. So I went from no babysitter to a full-time one. It was an easy decision to make. I could finish school, and I knew that Ray's parents would take good care of her.

Raven was born a month later, and they picked her up from the hospital. They wanted me to sign over my rights so they could adopt her. At first I was going to, but Aunt Rhonda told me not to sign anything. She said they could just raise her until I was older and had my own place, but that I shouldn't let them keep her forever. That was good advice, and I am so happy I listened to Aunt Rhonda. When I get a real job and my own place, I'm going to get my daughter and raise her myself.

I met my daughter and my baby's father's mother, Ms. Valerie, at the Cheltenham Mall. My day to see Raven was always conveniently during Ms. Valerie's hair appointment. She handed me my daughter's hand. Raven looked just like me; she even had a little shape at five, which I wasn't happy about. I hope she stays skinny and don't develop too quickly like I did.

Ms. Valerie gazed at me and Raven standing together. "So I shouldn't be that long. I'm only getting a wash and set. You're not going to leave the mall, are you?"

"No, we'll be right here."

It would be nice to take my daughter outside the mall on a bus or a train. Sometimes I feel like Ms. Valerie's trying to turn Raven against me. I feel like each time I visit with her, I have to start all over again. I wish I could just take her with me, but where am I going to take her to? She can't share my bed.

"Rave, what do you want to do today? Do you wanna see a movie or you wanna go to the pet store and look at the doggies?" I always took her to the pet store and let her look at the cute puppies.

"I want to see the doggies again," she answered. We walked to the end of the mall to the pet store, hand in hand.

* * *

Once we left the cute pups, we traveled to the food court and I got her chicken nuggets and fries. After she was done I was going to let her get on a few of the dollar rides across from the food court. There was a little merry-go-round and a car that moved up and down.

"Shani, I like the puppies. I wish I could take them all home."

"When we get our own house, I'm going to buy you the cutest puppy in the store. Okay, Raven?"

"I'm going to live with you, Shani?"

"Yes, one day. You are going to live with Shani."

While Raven was eating her chicken nuggets, Courtney called. I didn't answer fast enough, so she texted me. She had set something up for the night and I needed to meet her at the house by six. We had to get all the bill money up, before Aunt Rhonda began tripping on us.

Ms. Valerie texted me that she was ready and I told her we were by the rides. Raven was having a fun time and did not want to leave. Ms. Valerie located us and halted our good time.

"Your hair looks pretty, Ms. Valerie."

"Thanks."

"Mommy, Shani said she is going to let me get a dog and let her move in with her."

"Oh yeah? That sounds nice," Ms. Valerie said, smiling at Raven while giving me the side-eye.

"Thanks for watching her." Valerie tried to hand me a few dollars, but I didn't accept it. I told her to keep her money. Then I bent down to knee level and told my daughter good-bye.

"I love you, Raven. We had fun, right?"

"Yes, you'll take me to your house soon and get a puppy, Shani?"

"Yes, real soon." I kissed her cheek and told Ms. Valerie I would call them. Raven always cried when I left, and that made me happy. It let me know she still knew who her real mommy was. When I get in the right position, I'm going to get my daughter, I swear I am. I'm going to get us a two-bedroom apartment for just me, her, and our puppy.

I met Courtney at the house. Our bills were due, so we were meeting up with these guys Courtney knew. We were going to hang out with them. "Hanging out" meant that we would let them give us some money for the pleasure of our company. Later, we'd reward them with sex.

Courtney started running down who we were meeting up with.

"They from South Philly and they're both paid. My bull name is Quan, and you're with his friend, Marquis. They're from down Seventh Street and Quan's uncle was getting it back in the day. Quan got street money and a job. I was talking to him and he said he had to call me back because he was at work. He works at the airport, doing something. I was like, okay, do that . . . a job and a hustle."

Quan and Marquis pulled up in and we hopped in the back seat of the silver Crown Victoria.

"So where y'all want to go? We will take you wherever," Quan said, turning around and looking at us in the back seat.

"I want Red Lobster. I love they biscuits. You cool with that, Shanice?" Courtney yelled out.

"That's fine, I guess." I didn't care as long as it didn't take all night.

"All right. We're there." Marquis turned around and started looking at me. He was okay-looking. He just had a big lightbulb head.

At the Red Lobster on Roosevelt Boulevard, we sat at a booth and talked a little. Marquis was wearing jeans, a white tee, and the new Jordans. I could see his money on and off his body. He had a huge money roll imprint in his pockets. I needed that. I hoped he wasn't stingy. He wasn't much of a talker, but he seemed cool. We ate, drank, and now it was time to handle the other part of our night.

On the way to the hotel, we listened to Meek Mill and smoked a blunt they had rolled. We were all chill and Courtney was all up on Quan like they were really together. He was cute, but she needed to remember what we were there for.

They got us a room at this sleazy motel. Marquis said that they only had one room with two double beds. I love my cousin, but I don't want to see or hear her have sex. I was ready to say let's find another hotel, but everyone got out of the car.

In the room Marquis starting pouring peach Cîroc into clear plastic cups and handed them out. I took a sip and mellowed out. Marquis started stroking my arms, then he got up and kissed me.

Before things got too serious, I excused myself and pulled Courtney into the bathroom.

"Did you get the money?"

Courtney pointed to her shoe and said, "Yeah, I got the eight hundred right here, four hundred apiece."

I came out the bathroom, took another sip of my drink, and had a seat next to Marquis. Courtney pulled Quan over in the corner by the bathroom and I turned on the television to drown out the noise they were about to make. I had a seat on the bed with Marquis, and we began to get familiar with one another.

Marquis licked on my neck and ears. His tongue left a sour trash smell. I turned my face to the side so I didn't have to inhale it.

He pulled out a condom and strapped it on himself.

Without waiting, he popped his hard dick into my pussy. His dick was curved and leaned to the right. At first it was feeling okay, but then that crooked shit kept stabbing my insides. I clenched my walls together to make him cum quicker, but that had the opposite reaction on Marquis. The tightness made him more excited, and he kept beating it up like he was knocking on a door. Then he would stop for a little bit, try to control his release, then start knocking again. I think Marquis and Quan may have been in some kind of competition to see who could go the hardest. Courtney was moaning loudly on the other side of the room and I didn't want to make any noise, but I couldn't help but scream.

I didn't think I would like Marquis, but more

liquor and more weed made him more fuckable. What he lacked in personality and features, he made up for with his dick. He was feeling better and better inside me.

Once he was done, I was ready to rest for a minute. All I could do was stretch out and close my eyes. Marquis said he would be back; he was going to get more condoms. I wasn't doing anything else, but I told him okay. I was about to take a nap. Before I shut my eyes all the way, I noticed Courtney's boy, Quan, digging all in her purse.

"Yo, why you in her bag?" He acted like he didn't hear me, so I said it again when I saw him reaching for Courtney's jacket.

"I'm looking for her lighter," he said, still digging around.

Her lighter was right on the nightstand. I sat up and then he was digging around in her jeans pockets.

"What are you looking for?" I asked him as I got up from the bed, walked across the room, and looked out the window. I saw Marquis still sitting outside in the car even though he said he was supposed to be on a condom run. I sensed something wasn't going right. I nudged Courtney awake, and she snatched her jeans from Quan and asked what the hell he was doing.

"Yo, Courtney, where the money at?" Quan said in a gruff voice.

"Huh, what money?" she asked.

"You know what money. Your pussy wasn't worth no eight hundred. Y'all should have been doing tricks and bumping pussies with each other and giving us a show for that kind of money. You didn't do nothing special, so give me our money back."

"Shit, you lost your mind. We not giving you shit. Fuck out of here," I said.

"Look, we ain't giving you any money back. You got what you wanted and we got paid. That's what it is," Courtney shouted at Quan.

"Naw, that ain't what it is," he said as he picked up Courtney's shoes. She leaped toward him. He pushed her and I was ready to hit him when he pulled out a black .45 automatic gun. He pointed the gun at us and we both fell back. I stood still as he took our hard-earned money out of Courtney's shoe. He backed up out of the room holding a gun in one hand and our money in the other. I didn't think it could get any worse, but it did. After he shut the door, Courtney ran over to the door and opened it. She screamed, "You little pencil-ass dick bitch. I was faking it when I was yelling. I couldn't even feel that shit."

What Courtney was saying must have had some truth behind it because Quan came back and banged on the door. We were laughing until he shot through the motel window twice. We both ducked down and waited until we heard their car screech off. There were so many names I could have called dumb-ass Courtney, but I didn't. I was too drained and too angry to light into her ass.

"We have to get out of here before the cops get here."

"I know," I said as I hurried to grab my belongings and we ran out of the motel.

* * *

We were several blocks away and out of breath before we stopped running.

"Oh. My. God. He is crazy. I can't believe he shot at us and left us all the way out here," Courtney gasped.

"Yeah, this is fucked up. I can't believe he shot at us, either. We have to find out what bus runs around here."

My insides were on fire. That dry-ass condom and his crooked dick were not a good combination. I was fuming mad. Now that my high was blown, I could smell Marquis's stank blunt breath all over my skin.

"I wish we could call the cops."

"And say what, Courtney? You sound so stupid right now."

"Yo, I had no idea he was crazy like that," Courtney said.

I looked over at Courtney's face and knew that I was so tired of doing this bum bitch shit. Getting robbed and shot at by the dudes we were just fucking with. Sometimes Courtney was my best friend, my sister, and other times she was the dumbest bitch I knew. I didn't want to yell at her, but I couldn't hold back.

"Courtney, this was some real stupid shit."

"Okay, so you act like I knew this was going to happen."

"I'm not saying that." I knew Courtney was about to flip it back on me. She fucked up, but somehow it was about to be my fault.

It always started with, "Bitch, you ain't better than me." She was going to say that I was nothing because I let my daughter go to live with her father's family. If I was a real woman I would hold it down like she was doing with her daughter. She always brings up unrelated shit when we arguing.

Aunt Rhonda says we are water and oil and we will never be able to get along fully. Sometimes I think she is jealous that Ayana never met her grandparents and my baby lives with hers.

"Don't try to act like this is my fault, Shanice. As soon as you saw him near my bag you should have said something."

"I did. I woke you up."

"Well, you should have been more on point. All I know is, you don't have to act like you better than anyone. You not better than me or smarter than me. Yeah, it's my bad I fucked up, but you did, too."

I could argue with Courtney, but she would never get it, and all I cared about was getting home into the shower and into my bed.

CHAPTER 7

Zakiya

"Happy birthday, Aunt Kiya," my nephews yelled as they both ran downstairs with a white notebook paper homemade card sealed with tape.

"Open it. Open it," they both yelled.

"Okay." I sat at the kitchen table and opened the card and about three dollars in dimes, nickels, and pennies fell out. On the front of the card there was a drawing of me and them and a greeting that was written in sloppy cursive handwriting that read HAPPY BIRTHDAY WORLD'S BEST AUNT.

"This is so nice. Wow, I'm so lucky."

"We gave you that money for your birthday to buy a new computer," Miles said.

"That's so sweet. Give me a hug," I said as I extended my arms out wide enough to hug them both.

My sister, Lisa, interrupted our lovefest and told the boys to grab their jackets and book bags and head out to the car, so they wouldn't be late for school.

"So now that you're legal, what are you doing today?" she asked as she put her jacket on.

"Nothing special. Just going to the library to type my paper and then to class and that's it."

"Well, maybe we can go to Applebee's or something tonight. Hopefully my overtime is on this check."

"Yeah, I have to work, so don't worry about it."

"Well, when you get off, let's do something."

"Okay."

It was my birthday, but it didn't feel like it. I hadn't really celebrated my birthday since before my mom killed herself when I was twelve. A lot of things just didn't matter anymore once she was gone.

I grabbed a birthday vanilla frosted donut with sprinkles from Dunkin' Donuts and a large orange juice. That was my birthday breakfast before I went and typed up my English paper. My phone was at the bottom of my bag and it started ringing.

Once I finally grabbed it, I was surprised to see Jabril's name on the screen. "Hey, Jabril," I said as I walked out of Dunkin' Donuts.

"I just wanted to call you and say happy birthday. What are you doing?"

"About to go to the library so I can type my paper. My computer is broke."

"What's wrong with it?"

"My nephews did something to it. I think it has a virus or something."

"Wow, that's messed up."

"Yeah, it is, but it's done and I know they didn't mean to do it. Well, I'm having breakfast and then going to class. I'll call you later."

"You are always busy. Every time I talk to you, you're in school or getting ready for school, or studying for a test."

"I have classes Monday, Wednesday, and Friday all day. So call me on Tuesday or Thursday."

"What are you doing this weekend?"

"I don't know. My sister and nephews are going to take me out maybe later on. Other than that, I'm not doing anything."

"You should come and visit me."

"I can't until like spring break. Yeah, spring break I will definitely come."

"Do you promise, Zakiya?"

"Yes, I promise." I said anything to get him off the phone. I think I knew if I saw him it wouldn't be as easy to resist and say no to him.

"All right, well, I'll talk to you. Enjoy your birthday."

"I will. Thanks, Jabril."

I made it to class right as my instructor was writing problems on the board, which no one was copying. I must have been the only person in class who actually was there to learn something. Everyone else was there just taking up space. That's what I hated about community college. Some of the students were people who were in search of higher learning and wanted a cheap quality education like me, but then we were forced to learn with the thirteenth graders whose parents gave them ultimatums: go to college or get out.

One girl was sitting in class texting and another guy had headphones up all loud with his hood on his head. *Why bother even coming to class?* I thought.

The professor began explaining our lesson and I was so lost. I looked in the book and back at the board, but it wasn't making any sense.

I raised my hand and asked him to explain it again. Usually, things came easy to me. But for this math, I needed a tutor to help me understand. He ran back through the problem fast and I still didn't catch up. So when he turned and asked if I got it, I just responded with a head nod.

After class I tried to wait in line to talk to Professor Langer. I didn't want to be late for work, but I had just sat for an hour and was still clueless. By the time I reached his desk, he was packing his briefcase.

"Hi, I was wondering how I can get extra help in this class."

"They have tutoring in the library and I have office hours."

"Do you have any time today?"

"No, I'm sorry, I have another class. I can't discuss this with you right now. You can e-mail me."

I thanked him and gathered my belongings. Exiting the classroom, I heard a little commotion. I walked around the growing crowd until I saw Jabril standing there with three guys in tuxedos. Each man was holding a dozen red and white roses. Before I could react to Jabril or seeing the flowers, the men handed me the flowers and began to sing Stevie Wonder's soulful, a cappella version of "Happy Birthday." I stood still with my hand over my mouth in shock. Jabril came over and hugged me tightly as the men continued to sing in harmony. Tears dripped down my face. I hid my face in Jabril's side as he comforted me.

"What are you doing here?" I mumbled.

"I had to come and say happy birthday to my favorite girl." I couldn't believe Jabril was right beside me. I hung on to him, so happy, but also mortified that he had made this big spectacle at my school. I couldn't believe that he'd shown up on the day I decided to rock a hoodie and jeans to school. Students were snapping pictures on their phones and recording us. Then those who weren't taking pictures were asking Jabril for his autograph or to take a picture with him. I guess it wasn't every day a famous basketball player came on campus. A lot of guys automatically recognized him. It was hard to miss his six-five frame, chestnut eyes, and beautiful smile. He was wearing a fitted black shirt and jeans.

"Zakiya, I couldn't wait until spring break to see you. You know I love you."

"I love you, too, Jabril." I couldn't keep the tears back and could barely speak. Jabril ordered me to stop crying and pulled me to his side once more, and he walked me out to an awaiting black Cadillac Escalade. The driver opened the door and helped me in the car. People had followed us to the car and were waving as we drove away. I wiped away more tears and then punched Jabril softly in his side.

"Why you come up to my school embarrassing me?"

"I knew I was going to be in the city, so I had to see you. I wanted to take you out and surprise you."

"But I have to go to work."

"I'm not taking no for an answer. You're calling out of work and I'm taking you to dinner."

"This is all nice, Jabril, but I can't call out from work."

"So I came all this way, and you can't tell the people at your job that you are sick?"

I looked over on the other side of Jabril and saw more flowers and gift bags.

"Okay, I'll call out, but you are crazy. What if you hadn't been able to find me?"

"No, I knew where you were, in class. Why do you think I called you this morning? But then you were taking so long coming out, I was like, damn, I hope she came to school today."

"So how long are you in town?"

"Until the weekend, then I'm going back."

Jabril had done all of this for me, I had to be thankful. I didn't have a choice. I had to call out from work. I asked him to be quiet as I dialed my job. I never called out, so I didn't expect it to be a problem. Someone from the customer service desk answered and I asked to speak to Lenora. Lenora answered and I said, "Lenora, it's Zakiya. I'm not feeling well so I'm not coming in."

"Okay, I hope you feel better, but you know I had three other call outs today. But it is not your fault. Feel better. I have to call around to see who I can get to come in."

* * *

I made sure she was off the phone before I said, "Okay, are you happy? I'm not going to work."

"Yes, I am. Thank you for allowing me to kidnap you." He kissed me, his tongue tickling mine, going back and forth. I hugged him so tightly and kissed him back. Now that he was in front of me I couldn't act like I didn't miss and want him, too.

"Well, I need you to open your first gift." He handed me a box with a watch, then there was this huge brown, leather monogrammed Louis Vuitton bag and inside of that bag was a pair of diamond earrings in the shape of a butterfly, a matching bracelet, a watch, and an iPad.

"Thank you, Jabril," I squealed, looking over all my gifts.

"You're welcome, Kiya. My boy Lloyd told me I should get you a pair of red-bottom shoes, but I couldn't remember your size and I forgot to ask you."

"Jabril, I'm happy with all this. I don't need anything else. I wanted an iPad. Thank you so very much. All of this is so nice." I placed the watch on one arm and the butterfly bracelet on the other.

"And that's not all. I have one more surprise for you." He pulled out another box. "And remember this? You left this."

"My chain."

"Now, you have the earrings and bracelet to match it now. And I know I said that was it, but you said you needed something else when I talked to you this morning."

"What?" I asked as I watched Jabril pull a slim box from under the seat and placed it on my lap.

"A new MacBook Pro!" I shouted. "I needed a computer so bad."

"I know. That's why I got it."

Out of all the gifts he'd just presented me with, the computer was the one that made me cry. I didn't know how I was going to buy another one. "Thanks, Jabril. Really, thanks."

I reached out and hugged him again and then asked him where we were going. Through all the present opening I noticed the driver was crossing over the Benjamin Franklin Bridge into New Jersey.

"I'm kidnapping you."

"Kidnapping me to where?"

"Somewhere you said you wanted to go when you finally turned twenty-one."

"Somewhere like where? Do you know how long ago that was? My memory is not that good . . . tell me!"

"Atlantic City, because you said you wanted to walk the casino floor and when they asked you for ID you were going to flash it in their face."

"I did say that. You remember everything, Jabril."

Jabril had a suite waiting for us at The Water Club by Borgata. We spent the day talking and getting reacquainted in the spacious room and massive bed.

"I missed you," Jabril said, kissing my forehead.

"I missed you, too." I felt all kinds of emotions overtake me.

"So, what are we doing now?"

"We are going to dinner, but first we have to get you a dress." He called down to the concierge desk and this man came upstairs and asked my shoe and dress size and returned with five dresses for me to pick from and three pairs of shoes.

I showered and changed into everything and I felt like a princess—or Cinderella. I had all these new sparkling jewels on, a new dress, new shoes, and my prince, Jabril.

We left our hotel room and walked to the restaurant on the same floor. The restaurant was set by a pool and it was intimate. There were only a few other tables, and they were empty. It was like we had our own private restaurant.

"You know, they only let their high rollers up here. I heard you have to gamble at least five hundred thousand to be invited to this floor. I asked around and everyone said this is the best place in Atlantic City."

"It's beautiful," I said, looking around and admiring the scenery.

Dinner was a lavish spread of filet mignon, lobster tails, and sautéed spinach. Our servers attended to our every need. Once I took my glass away from my mouth, they were there to refill it or pick up my napkin when it fell off the table.

"So, how has your mom been?" I asked. Jabril's mother, Claudette, and I had become quite close when he and I were together, but I cut her off when I cut him off.

"She is good, going back and forth from here and Oklahoma. Always asking about you."

"Aw, really? Tell her I said hello. How about your uncle?"

"Oh, Wendell isn't living with us anymore. He's back out here. He has his own place. He still helps me out, but from a distance. I don't really need him all up in my business anymore. You know, telling me what to do. I'm older now. What about your sister and little nephews?"

"They are good boys. My sister is doing well."

After our meal, the waiters brought out a huge birthday cake covered with gold flowers and silver stars. It had huge sparkling candles like fireworks sprouting out of it, and they all sang "Happy Birthday" to me again. The cake read: HAPPY 21ST BIRTHDAY, BABY. I LOVE YOU!

I couldn't have ever dreamed of a birthday this great. I blew out my candles, and instead of wishing for anything, I simply thanked God for everything I had already received.

We took the elevator on to the casino floor. I was ready to show my identification, but I didn't get carded and was able to gamble without any problems. I didn't win any money, but it was fun. On the way back up to the hotel room, Miles called me.

"Aunt Kiya, are you okay? We were waiting for you to go to dinner."

"My nephews were waiting for me at home," I whispered to Jabril. "Miles, tell your mom I'm sorry I didn't call." Lisa came on the line.

"Is everything all right?" Lisa asked.

"Yes, I'm with Jabril. It's a long story. I'll be home in the morning. He showed up and surprised me at my school."

"That was nice. Well, enjoy yourself. Have fun and call me."

Once in the room Jabril hugged me tightly and would not let go. His body was warm and felt so good. "Thank you for all this, Jabril. No one has ever done anything this big or sweet for me."

"You're welcome. You know I can and would do anything for my girl. I always wanted to give you the world."

"I know. You almost did today. How did you plan all of this?"

"My boys Lloyd and Omar helped me out. We work out and practice together. Lloyd is cool. He's a little bit older. Him and his wife are good people. Then my other boy, Omar, be schooling me on and off the court. I asked them all the time, how can I get my girl back and what do you think I should do? And they gave me some pointers. I asked they wives, too."

"Well, they did a good job. Tell them I said thank you."

"I will, but I have to tell you, Zakiya, my life hasn't been right since we've been apart. I've been asking God to bring you back to me. I don't understand why you left me. But I know I'll do whatever I have to do to fix it and make it right. I can't believe God brought you back to me."

"I can't believe I am here." The entire day had

been full of surprises. I was still shocked that I'd left my house this morning in hoodie and jeans, was lost in math class, and now I was relaxing with the once love of my life.

"Zakiya, you don't understand what you mean to me." He took off his T-shirt, uncovering his muscular physique and his tattoo with my name, his name, and our son's name.

"You didn't cover the tattoo, Jabril." I touched the tattoo, and tears flowed out of my eyes.

"No, I wouldn't do that. I know we lost our first son, but I know one day we are going to have Jabril the second again. I know we will. Just not right now. It wasn't our fault . . . not yours or mine. You shouldn't have ever left. Why would you leave me, Kiya?"

I didn't want to cry again, but I didn't have an answer for him.

"I don't know why I left. It was just so hard for me, Jabril," I said, trying to hold back tears.

"We were being tested. God tests everyone. He wanted us to be a little more mature and married before he gave us our son. So, no, I didn't cover the tattoo because when I'm talking to our son one day, I'm going to tell him all it took for him to get here."

He grabbed me and held me some more. I cried. I let out every emotion that was pinned inside of me for all of this time. The hurt, the longing, the sadness. He removed my clothing and kissed me all over my body, and then moved to enter me.

"Jabril, you have to wear a condom."

"Why? I don't have anything. Have you been dealing with anyone?"

"No, but I just don't want to get pregnant."

"All right, fine. Grab one, it's on the side of the bed, in the bag."

I leaned over the side of bed and noticed in his duffel bag strips of condoms and all types of flavored lubricants.

Once the condom was on, he plunged deep inside regions and openings that hadn't been touched in over a year. It started out a little uncomfortable. I was on my side and positioned my body so he could reach the right spots. Back and forth he dove into my warm waters. I let out short moans of pleasure as he filled my body.

"Have you let anyone else in here, Kiya?"

"No, Jabril."

"You sure? You been keeping it tight for me? It's still mine?"

"Jabril, it is still yours."

"I want to feel it. I want to feel you. Let me see if it's still mine, Kiya." He quickly took himself out and slipped the condom off and then began going wild inside of me. "You better not ever let anyone near mine. You hear me?" His face was serious. Sweat beads poured off of him and onto me.

"Yes. Yes. Yes, Bril." I couldn't get it out. I was gasping for air. He was more forceful and aggressive and gave my body an hour's worth of ecstasy.

We showered and then I wrapped myself in him. Jabril made me feel so beautiful and special. We were reunited, and nothing else mattered.

He kissed my cheek. "Zakiya, I would have never come up to your school, if I knew this is all it would take to get you back."

"Whatever."

"You know I'm only playing. So are you going to start answering the telephone now?"

"I'll think about answering the telephone."

"You better." He playfully slapped my butt. He then threw on his boxers, walked into the bathroom, and came out with a Ziploc bag of weed. I watched him as he carefully picked out the seeds, poured the herb into a blunt wrapper, and then licked it closed.

"Since when did you start smoking, Jabril?"

"Since I needed to relax. Kiya, I was so stressed out. Now I can deal with any and everything." He lit the long brown paper, inhaled, and exhaled, then offered me some.

"No, I'm good, Bril. It is not making you slow?"

"No, not at all. It's actually helping me. When I smoke, I get relaxed, then I eat and it helps me build muscle to train."

"Just be careful. Don't they drug-test you?"

"Yeah, they do. They say it is random, but we all get a heads-up a few weeks before and I'll cut it out then."

CHAPTER 8

Adrienne

I walked into Ian's office and sat on his lap. It was the only way I could get his attention. He was in the middle of editing a music video he had just filmed. I played with his dreads and massaged his scalp with the tips of my fingers.

Editing was a complicated process that usually took days and days at a time, and I tried not to bother him. It took hours and hours of footage to make a four-minute video. Ian had amazing patience and was super-talented. I admired the way he was able to get it all done. He needed full concentration so he could precisely sync the audio and visual up so they would match. He was also looking for shadows and other things that most people wouldn't even care about.

I've been on the set with him and thought, *Oh, this is easy.* The first hour I was excited to get there and then it got boring as hell. In my mind, I thought, just hit RECORD, let the singer sing the song, and you have a video. However, I was so wrong. There were so many other things involved. Ian kept telling the actors to repeat themselves or do it this way . . . turn to the side and speak with feeling. Making music videos wasn't his passion, but it was the money that was paying the bills and would one day fund his film career.

"Are you almost done, babe?"

"Yes, almost. I have to go out and get more B-roll. Why, what's up?"

"I wanted to ask your opinion on something." He stopped moving his mouse and looked at me.

"What do you think about me opening a nightclub?"

"In Miami?"

"Yeah, I was joking with Angelique about it when she was here. But the more I think about it, the better of an idea it is becoming. I need something to invest my money in, right? And a nightclub is a sure thing. If I have the perfect location and people, it could be a success. I can charge people thousands of dollars a night to drink and be seen. I'll make so much money."

"Adrienne, you should probably start a business you're more familiar with, like a hair salon or boutique or something."

"I do know about nightclubs. I've been to enough of them. I used to go out all the time. I saw a few empty spaces when I was walking down Collins Avenue today."

"You know my cousin Keldrick is a party promoter in D.C. I can ask him and we can see what he thinks. But I honestly think you should come up with something else."

Later that evening, Ian set up a conference call with his cousin Keldrick. His cousin had this rough, country voice. He was from D.C. but sounded like he was from farther south. Ian told him about my club idea, and without even knowing me fully, he began ripping my dream apart.

"Thank you for speaking with us, Keldrick. So like I was telling you, my lady was interested in opening a nightclub here in Miami."

"Has she done any research on the club industry in Miami?" Keldrick asked with authority in his voice. Ian looked at me and then spoke into the phone. "No, we were just in the beginning stages of everything."

"Listen, Ian, tell her I know everything about nightclubs, and there are so many things you have to think about before you open your doors. You have to have a liquor license, and you have to hire staff. You need the right spot, and when all that is said and done, you have to create a buzz and get the word out about your club."

"I could hire a street team and web people," I said, joining in the conversation.

"Yeah, that's not all. In my opinion, Miami is too expensive to open a club, and there are enough clubs down there already. If anything, I would bring the Miami vibe up north."

"I don't want a club in Philly."

"No, I wasn't really thinking Philly. I was thinking the DMV area. Even though there's enough clubs up here, too, you have a better chance here than in Miami. What makes you even think you can do this?"

I stared down at the phone, annoyed and mad that Ian had even had me on the phone with this loser.

"I know it can happen. Your cousin contacted you because he thought you could help me."

"I probably could. I got friends, but you really need a team to open a club, and since you don't have a team, then you are wasting your time. One chick opening up a club by herself, I don't really see that happening. Let me ask you a question—how soon do you want to open up your club?"

"Like in the next couple of months, maybe by the spring," I responded.

"That's almost impossible, to get something open that quick. Do you know it usually takes at least nine months to get a club up and running?"

"It may take that long, but I'm really good at putting things together."

"You need to know more than just how to put things together. You need to sit down and write up a business plan. Start checking out your competition. And what type of money are you trying to invest? Your liquor license application alone can run thousands of dollars."

"I have money. That's not a problem. I have friends who know people and I can get them to come out. I partied with celebrities, and I can pay people to spread the word to anyone I may not know and get them to come to my club."

"Just because you know them doesn't mean they are going to come to your club. But, okay . . . Let me ask you, how are you going to get people who don't know your friends to the club?"

"You just asked me that, and I said I'd hire a street team. I'll use social media and word of mouth. Believe me, my friends will make sure to spread the word."

"There are guys who've been hosting parties and have followers for ten . . . twenty years, so you just can't rely on the people you know and some websites."

He was making me seem like I was a moron, like I hadn't weighed all my options and I didn't know what I was talking about. Which was true, but I didn't need him to emphasize my shortcomings. I didn't like the way he spoke to me, but it was obvious that he knew exactly what it was going to take to get started. The only reason I tolerated his know-it-all attitude was because he had information that I needed. I've learned that it's better to let someone underestimate you than to argue with them and prove them right. I already knew that I could pull this off, so Keldrick was going to be in for a surprise when he saw how successful my club turned out to be.

"What you need to ask yourself is, what's going to make your club different. If there are ten clubs on the same strip, why would the people come to yours?"

"They would come to my club because the entire club will be VIP only. And I will have an all-female staff. I do know that where the pretty girls are, the men will follow."

"You're not listening."

"No, I'm listening. I know I can get people out.

And I know what kind of atmosphere elite people want to party in. They don't want people taking pictures and being extra; they want their privacy and to be able to enjoy themselves."

"Let me ask you this: Are you interested in having any partners? I know people who would be interested in investing, possibly a forty-sixty split."

"Forty-sixty? I don't know about that. I'll be doing all the work."

"But you're going to need at least about a hundred to two hundred thousand dollars to get started, and I know you don't have that kind of paper."

"That's about how much I thought it would be."

"Then maybe you do have something. VIP-only sounds like something people will be interested in."

"Yeah, I know. Well, thanks for speaking with me."

He had given me a lot of information, but I was done hearing his voice. I got Ian's attention and told him that he could end the call. He got back on the phone and concluded the conversation.

"All right, cousin, we will look into everything. I'm going to talk to you." After Ian disconnected the call, he looked over at me.

"I think what he was saying is true. Like I said, you should probably do something that you know more about."

"I still think it is a good idea. We'll see." I couldn't let on to Ian that he was right.

Hmm, I suppose maybe I wanted to be too big, too soon. I wanted to go straight from sneakers to six-inch stiletto heels, and there were so many steps that needed to be taken in between. The more I thought about it, the more I really wanted it to work. I don't know, maybe I wouldn't be opening a night club. I had to meet DeCarious and pick up Malaysia in Gainesville, Florida, the exact middle of the road between Atlanta and Miami. I couldn't wait to see my baby and I could think everything over during the long drive.

When I arrived, they were already parked at the rest stop and I pulled up next to DeCarious's big navy-colored truck. I caught a glimpse of his fiancée, Cherise. She got on my nerves. Why was she always with DeCarious and my daughter? Didn't she have a job to do? Like go cover a news story or something? Why did she feel like it was necessary to have to drive with him to drop my daughter off? She probably thought I still wanted him, but I didn't. Looking at DeCarious, I felt not even a twinge of jealousy. If he tried to come on to me, I would be sick and vomit. I got out the car and waited for him to bring her over.

My baby, Malaysia, saw me and ran over to my legs and began hugging me. "Mommy!" I gave her kisses all over both cheeks. She was three, but she could talk well. She started forming sentences when she was one and she talked so much, we actually had to tell her to be quiet.

DeCarious handed me her suitcase. I snapped her in her car seat. His fiancée got out of the car and I gave her an *I don't really like you, but I'm going to speak anyway* wave.

"Listen, I wanted to talk to you about Malaysia

staying with me year-round for some stability," DeCarious said.

"Yes, we've been thinking—" Cherise butted in, but I looked over at her and cut her off with a look, then I rolled my eyes. She had nothing to do with the conversation, and she could get back in the car.

"That's not going to happen," I said calmly.

"You know everything doesn't have to be nasty, Adrienne," DeCarious stated.

"DeCarious, it is not nasty, but I don't have time for this discussion. I need to get on the road, and I don't see anything wrong with our current situation. I'll see you in two weeks." I left them both standing outside their car and pulled off.

Chapter 9

Zakiya

How did I go from Jabril surprising me at my school to me being back in Oklahoma City, Oklahoma, with him? I don't know. I don't know how Jabril swept me off my feet. It happened so fast, and we picked up right from where we left off. We had such a good time in Atlantic City that I agreed to skip my Friday classes. Then I told Lenora not to put me on the schedule over the weekend. But once I started saying yes to Jabril, he kept trying to see how much further he could push me. We went from him popping up at my school and taking me to dinner to asking me to come out to Oklahoma City for a week. I said yes to everything, and then out of nowhere, Jabril asked if I could transfer to a college in Oklahoma City so we could be back together. There is something very strange about loving someone. When you really love a person, months and years can go by without seeing or hearing from them, but you feel like nothing has changed between you when you see them again. Unfortunately, that's how I felt.

The crazy thing is, for about four seconds I thought about it. I actually thought about rearranging my life for him again. Then I came to my senses. Everything felt right, but it was time for me to go back home.

I walked into my former gigantic closet and began packing my clothes. All my clothes were still in place just like I had left them. The week was over and I'd really enjoyed myself, but I had to get home. We were still best friends and in sync. It was undeniable that I loved Jabril, I just didn't want to be with him—not right now. I told him to book my flight and I would be back in a few weeks.

I tried to stuff all my new and old things into my suitcase. Even with everything folded neatly, my things wouldn't fit. Claudette peeked in the room as I struggled with closing the suitcase.

"What time does your flight leave?" Claudette asked.

"I don't know exactly. Bril made the reservations."

"Okay, I'll ask him. We better get going soon. I'm sure it is an afternoon flight."

"I'm almost done packing. I only want to bring a carry-on on the flight," I said.

"Also, Zakiya, I just wanted to say it was good having you back. Jabril hasn't been this happy in such a long time."

"Thanks, Claudette, I'll be back more often."

"Good, well, I'm going to run out to the store, then by the time I get back we can go."

I finally closed my suitcase and carried it toward the door. I walked past the pool and found Jabril outside on the court behind the house practicing free throws. I called out his name and he didn't stop playing until I was standing right next to him. I acted like I was going to knock the ball out of his hands. He dodged me, then shot at the hoop again.

"What time is my flight? I need the airline information."

"I think it's United . . . or it might have been American. I'm not sure. I forgot." He shot at the hoop again, missing this time. He ran after the ball, grabbed it, and then had me check him and the ball and pass it back to him.

"Why don't you know anything? Did you make my reservation, Jabril?"

"What if I didn't?" he asked, throwing the ball at the hoop again.

"Jabril! Oh my God! I have to be back at work and I have classes. I hope you are joking, because this is not funny at all."

"Then don't laugh, because I didn't book the flight. We need to talk, Zakiya. You have to make me understand, what's so important back in Philly? There are schools out here, and if you really wanted to work, there are a bunch of grocery stores, too."

"So, that's what you are trying to do, Jabril, keep me here? You are really unbelievable. We were having a good time, and then you have to do this. I don't need you to make me a reservation. I'll do it on my own. I'll get my own flight home." I walked back toward the house, and Jabril chased behind me.

"Zakiya, I'm sorry. You are right. I shouldn't have done this to you. It's just like . . ." he stammered. "It's like, spending time with you reminds me of old times. I know I'm being selfish, but I don't want you to go back. I want you here with me."

"Why are you pushing so hard for everything all at once? Why can't we date? I can come out here a few times a month. Maybe meet you on the road . . . you know . . . we need to start slow."

"But that's not what I want," he said with his head down.

"Jabril, everything is not going to be the way you want it. This is hard for me, too. I still think about you every day. I think about the baby, too. I'm not sure if I'm ready for all of this."

"Zakiya, it hasn't been easy for you, but you left me. You made the decision to pack up and leave when I begged you to stay. You really act like I didn't lose a child, too. I got hit twice as hard . . . I lost you and my son. Kiya, I love you and have never stopped loving you. The only place you should be is here with me. Why do you think I went through all of this, this week? I did it for you and for him. Our son is an angel now. He is watching us, and he wants us to be together."

"I appreciate everything. Jabril, let me just think and get my thoughts together. I'll go home and think about it. I really think we should just go slower this time. I have to worry about my job and my family, my classes."

"Don't you get it, Kiya?" He was bouncing the

ball between his legs. "You don't need a job or classes. You are my girl; I'm going to support you. I'll make sure you have everything."

"So, you want me to drop everything for you?"

"No, I want you to drop everything for us. . . ."

"I need my own, Jabril. I don't ever want to have to depend on you. I don't like having to ask you for money."

"You don't have to ask. I'll put money in your account every week, like I do for my mom."

"Okay, fine, but money wasn't our only problem. What about all the cheating on me? Let's talk about that. All the parties and girls all over the Internet saying that they've been with you."

"Zakiya, I wasn't cheating on you before. I only want you. I dated people since we have broken up, but no one compares to you. No one, Kiya. If you come back to me, I promise, I will give you everything and be the man that you want me to be. I will never hurt you again. I just need another chance, please. Please come back to me. I want you to be my wife one day. You are the only girl I ever cared about." He took his whole six-foot-five body and smothered me with affection.

"I'm not letting you leave me again. You can't leave me," he said with a sincere look in his eyes. I knew that he loved me and I loved him. I had a decision to make, and I needed time to think it over.

CHAPTER 10

Zakiya

I managed to get back home even though Jabril tried to hold me hostage. I wanted to stay, but I couldn't. My sister needed me, and so did my nephews. When I finish this semester, maybe we can see what will happen.

Being home in Philly made everything normal again. I had my fun, now it was time to get back to my ordinary life.

At least I thought it would be normal, but this girl in my math class, the same girl I asked to look at her test a few weeks ago who gave me an attitude . . . she kept smiling at me and then she passed me a note. The note read: *Hey, I thought that was so cute what your boyfriend did for you for your birthday. I wanted to say happy birthday and maybe we can hang out. I can take you out for drinks. P.S. Does your boyfriend have any friends you can introduce me to?*

I didn't know this girl, and I wasn't interested in getting to know her. I sent her the note back saying I didn't drink like that and I didn't know any of Jabril's friends.

Then after math class, this oversized boy walked up to me and asked me if I knew who Jabril's agent was. I didn't, and if I did, I wouldn't have told him.

"No, I'm sorry," I said, shaking my head.

"Do you think you can give me his telephone number? I want to see if I can get a tryout with his team."

"Yeah, I'm sorry, I don't know any of that."

He shook his head and said, "My bad," and left me alone. I hoped no one else would recognize me as the girl whose boyfriend had come to the school and embarrassed her.

School was weird and I was so unprepared for it. I liked it better when no one said anything to me.

From school I traveled to work. It was funny being back on the bus after hopping out of luxury cars all week.

The aisles of the market were light with traffic, and that let me know it was going to be an easy day. I came in and looked to see what time I was on the schedule for, only to see that I wasn't on there for the entire week. That wasn't fair. I located Lenora in the bakery section to ask why she'd left me off the schedule. She was going over something with the baker's assistant. I stepped to the side and waited for her to finish talking.

"Hey, miss, are you feeling better now?" she said, touching my shoulder.

"Yeah, I am." I had forgotten about my little lie. "Lenora, I'm not on the schedule."

"Yeah, I didn't put you on because I wasn't sure what was going on with you."

"Okay, well, I'm feeling better, so make sure you put me on for next week and if anyone calls out, I'm available."

"Will do."

I'd needed the break and I had money. Jabril slipped a couple of thousand dollars in my bag before I left, so it was okay. I was able to sit still for the first time in almost a week and take in everything that had happened. I looked at pictures of me and Jabril in my phone. I missed him already. I had been without him for over a year straight, and now a week with him was making me question everything I was doing with my life. I was going to go back out and visit him again in a few weeks.

Once I reached home, Lisa was on the sofa folding clothes when I walked in. It was the first time I had seen her since I had been back.

"Hey, Lisa, where are my boys?"

"They went with Mikey to the library."

"I missed them, and I didn't have to work so I came home and they are not even here."

"They will be back soon, but tell me about your fantasy date. Miss I'm-not-doing-anything-for-my-birthday. What did y'all do? Where did he take you?" Lisa asked.

"Lisa, he took me to this restaurant by a pool, and it was so nice. There were only ten tables in the entire place. We had our own chef and waitstaff. And before that, he came to my school and surprised me. He had flowers and these men singing to me. Then, look—I have a new computer." I opened my new laptop and showed it to her. "If the boys touch this one, I'm going to knock them out. But anyway . . . me and Jabril had such a great time. Oh, look at my bracelet, earrings, and necklace."

"Are they real? Wow, Zakiya, you can't be walking around Philly in those big diamonds, girl. Everything sounds like it was beautiful. He is such a romantic guy."

"He is," I agreed. "I had such a good time, and he wants us to get back together and he wanted me to stay there again. I'm thinking about it."

"Why wouldn't you? What do you have to lose? He treats you so well."

"I don't know, I feel like I have school and my own life now. Then I know you need me to help you out."

"Zakiya, I love you, but I would never want to stop you from living your life. I have the boys enrolled in after-school day care, so don't use us as an excuse."

"I'm not making any excuses."

"You two went through a lot last time, but from what I know of him, he seems like a really good guy. All I'm saying is, don't make up excuses not to be happy."

"I do want to be happy, Lisa. I'm just so confused. I want to be with him, but then I feel like I've come so far. Why would I turn back now?"

"Turn back because you love Jabril and obviously he loves you. That's enough right there. Love can make anything possible. Like me and Mikey... we're going to make it work again. We're getting married, and he's moving back in."

"What! Are you serious, Lisa?" I said angrily. I knew something was up with those two.

"We've been going out on dates and seeing each other for months. He has changed, and he deserves another chance. And the boys need to have him around."

"Lisa, when were you going to tell me? I can't believe you are taking him back."

"You were gone last week. So I'm telling you now. Everyone needs their own happiness, including you. Maybe it is time for you to live your life and stop worrying about us so much."

"So, what are you saying, Lisa?"

"I'm not saying you have to leave, but I don't want to hear any negativity about Mikey."

I didn't have anything to say. I just didn't think I could watch when the bomb exploded again.

I walked out of the house and took a walk. I don't know why I was so angry about the reunion of Mikey and Lisa. It wasn't my relationship. But I know for sure that when Mikey is around, trouble was not far. I already know I'm not staying here with them. When they were together before, I had to referee their fights and arguments, and I wasn't doing it again. Maybe I should just go back to Jabril and worry about myself, like Lisa said, because she doesn't care how I feel. I walked a few blocks and then I called Adrienne. She was like my other big sister. I used to be her nanny and she's the only person who would understand my dilemma with Jabril.

"Hey, Adrienne, I really need to talk to you. I need some advice."

"Can I call you back? I just came in with Asia and need to give her a bath."

"Aw, give Asia a big kiss for me. Adrienne, it will be real quick. I have one question I need to ask you."

"Okay, go ahead."

"Well, it's about Jabril. He came to Philly and surprised me for my birthday. We spent a week together and had so much fun. It was like old times, and he wants us to get back together. But I feel like I want to go to school and have my own life. You know what happened last time. So I'm scared that I'm going to lose myself again. And I don't want to drop out of college."

"Um, that's a rough one. You two had something tragic happen, but I know he loves you. You can take the same courses there as you can here."

"I know I can, and I do see myself with him eventually. I just wanted to make sure I had my own career and money if we ever got back together again. And Jabril kept saying I didn't need school or money because I was with him and I'm going to be his wife."

"I really have to go, but, Zakiya, I will tell you this, nothing you go to school for is going to ever pay more than being Jabril's wife."

CHAPTER 11

Shanice

I sat on the bed and watched television. I needed to figure out what my next move was going to be. I needed to get to some money, but I was done with meeting people through Courtney. I did not want to get shot at again, and fucking old men was over, too. What would be next, getting kidnapped and tortured? I don't think so. My actions were about to change, they had to. This cramped apartment was making me miserable. Aunt Rhonda's aching and whining was making my ears and body hurt. Feeling hungry, I walked into the kitchen. Aunt Rhonda was sitting at the table separating her pills and placing them in a plastic container that had compartments for every day of the week.

"Aunt Rhonda, you going to make dinner?"

"No, I'm not cooking for you. You and Courtney are both trifling. You're almost twenty-five, and you're standing around waiting for someone to cook for you."

"I'm not trifling, and I'm only twenty-three. Every time you ask me for some money, I give it to you, don't I? Maybe you should use the money we give you and buy some real food instead of noodles and microwave stuff," I yelled, walking out the door and slamming it behind me.

I walked to the Puerto Rican corner store called Papi's to get a cheesesteak and fries. I needed my life to change, and now. I called my old head Tone while I was on my way to buy my platter. Tone was someone I used to deal with. He always looked out. He always got some kind of hustle and a way to get money. He has a girlfriend, but when I call him he drops everything. He's ugly and his dick is little, so that's why I can't really be bothered with him. Before he said hello, I said, "Tone, I need some money."

"What's up? How are you today, Shanice?" he said with a smile in his voice, trying to be smart.

"I'm fine, thanks for asking, but I need some money, Tone." I waited for him to talk but there was a long silence. I said hello again and then he said, "It's nice of you to call me, Shanice."

"Tone, come on, stop playing. I'm serious, I need some money. If you can't give me any, then tell me how I can get some."

"I can get you plenty if you let me put you on the track."

"What do I look like, going on the damn track? I'm not hoeing for you."

"I was only joking. What's up, Shanice?"

"I'm not joking. I need to get some money for

real. I'm trying to move. I'm tired of living with my aunt and cousin."

"Be with me then, I'll put you up somewhere nice." I frowned when he said that. No way I'd be laying up with him on a regular basis.

"All right, never mind. You playing too much. I'll talk to you later. Bye, Tone."

"All right, seriously, you can bust a script for me and I'll give you two hundred."

"Okay, I can do that."

I met Tone around the corner from the Rite Aid pharmacy. He handed me the prescription and someone named Edna Fenilli's prescription card. I got in the car so he could explain everything he needed me to do.

"All you have to do is go in and say, 'I'm dropping this off for my mom.' They going to fill it and you going to walk out."

"So, you going to give me two hundred dollars just to do this?"

"Yeah, I'm giving it to you to just handle that."

"All right, what kind of pills am I getting?"

"They Xanax and oxycontin. They go for like twenty a pop on the street."

I had heard of Zaneys but not the other pill.

"All right, I'll be right back." I jumped out of the car and walked into the pharmacy with the prescription. I handed the small piece of paper to the young, Indian-looking woman pharmacist and told her I was dropping it off for my mom. I hoped she couldn't tell it wasn't real. She looked down at the prescription, then back at me. Maybe she was trying to see if I looked like my name could be Fenilli. She looked down at the paper again, scribbled something, and then typed into the computer.

"What's the date of birth?"

"Mine?"

"No, your mom's date of birth."

"Oh, I don't know. My mom always be lying about her age," I said and smiled innocently. The pharmacist cracked a slight smile and told me not to worry. She looked it up in the computer and then told me I could return in a half hour for pickup.

Great—I had to sit in the car with Tone's ass for thirty minutes. All he was going to talk about was how I needed to be with him. When I got back in the car, I noticed he already had a bunch of pills and containers and baggies in the backseat.

"You better cover those pills up before a cop rides past."

"You right." He covered all of the drugs and then he said, "So, what's been up with you?"

"Nothing, trying to get a real job or something."

"A real job doing what?"

"I don't know, something like working downtown somewhere."

"That sounds good and all, but really working for what . . . minimum wage? Like eight dollars an hour times forty? That's not no bread. That's only like three hundred a week. You can just get with the right bull, he can give you more than that a week."

"Naw, getting with the right bull comes with a lotta bullshit, though." I laughed. In the middle of our debate Courtney texted me. She asked what I was doing and when I would be home. I texted her back, telling her about the little scheme I had going with Tone, and then she got me scared.

Girl you can get time for dat. Don't do it.

I texted her back: 4 REAL?

Yeah it's major. Tell Tone to go fuck himself.

Now that Courtney warned me that the small thing I was doing was a big crime, I was scared to go in and pick up what I had dropped off.

"Tone, what you got me into? My cousin just said this shit is heavy. I'm not trying to go to jail."

"Shut up, you not going to jail. They can't call and check up on every prescription. That's why we went after five anyway. The doctor's office is closed. They only fuck with people that look like fiends. You look normal, so you cool."

"Yo, if I get locked up," I said, shaking my head as I got out the car.

"If you get locked up, you don't know me. I'll bail you out, but don't say my name," Tone warned me.

"I know that. I'm not no snitch. I'll be right back." I had already dropped it off, so I figured I might as well finish what I started. I walked back in the pharmacy feeling nervous. I wondered if she had called the cops on me and was thinking I was about to be arrested. I looked up and down the aisles to make sure no cops were behind me waiting to cuff me. I reached the counter and stood in the now crowded area of customers. The pharmacist that had helped me before was in the back counting pills. A short Asian guy with glasses came to assist me. He asked me if I was there to drop off or pick up.

"I'm picking up my mom's prescription. The last name is Fenilli," I answered nervously. He looked in the basket beginning with *F.* I could tell he wasn't really paying attention. He was just trying to get rid of all the people waiting. He asked me to sign a small screen computer and moved on to the next person. I took the bag and nervously walk-ran out the store. I looked all around me to make sure no one was following me. They weren't. I gave Tone the containers of pills and he gave me two hundred dollars. There had to be an easier way to make money.

CHAPTER 12

Adrienne

When Asia was home, she gave the condo a whole other vibe. I would miss out on my morning runs and eating right. All my time went into chasing her around and eating French fries with her. She spilled her sippy cup, wrote on my love seat with pink crayons, but I wouldn't trade it for the world. I love my baby girl. She was watching her favorite show, *Max and Ruby*, while I cleaned up the condo a little. Ian came out into the kitchen and greeted us. He was getting ready to leave out. He said good morning to Asia and she smiled and asked him to have a seat with her and watch television. He said maybe next time. I stood up, kissed him, and told him to have a good day.

Ian and I've been together over a year, and he still hasn't connected with Asia. It doesn't bother me as much as it used to, because it is not her personally, he's just weird-acting sometimes. For some reason, she made him a little uncomfortable. When we first started dating and I told him I had a daughter, he was surprised and said he wasn't ready to be a stepdad. I laughed and assured him she had a daddy and I wasn't looking for another one for her, but I think he still is afraid of getting too close to her.

While Asia watched her shows, I closed my eyes on the sofa and thought about what I was going to do with my life. I had paid my bills yesterday and I hated to see a chunk of money being taken away from my checking account when I didn't know how I was going to put it back. I was still thinking about my club idea, but Ian's cousin made it seem impossible. Maybe I would just try something else like a clothing store. That would be easy. Or maybe I could sell clothes for little girls.

"Asia, girl, what are we going to do today? I think we should go to the park. Would you like that?"

"Mommy, sit. Let's play baby. Here." She put the bald-headed doll in my arms and made me rock her. I rocked the baby doll back and forth a couple of times and then laid her on the sofa.

"Okay, Asia girl, Mommy doesn't want to play baby doll anymore. The baby is tired. Let's get dressed and go to the park." I walked into Asia's sparsely furnished room. I needed to do something with it because it lacked color and decoration. It wasn't anything like her pretty room back home that was filled with purple unicorns and rainbows.

I readied Asia and myself for the park. Just as I

put on Asia's sandals, Ian came back in and asked, "Where are you going?"

"To the park. Why are you back so early?" Before I could speak, he picked me up and swung me around, then bent me back, gave me a deep, long kiss, and said, "I love you, Adrienne Sheppard."

"What's going on? Why are you so excited?"

"I have great news. That production company in California I've been going back and forth with? They called me. They read my script and they're interested. They want to buy *Falcon Hall Boys.*"

"They do, oh my God, congratulations, Ian, this is great!" I jumped up and down and gave him another hug. We were making so much noise we scared Asia. Ian picked her up and kissed her on her cheek, and said, "It's okay, Asia, we are just happy." He then patted her back to calm her.

"So, what happened? When did you speak with them?"

"The producer called as soon as I left out, and we were on the phone for an hour. He read my script a few times and passed it on to his partner. She loved it and they want to make the movie and get it to theaters. I could tell he really read it because he was talking about how much he loved Derrick's character and struggle."

"Baby, I am so happy for you. This is so big."

"I know."

Falcon Hall Boys was Ian's baby. He wrote the screenplay while he was in college. The script was based on his freshman-year experience. Ian and all the other freshmen in his dorm made the promise of not dropping out of college, no matter what. There were fourteen of them when they began, but only six of them graduated. It was really a good script. It detailed everything each Falcon boy had to face on and off campus to get their degree.

"So, what happens next? Are they coming here, or are you going there?"

"They want me to fly out to L.A. by Friday. I didn't even look into the flights yet. Adrienne, I want you to go with me. I need my lady by my side for my big deal." He put Asia down and began to walk toward my laptop.

"Okay, I'll book our flights. I'll go to Philly and drop Asia off at my mom's. She wanted to see her anyway, and then I'll meet you there."

"Babe, this is our beginning."

"Yes, our beginning. I'm so proud of you, Ian."

Asia was in Philly with my mom, and I was on my way to the City of Angels. I like L.A.; it has all the movie stars and warm weather, but every time I'm there I feel like I didn't get to experience everything. It was probably because I was always drained from the five-hour flight and everything being so far apart.

The plan was that after I landed, I was to go to the hotel to change and then we would go to his meeting. Instead, Ian was at the hotel waiting for me. My flight sat on the tarmac for an extra hour. They had to find a gate for us to park in. I called him, apologizing.

"I don't want to be late for my meeting. I know

you can't help that the plane is running late, but I—"

"If you have to, you can go without me to the meeting. That's fine. Maybe I'll meet you there."

"No, what I'll do is just come straight to the airport and you can change in the car."

"Okay, I'll do that."

As soon as they opened the doors of the plane, I pushed my way off and ran to the baggage claim gate. Ian was right there, and we drove straight to his meeting with the film company.

"Baby, I'm so sorry. That stupid flight." I threw my luggage in the back seat of the Ford Taurus rental car and began changing my clothes.

"It is not your fault. You are here now, let's just get there. Can you look up the directions on the phone? I want to make sure we are taking the quickest way. The guy at the hotel gave me directions that are saying to take the 405."

I typed the address of the restaurant into the GPS system. And it gave different directions.

"Ian, it says to take La Cienega Boulevard and we will be there in twenty-two minutes."

We pulled up to Spago in Beverly Hills with five minutes to spare. We entered the restaurant, and the hostess walked us to the table of Sydney Harris. She stood up and greeted us. She was in her early thirties and had a blond bush. She was wearing tights and stilettos with a T-shirt exposing her flat stomach and pierced navel. Also at the table was an older black college-professor-type guy. He introduced himself as her partner, and his name was Arthur Harrington. They both had cocktails in front of them that looked like they hadn't been touched. I was usually a good judge of what people were thinking, but with them all I read was kooky. They didn't look rich or poor, and their serious expressions never changed. After our introductions, I sat quietly while they discussed the script. My only job was to be there for support and to be the pretty, attentive girlfriend.

Sydney and Arthur owned the production company Black Ground Productions. They had a lot of films that went straight to DVD, but they had branched off to limited theater releases. They were good at what they did, and I hoped they gave Ian the opportunity he deserved.

"So, we are very interested in your script. We loved it, we want to see it on the screen, and we think it is going to be a hit," Sydney gushed.

Arthur took over and said, "We are really excited about this project. And we like just about everything. However, there are a few things we would like to change about the script. We want you to meet with our screenwriter and tweak a few things."

"Change? Tweak? What type of things are you talking about?"

"Don't worry. Nothing big. Simple things," Sydney said.

"I think my script is damn near perfect. Everyone that has read my script loves it just the way it is.

So I'm not interested in changing anything, really," Ian said. Which surprised me. He was acting kind of rude to people who wanted to help him fulfill his dream.

"We just want to make the script more commercial. The message itself is wonderful, but we need to maybe add a Hispanic and a white Falcon brother. And the college doesn't have to be a historically black college. They can attend a college in a small town, which makes their bond stronger."

"You are talking about changing the most important part of the script. You want me to change who they are and what they represent. I thank you both for your time and this meeting, but no thank you." Ian surprised me again and shot up abruptly from the table, leaving me behind. They both looked at me like I had an answer for why he was so upset.

"Maybe he'll reconsider. Thank you for your time and consideration. I'll talk to him," I said and thanked them again. I couldn't believe we had flown across the country for a ten-minute meeting.

I caught up with Ian outside the restaurant. He was already on his phone.

"Ian, that was so rude. You could have at least finished hearing what they had to say. You don't even know how much they were willing to offer you."

"I don't care. I'll finance my own movie before I give creative control to anyone. That's an insult. They want to hire a screenwriter to help change my script? The script that I wrote? No, that's not happening."

"But maybe you could have compromised on some things, letting them have this movie to have more control on your next project."

"Why would I do that? The first movie sets the precedent, Adrienne. How about if there isn't a second movie? I have to make my first movie my best movie."

"If that's the way you feel, just wait for someone else to come along and buy it, then. I don't know about the movie industry. You do."

"You're right, I do. Do you know how long people with great scripts wait to go to film? Sometimes forever. I'm not sitting around waiting for someone to come and do my film. Forget that. I'll make my own movies. I'll get the funding."

Ian didn't talk to me during the drive back downtown to our hotel. He was talking out loud while he tried to figure things out for himself.

We entered our room at the Omni Hotel, and I sat on the bed while Ian took a long shower. I just assumed that Ian was going to be upset about the results of the meeting, but he wasn't. He came out the shower renewed, talking on his cell with the towel wrapped around his waist. I kept hearing him say, "Okay, yeah, exactly," and I heard him mention his cousin Keldrick's name a few times. Instead of being devastated, it was like the disastrous meeting just gave him a boost to move forward. He asked Keldrick if he knew of anyone that might be interested in investing in his film.

He finally hung up and said, "I talked to Keldrick and he said he can find me some investors and we are going to make *Falcon Hall Boys* ourselves. We are going to go the film festival route. And we can premiere it at all of the festivals and then get distribution."

"That's good, Ian. That sounds like a plan. I want to open my club, too. Do you think your cousin can get those investors he said he had for me still for my club? Think about it. If we had our own club, you could film your movies. But we can also charge artists to shoot videos in the club. It would be perfect. If your cousin can't get investors for my club, I think I'm just going to use my own money."

"Well, Adrienne, you can invest in my movie. And then we can sell the movie and open the club."

"No, I'm going to open my club first, then maybe I can invest the proceeds from the club into helping you with your movie. The movie can flop, but the club is a sure thing and can bring in money on a weekly and monthly basis."

"Yeah, we'll open the club first, and then I'll get investors for the movie. We are going to make it happen."

Ian and I spent the rest of the weekend making love and mapping out how he was going to get his film funded and how I was going to open my club. We arrived in L.A. with one set of expectations, and we left with new business plans and visions. We were about to be a power couple. Team Us!

CHAPTER 13

Zakiya

I'm twenty-one, and if I decide to go back to school later, I can. I'll always have a home to go to if I ever need to come back to Philly. My sister can have her space and work things out with Mikey if she wants to, and I'm going to live my life and put Zakiya first. I still love Jabril and I know that he loves me. This is what I kept telling myself about my decision to give in to Jabril. I needed a logical reason to leave my life, my job, and my family. If that wasn't good enough, then it was that I didn't want to be without Jabril anymore.

Life is so surreal: One week I was home in Philly and the next week I'm rooting Bril on at a home Oklahoma Thunder game. OKC was crushing the

Mavericks by fifteen and the arena was filled to capacity with everyone screaming, "Thunder up!" This team had come a long way from the one I watched two seasons ago. Jabril kept bringing the ball to the net and scoring. He had ten points and four assists.

At the end of the game, we were up by twenty and won. I was so excited for him and couldn't wait to congratulate him on his win. I waited for Jabril outside the locker room. There were some other wives, girlfriends, reporters, and lucky fans scattered about. I stood patiently; I didn't mingle with anyone, even though people spoke to me and were being polite.

All the women I had met before seemed fake and phony. I always felt like their eyes were scanning and checking for the label on my shoes and my bag. This time I told myself I would make an effort to look a certain way because I was representing Jabril.

As I waited, a petite woman with tanned brown skin and flowing, naturally long, thick brown and blondish hair and eyebrows approached me.

"So, who are you waiting for?" she asked, staring me directly in my eyes. Damn, the first game and it was starting already. Either she was someone who knew Jabril or wanted to get to know him. I knew I might encounter situations like this, but not so soon. I put on a mean face and answered her question.

"I'm waiting for my boyfriend. Why do you want to know?" I asked angrily.

Another woman approached, toting a big round

stomach on a miniature frame and spoke with an accent that didn't sound southern or Midwestern, but was unique. "Who is your boyfriend?"

I wasn't sure what these ladies thought they were going to do to me, but I prepped myself for a full confrontation. Without pausing, I told them I was there for Jabril.

"Jabril, right. What's your name?" the brown-haired woman asked.

"My name is Zakiya. Why exactly do you want to know?"

"Zakiya," they both squealed in unison, startling everyone around us. Then the one with the long brown hair gave me a hug and the other big-bellied woman joined in. I was so confused and didn't know who the women were that were engaging me in an uncomfortable group hug. I pulled back, and the woman with the brown hair started speaking again.

"Oh my God, Zakiya, Jabril has told us everything about you. I feel like I already know you. He asked us how he could get you back, and now you are here. It worked," she said to the petite woman with the stomach. "Sorry if we are frightening you. We are friends of Jabril. I'm Nichelle and this is Christie. I'm married to Lloyd DeBurrows—the guard, number five—and her boyfriend is Omar Mathis—number seventeen, the forward."

"Oh yes, he did mention you. Okay, you did scare me. I was wondering what was going on," I said, relieved. I wasn't really prepared for drama.

"Wow, you are so cute. I can see why he was so desperate to get you back." The big-bellied lady named Christie said.

"Thank you."

"You're welcome. Well, it was great to finally meet you."

I saw Jabril coming down the corridor. He was dressed in a navy blazer and dress pants. He gave me a hug and pecked me a couple of times on the cheek. He wrapped his long arm around my shoulders.

"Good game, number forty-one. I saw you showing off."

"I had someone to show off for." Jabril kissed my cheek again, then placed his duffel bag on his right arm, took my hand, and led us to his truck in the parking lot of the arena.

Coming out of the garage parking lot, a young boy and his father spotted Jabril in the SUV's passenger seat. Jabril rolled down the window, and the man said, "Excuse me, Mr. Smith, can my son have your autograph?" Jabril signed the jersey. Then the man said, "How about a picture? It would mean so much." He then turned to me and asked if I could take a picture of his son, Jabril, and him. Jabril got out of the car and I placed the car in PARK. I snapped a couple of pictures of the father and son and they both thanked Jabril.

"Doesn't that make you feel special?" I asked as we made our way out of the underground parking lot.

"It does. That's why I always stop and talk. When I was young, this basketball camp in Camden took us to a Sixers game. And when it was over, we got to meet the team. When I saw Iverson up close and in person, it was the best feeling in the world. He shook my hand, and I literally didn't wash it for a week. I was talking to my uncle about that. I want to find a way to give back to kids and start a group like the one I was a part of. I want kids to see they can make it like I did, no matter what."

"So, you want to start a foundation or organization or something? I can help you run it."

"Yeah, a foundation. I want one here and one back home. I'm going to ask other guys that have them what exactly you have to do."

"That would be really good, Jabril. Which way do you want me to go? You know these roads out here still confuse me," I asked, turning in to the busy traffic.

"Make a right. Are you hungry? Because I wanted to meet up with my man Lloyd and his wife, Nichelle."

"That's fine. I think I just met her. She came over to me, asking all these questions and hugging me, saying she was so happy I was back."

"She did? Nichelle's cool. Remember I said I was asking them what did they think I should do to get you back? You know how ladies are . . . so every time they seen me, they would ask me about my progress with you. And I would say not yet, but now I can say it worked."

"Really? You have me? How about I have you?"

"You do have me. You have always had me," he said as he lovingly stroked my face. "Nah, Kiya on the real. You don't know how happy I am to have you here."

"Well, I'm happy to be back."

* * *

We met Lloyd and Nichelle DeBurrows at the Skky Bar, which was a restaurant and nightclub. They were already seated at a booth in the corner. They stood up to greet us. Lloyd was a little taller than Jabril and very handsome. His wife, Nichelle, matched his good looks, and together they were a beautiful couple. They were in their early thirties, but both could pass for younger. He had dark walnut-brown skin with closely shaved black hair.

We ordered a round of drinks. While Jabril and Lloyd discussed their win and next game, Nichelle leaned over to me and said, "Sorry if me and Christie scared you earlier. It's just that we were like, is that Zakiya? Jabril has been showing us pictures and telling all of us about you for forever. He was obsessed."

I laughed. "It's okay. I was just confused. Like, who the heck are these ladies and what do they want with me?"

"These two are so tight now, like big brother, little brother. So, where are you from? I'm from Vegas."

"Philly."

"That's right. The East Coast. I have some friends in New Jersey. So, how do you like it out here so far?"

"It is okay. I'm getting back used to it. It is very quiet and a lot slower than what I am used to."

"I know no one here is really trying to be Okie. This city is boring as hell, but I say I'd rather be here with him than at home alone. Lloyd has been in the league eight years, and this is our fifth city. Every February, it's crazy when trade deadlines come up. I'm like, God, where are we going now, but he signed for two years with the Thunder so we are good for now."

"Wow, that's a lot of moving."

"It is, but you learn to just handle it. We have our house here and another in North Carolina that I barely get to see."

"Well, I guess that's a good problem to have."

"Yeah, you are right. I never thought about it like that."

"I like your hair, the colors are really pretty," I said, admiring her toasted brown and blond locks.

"Thanks. I do hair and makeup. I'm also a stylist. I can hook you up with some highlights. Take my number, call me, and we can hang out. I know everyone here. I try to make this place fun. Do you drive?"

"Yeah, I do."

"Oh, then, we are going to best friends. I really don't like driving on the highway, and I've been dying to get to Dallas."

"What's in Dallas?"

"Good shopping. I love the Galleria mall." There was something about Nichelle I liked. She seemed really sweet. She was beautiful but friendly, and those two characteristics don't usually come together.

Chapter 14

Adrienne

When Ian and I returned from L.A., we went right into business mode. He began finding investors for his film and launching a donation website. I started to look for clubs in Miami. I hit up several upscale locations like J-Bar and Kelly Beach Club. I arrived early, when they were setting up, and instead of partying I studied and asked questions. I took their drink menus and stuffed them in my bag. I talked to everyone. I spoke with the hostesses, bouncers, bottle girls, and even the patrons. I asked them what they liked and what they didn't like. I even asked them what they would do differently if they owned a club.

Everyone gave honest answers, and I noticed that the men I spoke to thought it was sweet that I wanted to open a little club. They didn't view me as competition or a real threat, so they gave me all types of information. One of the club owners even gave me copies of his business plan and the numbers to some of the vendors he used.

I knew opening a club would work and no one was going to stop me. I just needed the perfect place. I wanted something in South Beach, but then I had an epiphany—it came to me when I called and got quotes on renting a building. I couldn't afford a club in Miami. The rent was twenty thousand dollars a month. That just didn't seem realistic. What if I had a bad month? They wanted six months up front and a deposit. Even if I charged thirty dollars a night and was open Wednesday through Saturday with bottle service it would be difficult to accomplish. I knew I had to rethink my plan.

My thoughts were interrupted by a call from Cherise. I frowned at the phone. I didn't like her, and I'm positive I wouldn't be interested in anything she had to say, but I answered anyway.

"Hello."

"Adrienne, this is Cherise. I'm calling to talk to you about Malaysia."

"Hey, Cherise, listen, we don't have anything to discuss. Have your fiancée call me. I don't talk to third parties. Bye."

"But . . . I . . ."

"Whatever it is, Cherise, I don't care." She was so prim and proper, and she didn't know how to handle my hood side. But I really couldn't talk to her. I had to figure out how I was going to get my club open.

Chapter 15

Zakiya

Jabril was back on the road for three games, and it was just me and his mom in the house. This was the part I didn't get. Jabril wanted me here, but he was barely here himself. I missed him a lot and wondered what he was doing when he was away. This time around I promised myself I would stay off the Internet and gossip websites. They were all full of lies and never made me feel good reading them. And I knew Jabril was a different guy now. Not only did he tell me, but he showed me by spoiling me with gift after gift.

That was the only good thing about him going away, he always came home with earrings, bracelets, and bags for me. I now had a collection of Chanel, Celine, and Louis Vuitton bags.

He has been so loving and caring, always calling

and texting me throughout the day no matter where he is. Then I also like that he is hanging out with a veteran player like Lloyd. Lloyd is a good family man at home and a model player on the court. Nichelle's husband was just an all-around good guy. Jabril is learning a lot from being with him and is doing great, with the exception of his little weed habit. I don't know where he picked that one up from, but I wish he would put it back down. He smokes everywhere, all around the house, like a pothead. His eyes are always red, and the other night he fell asleep smoking a blunt. That could have caused a fire that killed us all. My solution to that is to keep hiding his weed from him until he quits.

Claudette seemed to be very happy I was home with her and had been attempting to fill my days with activities for her and me. Claudette needed a boyfriend or a hobby. She is almost forty, and it seems like her life is more consumed now with Jabril and what he is doing than ever before.

"I want you to take a ride with me, Zakiya," Claudette called out to me.

"Where to?"

"To this place with this really good chicken."

"Claudette, I'm not pregnant anymore, so we can't go out to eat all the time like we used to."

"It doesn't matter. You won't gain any weight anyway. Look how skinny you are still. Come on and take the ride with me. Eichen has the best fried chicken anywhere. There isn't anything else to do here but eat like you're pregnant."

"No, I'll pass."

"Well, speaking of babies, when do you think you and Jabril will be giving me a grandchild?"

"Are you serious, Claudette? Are you really ready to be a grandmom?"

"Not really, but I know it is no time like the present, and I'll be a Glam mom. What I do know is Jabril lost you and his firstborn. He was pretty messed up about that. And now that you two are working it out, it is only right if you give him the child that he lost, too."

"I'll keep that in mind, Claudette."

"Please do. I'll see you later. I'll bring you some food back so you can get some weight on you to carry my grandbaby."

Claudette left out and paid very little mind to our conversation. If she wants Jabril to have a baby, she can have one for him. Before I came back here, I made sure I was on birth control. There will be no babies anytime soon.

With the house to myself, I was going to clean up some and relax. They have a housekeeper who comes a few times a week, but Jabril doesn't allow her in his room. He says she moves things and he can't find his stuff. He'll probably be mad at me, because I've been organizing and sorting his stuff. He had so many jeans and shirts and sneakers that he doesn't even wear. I was thinking about giving a lot of his things to a shelter or something.

During the cleaning, I called Lisa, Miles, and Kyle. Afterward I returned Nichelle's call because she'd been calling me.

"Hey, Zakiya, I was waiting for you to call me. I wanted to see if you wanted to go to lunch with me and Christie, Omar's girlfriend. You know, the one that was with me at the game."

"Jabril's mom is going to kill me. She asked me to go out with her, but I said no."

"Come on, we want to get to know you more. I can come and pick you up, or you can come and get me, and then we'll drive over to her house because she is over in Edmond. It is like ten minutes away."

"Okay, I'll come get you. What is your address?"

The DeBurrowses' compound was huge, with a round, asphalt driveway with trees in the center. There were three cars parked in the garage. Nichelle met me at the large mahogany double doors. She was still getting dressed and told me to come in. We walked up her staircase. I admired the large, sparkling chandelier that set in the hallway that led to a kitchen and dining room area. Down the long hall, she stepped inside of her bedroom, and we entered her closet, which looked like a small boutique.

"This closet is huge. Wow," I said, looking around.

"Thanks, but this house is a rental. Our real house in Charlotte is way bigger." I admired all of her clothes, belts, and shoes neatly displayed.

"You can borrow something if you like. I'll take you shopping and pick out some things for you. I told you I'm a stylist and I do makeovers. You are going to need my services sooner than later. My salon is in the basement."

"What's wrong with what I have on? I thought I did a good job dressing myself." I laughed even though she was politely insulting me.

"You did, I suppose. You just look a little plain. You need some pop. Don't worry, we'll go shopping."

We drove to Christie and Omar's grand-looking house. It set alone in a fairly new development. As we approached the door, I smelled a strong, disgusting animal scent.

Nichelle knocked on the door and said, "I'm warning you now, her house is always a mess. But don't worry, we won't be here long."

I said okay, wondering how bad of a mess this beautiful house could be, but once Christie invited us in, I saw instantly what Nichelle meant. Christie was tiny, cute, and pregnant, and her house was a beautiful mess. The entire downstairs was painted a light yellow with white trim, and all the windows were open big and bright, letting in the natural sunlight. The window fixtures and furniture weren't modern but elegant, but none of that mattered because the entire house was in need of a deep cleaning.

How could a mansion be so filthy? There were piles of clothes on the floor, like someone was sorting clothes and was about to wash them but then decided they weren't going to. It smelled like a few dogs inhabited the premises. I saw miscellaneous dishes on the dining room table. There were visible stains on the wall and on the tables. In the dining room, there was a picture half of the size of a wall of her and her man, Omar. He had a nappy bush and looked more like a person who asked for change on the street than a multimillionaire basketball player. He looked like all he did was get high. His tattoos were bright and colorful, like Jabril's, but many more and larger. She greeted us, then removed boxes from the chairs of her dining room table and told us we could have a seat.

"Does it smell?" she asked and sniffed, then grabbed a bottle of air freshener. "Omar keeps those dogs caged up downstairs, and all they do is poop. I refuse to go out and walk them, they might bite me."

"Girl, how are you living with animals you can't even maintain?"

"I don't know, I guess the same way I'm dealing with his kids. Nichelle, I meant to call you back to tell you I can't go. I'm babysitting. His kids are here." As if on cue, three children ran down the steps, screaming and hollering: two identical-looking boys about seven and one little baby girl who looked to be around three.

"How did his kids get here?"

"His baby mother left them on the steps. I don't know what she was thinking. She came over last night, rang the bell, pulled off yelling for him to spend some time with your kids. She didn't know he wasn't here. I go to the front door, and they are standing there with their bags."

"What! Oh my God. She is crazy," Nichelle said.

"Right, because doesn't she know when you give up the kids, you lose the child support check? She gets twelve thousand a month."

"That's a shame. What kind of woman leaves her children on the steps?" I added, shaking my head.

"The kind that wants a babysitter. But you know, Omar is just like, whatever. She is making him appreciate me even more." She grabbed a small shoe box off the crammed table and said, "Oh, look what Omar brought the baby. Mommy and baby are both going to be rocking Dior. My daughter is coming out with a mean shoe game."

"You are so tacky. They are cute, but not because they are Dior," Nichelle said, glancing at the shoes.

"How many months are you?" I asked, admiring her stomach.

"Six months."

"I knew you were getting big," Nichelle said. "That stomach just appeared out of nowhere."

"I know. Omar was just talking about that. He was like, one day you tell me you missed your period. Then the next day your stomach is poking out."

"I know you are so excited." I smiled, still focusing on her belly.

"We are," Christie said. She looked over at me and placed my hand on her firm stomach. "Go ahead, you can touch it." Her round stomach was so perfect and cute. It was the first time I was ever interested in a pregnancy.

"Wow, you are so big. I carried big like that, too."

"You have a baby?"

"No. We had one. Me and Jabril lost a baby. It wasn't full term."

"I'm sorry. Jabril told us that. I forgot." She approached me and rubbed my back.

Just like Nichelle told me, I needed a makeover. She changed the subject and put Christie on the spot for her lack of cleaning. She was very direct, but cute and funny so Christie couldn't be offended. "So, Christie girl, what's up with this house? Are you going to allow the dirt to take over? You really need to clean."

"What I need is his kids not to come here and for his family to stop calling me, asking me to Western Union them money every day. Then maybe I could sit and think about cleaning up."

"Why don't you just call an agency to come?"

"You right. That's what I'll do."

"Yes, they will come and clean this dirty place up, or run from the challenge." Nichelle laughed and I tried not to. "When Omar gets home off the road, this place should be spotless. A man doesn't want to come home to a dirty house, Christie."

"You're right. I have to get everything ready for the baby anyway. You know, I'm breast-feeding my baby. I'm not running all around. A mother is supposed to be in the house with their child. Omar already said he is going to be a hands-on father. I'm happy about that, because I don't want to be the chick that has to be following my man all around the country." Christie sneered.

"Yeah, I don't want that, either. That's why I'm glad my man invites me to meet him on the road. A bunch of babies would stop all that. You don't have to be that chick, but you keep up on what he is doing," Nichelle shot back.

"No, Nichelle, I was just saying we have to be smart when it comes to these men. If we don't do our job, there are groupies ready to do it for us. And they won't complain about doing a bunch of whore activities."

"Whore activities! You are so funny, Christie," Nichelle repeated, and I laughed, taking in all the information she was giving.

"No, I'm serious. Even with this baby in my stomach, I'm still dropping it every time he asks in a new, exciting way. I never say no. You better get you a pole and get to bouncing." Christie began bouncing her hips and butt at us inappropriately.

"You are not lying. Remember we were all out in New York and that random chick was all over Lloyd after he said, 'I'm sorry, I'm not interested,' and pointed to his ring? She still came back all persistent with her little New York voice saying, 'You ain't never have it like this in your life.' I had to stand up and say, 'Hey, hello, um, I'm his wife; he's married, and I'm sure he has.' Then she said, 'Oh, my bad.'"

"Like I don't know what would make someone want to be with someone's husband or boyfriend. I would feel so bad," I said, joining in the conversation.

"These groupies don't have a conscience. You have to watch them, especially with your man, Zakiya. Jabril is handsome, young, and still fresh meat, and they are going to be all over him," Christie added.

"I know, the last time we were together these girls I didn't even know were calling me ugly and talking about me on the blogs."

"You're beautiful. Do not waste your time reading any of those sites. I can't read them. If I did, I would go crazy. Once I saw this blog, where they were discussing how long Lloyd and I have been together. They even had pictures from my wedding. It was insane. The entire time I'm reading the site, I was thinking, *Who has enough time to sit around and come up with this stuff?* Get a life," Nichelle said.

"The girls on that site are the ones you have to watch out for. They are all envious wannabes. All I say is, handle your business before someone handles it for you. We have to keep them satisfied and they won't cheat," Christie said, bouncing her butt in our direction again.

"You are really crazy, Christie. We are out of here. We're hungry. Go back to watching your stepkids."

We left and were on the way to our late lunch date. Nichelle must have read my mind. I was thinking about everything Christie had said about making sure I keep Jabril satisfied or someone else will.

"Don't pay Christie any mind. She has issues. What she said is only halfway true. As insane as she is, she knows Omar does not cheat on her. Don't worry. I haven't heard anything about Jabril, either. So you are good, but my husband—that's another story. He's cheated before. That's why we are always going out and taking trips. I try to keep him so busy that he doesn't have the stamina or the time. Zakiya, believe me, you can't play detective. It doesn't work. That's why I just let Lloyd know I'm here, but I don't wrap my life around his. I meet Lloyd on some road games, but the truth is, some of them cheat. We've been together for a long time, and if he is ever ready to go, I will open the door for him and say good-bye. That's why we don't have any children yet, because that would make it harder to work on us. When he retires, we may start trying, but it is hard to raise a child when the father is never home. All I can say is, make yourself happy and you have to remember who you are. That's the key."

"You're right," I said, taking it all in.

Nichelle and Christie said a lot, and I tried to file all the information they gave me. I had so much in common with Nichelle and Christie. They knew exactly what I was going through, and because of that I felt an instant connection with them.

This time would be different than the last, because Jabril and I had an unofficial pact. He wasn't going to cheat again, and I would make sure he had no reason to. And if he did, I was going to leave.

Chapter 16

Adrienne

Ian's cousin Keldrick was an asshole, but he was right: I couldn't open a club in Miami. It wasn't my city, and I didn't have the capital or enough connections. Instead of opening a club in Miami, I am opening a club in Philly with a Miami feel.

I found a small club in Philly that holds five hundred people. It is perfect, not too small and not too big. It is around the corner from the SugarHouse Casino, tucked away on a small street.

The previous club hadn't been open in a few years. It had been closed down for allowing underage drinking. The club owner wanted to reopen, but he didn't have the money. He was happy to lease it to me for one year. A year is enough time to know if I want to keep going. I'm not getting any investors or going to any bank to get a loan.

This is all on me. And the club's success will be all mine, too.

I've decided I want to only attract a certain affluent clientele. So my club will be an all-VIP-exclusive club. I'm going in business to make a profit, so I only need people with an annual income of over a hundred thousand coming to my establishment. I want my club to attract celebrities, powerful businessmen, athletes, singers, rappers, doctors, lawyers, and political figures. The motto of the club will be, "If you are not someone, you have to know someone to get in." Elitism at its best.

In order for the club to be a success, I must have the best of everything. The best liquor, the prettiest bottle girls, the right atmosphere. I'm placing ads with some modeling agencies, on college campuses, and online. I want my bottle girls to have great shapes and beautiful faces. And I'm getting a mixture of all sizes and colors.

We will be the place where the cool kids party, and I'm going to be one rich bitch.

Chapter 17

Shanice

I needed to be working somewhere. I'm twenty-three and I never had a real job. I'm not doing any more little hustles for Tone, and no "dating" with Courtney. I did graduate from high school, so I should be able to find something. I know how to speak, but I'm not that good with my writing. I never was. Back in school, I just learned if you were quiet and nice to the teacher, they would pass you. If that didn't work, I would just tell them about my mom being in jail and they would feel sorry for me and give me a good grade.

I know I'm not dumb, but sometimes I don't spell things right. I remember my fourth grade teacher telling me to sound things out, and that usually works, but a lot of words don't sound like they are written. And I don't want to get a job and be spelling things incorrect and get fired.

I walked to the corner store to get a newspaper to look in the job section. There were a lot of jobs, but you had to fill out the applications online.

I want to work in a hospital or downtown somewhere, maybe in an office. I know them kind of jobs pay money. I hear even the cleaning people get money at the hospital. If I was to get a good job like that, I'll have enough money to get my own place.

I was sitting at the kitchen table, when Courtney came in the apartment, disturbing my finding-a-job flow. She had three big department store shopping bags. I knew she wasn't out shopping without me.

"Where you get money from?" I asked.

"My friend."

"Your friend who?"

"This older guy I met. He's married, but he out on disability and got this cleaning company. I tried to get money from him, but he said he only had credit cards. So, I had to get what I could. He was the worst, telling me how his back hurt, but you see, I got him right in the mall. So, you going out with me tonight, right? I'm going to put Ayana to sleep and then I'm out."

"Probably not. I'm tired."

"You sure you don't want to go?"

"No, I said I'm tired. Bitch, stop asking me." She was working my nerves, all happy because she had new stuff from the mall. I didn't have time for her and focused my attention back on my job search.

"So, did you give my mom the rest of the money?

I told my mom we was going to give it to her tonight." I knew she wasn't asking me for my half of the rent when she just got me robbed and was coming in from a shopping trip. I stood up and peeked in her bag. She had a new pair of Louboutin shoes. I held up her one and said, "You could have paid the rent twice with these."

She snatched her shoe back and said something dumb. "I need those shoes to go out tonight, and I told you he only had credit cards."

"Well, you could have got him to give you gift cards and we could have sold them."

"I'll get my money, and you need to get yours. So, why don't you come out with me?"

"No, I'm tired, and I don't have anything new to wear or anyone to take me to the mall."

"Why you ain't call one of them guys we met the other night, or ask Tone for some more money?"

"I'm done with all of that, and I'm not meeting anyone with you. I don't feel like getting shot at again."

"Bye, girl, that was a onetime thing. You didn't get shot, did you?"

"Who says next time I won't?" She couldn't answer that question. She went in the room, and I returned to looking for jobs. All of them wanted a résumé. I didn't have one of those. What was I supposed to put on a résumé if I've never had a job? I would have to make something up.

I didn't see anything worthwhile until I reached the *W* section and saw jobs for waitresses. I could be a waitress and give people they food and talk to them. I remember this girl, name Char, we went to school together and she said she made money every day. I saw her in the mall once and I thought she was a stripper because she had all these one dollar bills, but she said she got tips. I searched in the waitress section of the want ads, and there was a job for a Waitress/Bottle Girl for a new night club on Delaware Avenue. The job description read: *Bottle Girls needed. No experience necessary. Requirements: Pretty, Great Body, Hardworking and ready to make $$$. Must be familiar with serving and selling alcohol.*

They were having interviews from three to six tomorrow. I needed to be there. What was I going to wear? How would I wear my hair? Somebody had to give me some more money. I dialed Tone, and he answered the phone sounding hype.

"Yooo, what's up?"

"I need a ride tomorrow and I need some money to get my hair done for this job interview."

"Larry, yeah, you caught me at a bad time. This shit out here is a little light. Hit me up next week and I'll have it by then."

"Huh? Who you talking to? Who is Larry? The interview is tomorrow. I can't wait until next week."

"Yeah, Larry, man. Yo, holler at me later. I might be able to help you out." After the third time he called me Larry, I realized he must have been with his girlfriend and he couldn't talk.

The next morning I got up and was trying to figure out how I was going to make myself look like something with nothing. My weave was all tangled and messy. I should have wrapped it before I went to bed. Then my nails were chipped, but somehow

I had to get it together. I was going to stand out and they were going to hire me.

Looking down at the time on my phone, I realized I didn't have enough time to get my hair done or throw another weave in. I jumped up out of the bed and started pulling out my tracks and finding something to wear.

"Where are you going?" Courtney asked.

"To this interview at this club to be a bottle girl. All you have to do is just walk around the club and give out the drinks. It said no experience needed, just be cute and ready to work hard and make money. You should go with me."

"Um, no, that don't sound like something I would want to do. I like popping bottles, not serving them. You going without getting your hair done?"

"I was going to try to go run and get a wig and a refill on my nails. I have to figure out a way. I'm not really trying to spend my last."

"Um, you look a mess, but good luck."

I left out the room and down the hall. Aunt Rhonda was sitting on the sofa. It was going to be hard to get out of the house without her asking me for some money. Ayana was sitting in the living room playing with her puzzles.

"Ayana, go in the room with your mom." Ayana followed her grandmother's command, but on the way down the hall, she asked me to take her to the store. I dug in my bag and gave her two dollars. I shouldn't have pulled out any money because Aunt Rhonda was counting what was left in my hand.

"Leave Shanice alone. Shani, I need a beer. Let me get three dollars."

"I don't have it."

"Yes, you do. Come on, help me out." I pulled out ten dollars and handed it to Aunt Rhonda. It was funny how she always nickeled and dimed me, but never asked her daughter for anything. She was one of the other reasons I needed to move out.

I left out the apartment and began walking to the subway. I had to walk to the sub and then get on the El. There were guys all on Girard Avenue, standing around saying ignorant stuff as I walked past. I learned to ignore them since I was young. If you say thank you, then they would take it a step further, and I didn't need any drama.

My phone started ringing right as I was walking down the subway steps. I thought it was Courtney, saying that she changed her mind, but Courtney's voice wasn't that deep.

"Who this?"

"It's Tone, yo, I got some money, I can help you. I'll be there in a few, and I'll drive you where you need to go."

"Naw, you was fronting real hard last night."

"I had to do that for my chick. I was at her house last night. Where you at?"

I did need a ride and money, and Tone could supply me with both. I told him to meet me in front of the KFC.

* * *

He pulled right up to the curb in his navy blue F-150. His engine was souped up and making a lot of noise. I got in and started giving it to him.

"I'm still mad that you was calling me Larry last night. Talking dirty to me for your chick. I don't play that shit."

"Be quiet, Shani. If you was doing what you was supposed to do, I wouldn't have to mess with nobody else."

"Whatever."

"So, where do you need to go?" he asked, eyeing my curves.

"Stop looking at me like that. I have to get ready for this interview. I need to get a wig and my nails done real quick."

"How much you need?"

"Enough to buy both." He handed me four hundred dollars, which was love. I only needed like a hundred. I was going to use some of that on my nails and wig, and the rest would land in Aunt Rhonda's hand so she would leave me alone.

We stopped at the Sophie Beauty Hair Store. There were wigs on mannequins with blank expressions in every direction and a variety of colors. I touched a wig I liked. It was cute, but too basic. The girl who worked there asked me if I needed help. I told her I did, but I would need a little bit more time. I just wanted to get something that was long and sexy, but sophisticated, also. I looked up and down at the rows of wigs, and when I found the perfect wig with a straight bang, I asked the salesgirl to grab it. She told me that I had to buy a stocking cap to try it on.

I purchased the cap and had a seat as she fitted

and styled the wig on me. It was pretty on me, even though it wasn't the best, but it would have to do.

After getting my wig, I got my nails done and my eyebrows arched and then got Tone to take me downtown.

The club was in a warehouse building on a small block down the street from the casino. I rang the bell and knocked on the door. No one answered, and then a handyman was walking out and I walked in. The club was in the process of being renovated, and there were workers all around hammering and power-drilling things together. There were a few people walking around the club. Looking around, I talked to the first person I saw.

"Hi, I'm here for the bottle girl position."

"You have to talk to the woman over there." He pointed to a pretty woman with curly hair pulled back into a bun. She had golden yellow skin and appeared to be about twenty-five or so. She looked over and told me to have a seat, fill out an application, and someone would interview me. There were a few people ahead of me. One was pretty with dark chocolate skin; she was wearing a navy suit and black business pumps. Looking at her, I wasn't sure if my jeans and shirt were dressy enough.

"Excuse me, are you supposed to be dressed up?"

"No, you don't have to, but I was coming from another interview and I came straight here so I didn't change. Don't worry. You look nice enough for this job."

"Oh, okay, thank you." She was real professional and seemed like she might work at a bank or something. We started talking. She was from New York and her name was Darcel. She was in school at Temple University. She said she was looking for a job because her scholarship money was short. She was a college girl, but I liked her. She was confident but not cocky.

Me and the girl Darcel talked some more until it was her time to interview. Even though the club was still being fixed up, I could see myself working there. I hoped I got the job.

Darcel came out of her interview and told me she got it and good luck. They called me into the interviewing area. I stood up, walked over, and smiled. It was the woman from earlier and a guy with dreads. He looked kind of mean. I asked them how they were doing and told them it was nice to meet them. The woman asked if I had any experience.

"Yeah, at this place around my neighborhood called Limelight. It's like a neighborhood place that everybody goes to," I lied.

"So, you've served drinks before?"

"Yeah. I mean, yes, I have." I was getting nervous. They both were staring at me. I just stood there, waiting for them to ask me the next question and trying not to mess up. The woman looked down at a yellow notepad and then she said, "This is a copy of your drink menu. Your job will be to service our guests and get them to enjoy themselves, but spend money in the process. If someone orders tequila and if they don't ask for a specific brand, you have to be ready to convince them to buy the most expensive bottle of Patrón. Do you think you could do that?"

"Yes, if you hire me, I can do that. Definitely. Like, I'm real good at talking to people and meeting people and when I smile at a dude, it's a wrap." The man stepped away to answer a call.

The woman laughed a little, and then continued, "Okay, that's good to know. You seem outgoing, but what's going on with your hair? Is that a wig?"

"Yes, it is."

"I don't like it, it looks cheap. You are cute, but you need to get your hair done."

"To be honest, I didn't have time to get my hair done and put my lashes on. I look a lot better when I'm dressed," I answered, feeling insecure.

"Yeah, and that earring in your eyebrow has to go, too."

I reached up and took it out. "No problem, I just really need this job, and I promise if you hire me, I will sell and keep your customers coming back. I'm going to make them buy bottles, trust me."

"So if you want the job it is yours, if you get your hair done. We want stylish, pretty girls in our VIP, none of those bright-ass color weaves. The whole entire club is VIP. Nothing about my club is ghetto."

"Oh, so this is your club. That's good. You look young yourself. That's what I'm talking about, women handling their business. What you like, twenty-five?"

"No, I'm almost thirty. And yes, it's my club. And we are opening in a couple of weeks. You will get a call to come in for a fitting for your uniforms. Do you know your measurements?"

"No, I don't have no measurements."

"Your bust, waist, and hips."

"Oh yeah, them, I got measurements. I got a lot of them. I'm sorry I didn't understand what you were talking about. I don't know them offhand but I can find out."

"Okay, well, I need you to get them to me as soon as you can. You are hired."

"Thank you so much," I said, running up to her. I was so excited I was about to hug her. I didn't know if that was professional or not, so I stopped myself and shook her hand. I couldn't believe I had a real job. I went back out to the truck, so excited. I told Tone the good news and thanked him for bringing me. He said it was cool and that I owed him one.

CHAPTER 18

Adrienne

Sometimes you have an idea that you think might be good, but then when things start moving so fast and get put in motion, before you can blink you know it is your destiny. That's how I felt about my soon-to-be club. Belize was meant to be, and I was about to come up.

I invested over a hundred and fifty thousand of my own money in this club. I had only thirty thousand dollars left in my account. Taking that big chunk out was painful, but I believe my club is going to take me to another level.

Belize Lounge was named after a Central American country, and Ian couldn't understand why. He didn't think it made sense to name the club after a place I'd never been to that did not hold any significance. He was right. It didn't hold any significance; honestly, I just couldn't think of any creative names that weren't already in use. I saw Belize somewhere online, and I liked the way it rolled off my tongue and sounded exotic. So that's the name I picked. We also disagreed with the club being all VIP. He hated my motto, "If you are not someone, you have to know someone to get into Belize."

Ian believes it is a horrible idea to be a pricey club in this economy and that I am leaving out the everyday working person who wants to have a good time. To that I say, who cares about the nine-to-fivers. My club is not for them. If they can't afford to buy a drink, then they can stay home and order a pizza and drink a beer.

Ian has really been getting on my nerves a lot lately. Moving from Miami to Philly has not been easy, and it was kind of unexpected, but he didn't have to come with me. He said until Belize is up and running, he's going to come back and forth to help me. I would have understood if he didn't. I know he has so much going on himself. Ian has already raised forty thousand for *Falcon Boys.* He needs about sixty thousand more to start filming. I thought about loaning him some of the money, but decided against it.

To be honest, I don't really think it is the move that is bothering him. I think it is just hard for him to see me get up and make moves and be business-minded. Since we've met, he has only known docile Adrienne. The Adrienne who wasn't on her grind, the Adrienne who was always going to the beach, relaxing in the condo, and always had time to watch his clip or take his call, but right now I'm busy. I'm trying to make something big happen, and he just has to understand. I feel like we are somewhat of a team, but then I feel like I have to make things happen for myself first, Team Adrienne.

Belize's color scheme was deep purple, white, and a light purplish-pink color. The club's trendy tables and long, white cube sofas were shipped from a company in Sweden. The chandeliers and lighting was done by a local company that specialized in huge events like weddings and concerts. Belize was costing me a small fortune, but in the end it will be worth it. I paid attention to every detail, from the glowing purple bar to the lit dance floor. The ceiling and wall panels resembled lavender crystals and illuminated the long white sofas. The white translucent drapes throughout the club gave it a sexy ambiance and mystique. I had three sections: the blue section, the rose section, and the yellow section. The sun, the sand, and the sky of Miami. The blue section was reserved for my ultra-VIPs, the rose section for mid-level patrons, and the yellow would be for people just happy to be in the club who didn't have bottle service. I still needed the city's License and Inspections to come out and approve a few things, but so far we were on track. I didn't want a kitchen in the club; I would just hire a caterer for special events.

Belize's security was made up of big, muscular men. One in particular was my big guy named Mack. He was six-six and diesel. His arms were ripped like weapons. I don't think anyone would dare to get rowdy with him. If they tried to step to him, they would be kissing the sidewalk with just one punch.

Then I have really cute bottle girls. They are going to be the nucleus of the club. I know that if I have beautiful women in my club, the men will come just to look at them. My bottle girls are like Playboy bunnies, but in all shapes and sizes. Their uniforms are short purple and black corset dresses with straps, which match the décor of the club. I only hired four girls for now; when I expand, I'm hiring more. My first Belize beauty is Darcel; she is in college and has beautiful cocoa-brown skin and jet-black hair. Darcel is beauty and brains in one. Next there was Summer; she has a blond straight, long bob that stops right above her boobs. She has green eyes and never-ending long legs. The other girls on my team are Joi and Shanice. Joi has a shape that she doesn't hide and kind of exotic features; she's a little weird but sexy. Then there is Shanice; she is really pretty with dimples. She's a little ghetto, but I saw this hunger in her, so I hired her. She reminded me of my younger self. I think she is going to be good. I know all of them are. Then I have my bartenders, Terrance and Waliq; they both look like baby bodybuilders. They will hurry and make the sexy drinks, and the girls will take them to our guests.

Being back in Philly was perfect: I could stay in my first house and my mom could help with Asia when she wasn't with DeCarious. My mother has been very happy since we've been back. She has taken Asia to the zoo, museums, and the aquarium. Her being around has been a tremendous help, because opening a club is not easy.

CHAPTER 19

Zakiya

I was dressed in a Victoria's Secret black cut-out teddy that I ordered online. It was borderline slutty, but I knew Jabril would love it. I was trying to step up my game and keep it sexy for Jabril. I heard the other ladies discussing what they did for their men before a long stretch of away games. Christie said it would keep their minds on you and their hands off any random chicks. Jabril is the only man I have ever been with, so I have no experience with giving him *head*, as he says. I kind of wish I was doing a little something while we was apart, because now he seems so much more advanced than I am. He wants to have sex all the time. He is asking me to try all these different positions and to take it from the back. I'm not complaining, it feels good, but I just want to be able to keep up with him.

My goal and my intentions were to be sexy and give Jabril something to think about, but my gag reflex kept being set off every time I placed Jabril's manhood in my mouth. I made horrible noises, and tears were forced from my eyes.

"Watch your teeth. Ow, Zakiya, stop." He pushed me up. I had bitten him accidentally again.

"Are you okay?" I asked, jumping up.

"I don't know, watch out. It hurts. Get me a wet washcloth." I ran in the bathroom, ran cold water over a cloth, and came back and applied the cloth to the tip of him.

"I'm sorry, Jabril. I didn't mean to bite you. I just don't know how . . ." I said as I wiped away the few drops of blood.

"I know you are. You'll learn, it is no big deal. I love you regardless. Ask one of your girlfriends how to do it."

"Lie back down. I want to learn now. I can do it, I know I can." I looked at his hard, long erection and attacked it again, trying to conquer it. Two minutes later it happened again. I felt like I was choking and I started almost throwing up.

"Is everything okay? Who's sick? Jabril, are you okay?" Claudette asked, knocking on the bedroom door.

"Yeah, Mom. We are fine," he yelled out. He leaped up from the bed and said, "I have to go. It's okay, Zakiya, I love you."

"I know you do, but I want to do it well for you before you leave." I sighed, defeated.

"I can't. I have to go. We'll continue when I get back, so be ready. I'll be back on Saturday." I just sat on the bed in my lingerie, looking sad. "Zakiya, come on, it is just a few days. Kiya, don't act like that."

"A few days for you, Jabril. It seems a lot longer for me." I don't know why saying good-bye never got easier, but it didn't.

"Wendell already transferred the money into your account. Go shopping or something. If you don't have enough while I'm gone, just ask my mom," he said as he dressed.

"I'm not going to spend eight thousand dollars in four days, Bril. I told you I still have money from the last time. Wendell doesn't have to put money in my account every week. I don't need anything else. I have enough." Every week at the same time Wendell had been putting money in my checking account. I had sixty thousand dollars just sitting there that I really hadn't even touched and Jabril still gave me cash and his credit cards to use.

"You're my chick, Kiya. You are going to stay with the best. All right? I love you. See you when I get back." He slapped my butt and said it was getting big.

"Is it really?" I jumped off the bed and looked in the mirror at my butt. "Your mom said the same thing, and then asked if I was I ready to have her grandchild. I told her she was crazy."

"Why is she crazy? You do want to have my baby again, right?"

"Yeah, I do, but not right now, Jabril. I mean, one day."

"Yeah, we will have to talk about that waiting," he said as he gave me a big smooch on my lips and whispered, "Please have my baby. Please, I want my son so bad, Kiya."

"JabriI, I want to finish college one day, and I want us to be married."

"We will get married and right after you have the baby, you can go to school. I'm going to get you a nanny. I'm going to get two nannies and then my mom will help us, too. Kiya, I can buy anything I want in the world, but the only thing I want is for you to give me what I don't have already. And that's a baby, a family with you." Jabril was making a baby sound so great, but there were so many other factors involved. I temporarily satisfied him with an *I'll think about it* and that was as good as a yes to him.

He and Claudette exited the house, and once again I waited for him to return.

CHAPTER 20

Zakiya

With friends here in Oklahoma City, life was so much easier. I didn't have to worry about being bored and hanging with Claudette every day when Jabril wasn't here. Nichelle and Christie kept my schedule busy. We did everything together, from shopping to spa days. We even took a road trip to the Galleria mall in Dallas last week. And, of course, we hang out with our guys, too, for dinners, the movies, and date nights. When they were in town, we ate at the best restaurants in the city. They had the money to pay, but the restaurants would always comp our meals, just to get a picture and an autograph to say players from the Oklahoma Thunder ate there.

I finally met Omar and I don't really like him. He is mean and just looks like a true drug-addicted-looking weirdo. Christie says he doesn't do drugs and is a health nut, but I don't believe it. I swear I counted thirty tattoos on his body. I don't know what Christie could see in him other than his paycheck. He should be so happy, that he has a good woman in his corner who puts up with his baby's mother and his crazy family.

Nichelle reminded me a little of Adrienne; she was just so together and knew a little about everything. What I really liked about her is that even though she had Lloyd's money, she still had her own passion. She did hair and styled people by appointment only. She had a small client list, but she still was working. And I loved the way Lloyd treated her, too. He kissed and complimented her in front of everyone. I want to one day have my own stuff going on like her, La La Anthony, or Shaunie O'Neal. I want a makeup or clothing line or something. Something that could keep me busy and make me rich on my own. And I really want to start on Jabril's charity and go back to school. I had so much I wanted to do, but I do still have plenty of time to do it all.

Nichelle and I were going to Christie's house. After we picked her up, we were all going to have lunch downtown and maybe do some light shopping at Quail Springs Mall. Nichelle had become my stylist for both my hair and wardrobe. I have something to wear for any and every occasion now.

She picked me up, and we drove to Christie's house, and from the looks of things, she must have taken Nichelle's advice and hired a housekeeper. Christie opened the double doors in a tangerine dress that dragged on the floor. She gave us both cutesy hugs and ushered us into her immaculate house.

"It looks wonderful in here!" Nichelle exclaimed.

"It does," I agreed.

"But it smells like she used a tad bit too much bleach," Nichelle said, looking around.

"I'm glad you said something. I thought so." Nichelle had just unknowingly given Christie the signal to go off. Christie grabbed the bottle and walked over to her new housekeeper. She kept pointing at the bottle. "Too much bleach. You understand?" Her housekeeper kept saying "*Si, si, señora.*"

"And you need to move everything, okay? Get behind the sofa and mop under the furniture. *Magna* clean, clean, clean. I want clean."

"Calm down and don't talk to her like that," Nichelle said.

"I'm trying to calm down. It is just me and Omar got into this huge fight about me not being clean enough. So, I want to have this place spotless when he gets back. Oh my God, I'm so stressed out. I feel like I have to clean behind her. God, why do I have to live like this? I just can't take all this stress. I hate when Omar stresses me out like this. Now she is not cleaning right." *How did she go from a crazy messy house to a neat freak fanatic?* I wondered.

"Sit down and relax, girl, and let her do her job. Get your keys and bags, and let's get out of here."

"Okay, but I want my house cleaned properly. I'm going to call the agency if she can't get it right by tomorrow." Christie began spraying Febreze around the living room to cover the bleach smell as we went out the door.

"Let's just go."

We all climbed into Nichelle's black Porsche Cayenne truck. I told Christie she could sit in the front so she could have more room for her baby bump. I sat comfortably in the back and checked on Lisa and my nephews. Lisa texted that she was fine and everything had been surprisingly working out with Mikey. She said they weren't having any issues, but just that she needed to make more money so they could do more. She didn't ask me, but I told her I was going to the bank tomorrow and wire her a few thousand dollars. Lisa called me crying as soon as I completed my text.

"What's wrong, Lisa?"

"I don't want you sending me any money."

"I know, but I want to. Jabril doesn't care if I give it to you or spend it on bags and clothes. Please, I'm sending it tomorrow as soon as I go to the bank. Okay?"

"Okay, then I'll pay you back."

"You don't have to." She thanked me once more. It felt good to be able to help my sister with no hesitation.

I had the most relaxing pedicure and manicure I'd ever had. My feet felt so soft and the color on my toes was bright and glossy like wet paint. I'm glad I took Nichelle's advice to try the gel manicure.

After the nail salon, we arrived at the restaurant and immediately after being seated we ordered our appetizers and beverages.

"I can't wait until I can drink again, but I have, like, two years." Christie sighed.

"Why two years?" I asked, sipping on my martini. I usually ordered what Nichelle ordered. She always ordered great tasting drinks.

"Because I'm breast-feeding."

"Oh wow. Well, cheers to you." We both drank our martinis, and she had a Shirley Temple.

The waiter delivered us a colossal order of nachos. The crabmeat and cheese covered the black and red tortilla chips. It was really good, but we didn't need two. Christie ordered another one while we were all still eating the first one. She took big lumps of the nachos and pushed it in her mouth, smearing cheese all over her lips.

"Your baby is going to be so fat," Nichelle joked.

"I'm hungry, and I don't know what it is. But sometimes I just can't stop eating. Omar can't wait for this to be over so I'll stop eating off his plate."

The waiter came back to take our dinner order and asked if Christie was serious when she ordered two entrées. He insisted that it was too much food for one person. She closed the menu and said, "I know what I have an appetite for, so don't try to tell me what I should order. I'm going to eat it, and whatever I don't eat I'll just take home."

"Sorry, ma'am," he said as he scurried away from the table.

* * *

Christie ordered so much food there wasn't enough room on the table, so they had to remove some of the condiments and the waiter needed help bringing all the plates.

"Is there a person missing?" the extra waitress asked.

"No, that's for them, all her." Nichelle and I laughed at the same time.

Finally satisfying her inner hungry beast, Christie started talking about something she loved more than food, and that was sex. "So, last night I swung on my swing, and Omar went crazy. Y'all should both get one. They only cost two hundred dollars. Between that and back shots, I swear, you will have to push your man out the door."

"Hold up, back shots? You mean anal?"

"Yeah."

"Oh girl, you are crazy. You let that big-ass Omar in your small booty?" Nichelle asked as she rose from the table like she had to run from disgust.

"Absolutely, girl, I'm telling you, I can teach you a few things. It doesn't hurt. You just have to relax."

"Well, I don't need a swing, Christie, but I do want some lessons on how to give better oral. Teach me how to do that," I said. They both looked at each other, and now everyone at the table was laughing at me.

"What?" Nichelle was laughing hysterically. "You don't know how to do that? Poor Zakiya, my poor baby girl," she said, bringing me into her shoulder.

"She's only twenty-one. I didn't know what I was

doing at her age, either. You have to live and learn. Zakiya, I can't show you exactly how, but I can tell you about this website I know about. You can practice on a banana. So, is Jabril complaining?"

"Not exactly. Well, he said he loves me regardless, but the other day I made him bleed. I kinda cut him with my teeth." They both looked at each other and laughed again at my expense.

Christie said, "It is not that bad, once you get the hang of it. I think you will actually like it. How about after lunch we go and take you to a toy store?"

"I'm not going to a toy store with you, freak girl," Nichelle quipped.

"Don't worry about this prude. I'm going to hook you up. Okay, when you on top riding him, stop right in the middle and just take it out," she said, demonstrating by bouncing her miniature body up and down. "Then you take a hold of the bottom real tight, and—"

Interrupting her, Nichelle said, "Zakiya, do not listen to her. You never suck after you fuck. You hook him up in the beginning during foreplay, when you first get into it. I'm telling you, I've been married how many years. Then if he wants more afterward, he needs to go take a shower and then you can give him more." I didn't know what to believe, but I did need advice on how to do it right.

After our heavy lunch, we all were too tired to do anything else, but Christie did pass me a note of a website to try out. I thanked her and put the note in my pocket.

* * *

Once I was home, I showered, wrapped my hair up, and turned on the television. I called Jabril, but he wasn't back in his room yet. The game wasn't playing here, so I looked online to see what the score was. They were trailing the Heat by six in the fourth quarter. He wouldn't get back to the hotel for another hour or two. I was going to stay up so I could talk to him, but in the meantime, while waiting, I typed in the website Christie gave me. An interesting, normal-looking woman appeared on the site dressed as a schoolteacher, saying she was the Queen of Fellatio. I didn't know what she could teach me, but I pressed PLAY anyway. The beginning of the video clip instructed me that I would need a banana or a cucumber to continue. I paused the video and ran downstairs to grab a cucumber out of the refrigerator, and then began practicing the technique from the video in the mirror. I felt silly, but I knew I needed to get it down pat. I followed along with the video as the lady kept saying to close your eyes and imagine that you were licking and sucking on a lollipop. I closed my eyes and followed along and felt like I was getting the hang of it. Then my cell phone rang, startling me. I answered. It was Adrienne.

"Hey, Adrienne, what's up?"

"I was calling to see how you are making out."

"I'm fine. I think I made the right decision coming back to Jabril. He has changed so much, and we are so happy. I feel like we both have grown some, and I have friends out here now."

"That's good. Yeah, I want you to invite Jabril and all his teammates to the grand opening of my new club, Belize. I'm looking at their schedule and see that they are in town that week, and I'll have a table and everything waiting for you."

"Okay, a club. Adrienne, wow. What made you decide to do that? You're always doing something big."

"I just wanted to try something different."

"That's so good. Of course I'll be there, and I'll make sure my friend brings her man, too."

After I hung up with Adrienne, I went back to learning how to please Jabril. The video seemed easy enough. I thought I was getting the hang of it, and I couldn't wait for Bril to come home to try it on him.

CHAPTER 21

Adrienne

In less than two months I had accomplished my goal of opening up a nightclub. I put in the work, did the research, and now it was my time. All my permits were approved, and we had our liquor license. People can say what they want, but if you have a dream and are determined, you can make it happen. Tonight is proof of it. I was beyond excited about Belize and tonight's grand opening. I'm way over budget, try like twenty-five thousand, but I know this club is going to make money, so I'm not going to allow myself to worry about it. And I'm not going to worry about Ian, either. He's been acting a little strange, too. I know he is pressed about the rest of the money for the movie. I told him he should tap in to some of these athletes and other famous people with money to get his project funded.

Ian's cousin Keldrick came up from D.C. to help with promotions, run the door, and monitor security. I also hired an amazing PR girl named Tamara Murphy. She was an "it" publicist from Atlanta who had done great work at this nightclub in New York for the Harold Brothers. She has been so on point with everything and has garnered us so much pre-publicity, that I have other publicists calling me, asking for their clients to attend our grand opening. Belize has been featured on every website and every paper in town. I know everything is about to take off for me. Tonight is the night.

I dressed in the mirror in a white, short mini-dress that draped in the front and had an oval, circular cutout in the back. I wore a big, glittery violet and silver necklace, bracelets, and long, amethyst-colored, sparkling earrings that accented my violet Jimmy Choo shoes. I went to the hair salon and had the stylist pull my hair back into one big, off-the-shoulder, wild, loose ponytail that trailed down my neck.

One last glance in the mirror and I was ready. Now, it was time for me to dress Ian. I heard him turn off the shower. I called out to him, "Ian, baby." He didn't answer, so I called out to him again: "Ian, sweetheart." He stepped out of the bathroom, drying off his ripped abdominal muscles. I almost forgot about the grand opening momentarily. I walked over to him and massaged his package. Ian stopped me, removed my hands from his waist, and said, "I have to get ready. Why are you being sweet? What do you want from me, Adrienne?"

"I don't want anything from you, babe, but I did buy you something to wear tonight." I pulled out the black suit, shoes, and purple tie I had bought him from Boyds.

"So, this is what all of this is about. All the sweet talk, you are trying to dress me. No, absolutely not. I'm not wearing this."

"Please, just put it on. I wanted us to be coordinated. You know, his and hers. We both will be wearing the same colors of the club." I hoped Ian was buying it. I not only wanted us to be coordinated and complement each other, but I also was afraid of Ian dressing himself. He looked over at the hideous gray pants and blue oxford button-down shirt he'd bought and decided I might be right.

Ian reluctantly picked the suit up and trudged into the bathroom. He was in there for over ten minutes, so I finally tapped on the door and demanded that he let me see what he looked like. He came from out the bathroom, straightening out his tie. He was acting as if I was his mom making him wear the ugly sweater that all the kids at school were going to tease him about. He kept complaining about everything, the fit, the color of the tie. His complaining didn't stop until he saw how good he looked in the mirror. He turned to the side and cracked a slight smile.

"See, babe, I told you. You look so handsome." I patted his back and smoothed out his pants.

He stared in the mirror and said, "I look okay, I guess. I'm only doing this for you, Adrienne. Otherwise I would never wear something like this."

"Well, thank you for pleasing me, because you are making that suit look good. We both look nice."

I gave him a quick kiss, and we made our way to the club.

We arrived at Belize, and I walked around my beautiful club and checked out everything. Keldrick and Mack had the security team lined up. Keldrick wasn't the big, horrible person I had met over the phone months ago. He had a big presence but he was short. He only stood about five foot four, and though he did talk over people, he knew his stuff and you had to respect him.

Tamara was outside with the red carpet and with a white and purple Belize logo backdrop. The photographer had arrived, and the caterer I'd hired was setting up. Everything was ready, and now all I needed were all my patrons to walk in and keep coming back every week.

I stood at the top of my VIP section steps and took in the beauty of Belize. Everything was just as I had imagined it would be. At that very moment it occurred to me that I had invested practically everything in my bank account in this place. The thought made me weak. I sat down, and my mind began somersaulting with horrible thoughts. In the slim chance that Belize didn't work, I would have nothing and would have to start all over again. Just that thought made me extremely nervous. I ran over to the bar and asked Waliq to pour me a vodka and cranberry to calm me down. Ian and I had made a promise that we wouldn't drink tonight, because we had to have clear heads and see everything going on in the club. I had broken that promise already and was about to break it again when I asked Waliq for another one. I was thinking about all the things that might not go right. *What if no one shows up? What if people come, but don't buy any bottles? What if the club is not as nice as I think it is?* I drank the vodka and cranberry, then counted to ten and took a deep breath. I walked over to our appetizer table and grabbed a few cocktail shrimp. They were good, but they still couldn't calm me.

Ian could tell my nerves were getting the best of me. He came over and had a seat next to me, then took my drink out of my hand.

"Don't worry, Adrienne, everything is going to turn out great."

"Ian, I'm scared. This is a lot," I said, surveying the club's elaborate design.

"Baby, you look beautiful, and look around at your dream realized." Even with his reassurance, I was still scared. My mind was only focusing on, what if he was wrong and I failed?

"I know, but I have so much money on the line."

"You have this. It's going to work. Just say, 'I got this.' " I looked at him and repeated, "I got this" to myself. Even though I echoed his words and it sounded very good coming out of my mouth, I still didn't fully believe. I put my head down again.

I heard Keldrick walk up and ask what was wrong with me.

"Nothing, I think she just has a little jitters," Ian said, rubbing my back as he squeezed my body sideways.

"Adrienne, you have nothing to be worried about. You definitely have a hit on your hands," Keldrick said. I brought my head up and asked Keldrick if he really thought so.

"Yeah, this place is nice, for real."

"Thank you so much." This place had to work,

because I needed all my money back and then some.

It was still an hour before the doors opened, and I was frantic. I resisted the urge to have another drink. I walked out of the club and down the street. My stomach was still cramping up. I didn't have time to tend to it, because Tamara called my cell phone and said she had more confirmations coming in. She thought we were going to be well over our 508 capacity.

"I'd rather have that problem than it not being crowded enough," I said, unfazed by her news.

"Do you know how pissed people are going to be that they can't get in, Adrienne?" Tamara huffed.

"I don't care. Just keep saying yes to everyone to ensure that we have a great night."

After I hung up with her, I walked some more and said a silent prayer. I prayed for Belize to be successful and that I would recoup all my money.

I returned to the club and transitioned into boss mode. I was now ready.

"Summer, gather everyone and tell them to meet me in the yellow section now," I commanded. I walked to the back of the club and prepared to have a pep talk with my staff. They needed to know what my expectations were and how to handle our guests. What they did tonight would determine whether I passed or failed.

Everyone congregated around and listened attentively. As I began to speak, I noticed Joi wasn't there yet.

"Where is Joi?"

"She is running a little late," Darcel answered.

"Okay, see, this is what we can't have, people running late on our first night." Instead of waiting for her to arrive, I began my meeting. "Let me just remind you guys that the people who are coming tonight are people who are used to the finer things. We have to show them that Belize is the best. They are coming to enjoy themselves, and it is all of your jobs to make sure they do. Waliq and Terrance, you have to be fast. As soon as one of the girls brings you an order, fill it. Keep their drinks flowing. Ladies, my Belize Beauties, you are the pretty girls in the VIP. You ladies must be on point. I want you to keep your appearance up. I don't want a hair out of place. I also want you to make sure our guests have what they need. If you wait until the glasses are empty to ask if you can get them anything else, then you are too late. Try your best to be a mind reader and be on task. You guys need to recommend everything expensive. If they ask for vodka, always sell them the Grey Goose over the bottle of Absolut. The higher their bill, the more money you make. Remember, you're getting an automatic twenty percent of the total bill. I'm giving bonuses to everyone whose guests spend more than three thousand dollars tonight. And if you suggest the right things to them, that won't be hard. Also, if you see anyone too drunk, notify Keldrick, Mack, or myself. We can't have anyone stumbling around this club. It becomes a liability." They all were taking mental notes and hanging on to my last sentence, but I was for the most part done. I was no longer scared, and I was ready to get the night started.

"That's it for you fellas. I need to talk to the ladies." Waliq and Terrance got up from the table and Joi rushed in.

"I'm sorry I'm late," Joi said, trying to catch her breath. I didn't even bother acknowledging her. I continued with my speech. My ignoring her sent a loud message that I disapproved of her tardiness.

"Now, ladies, you all are very pretty women. You all have great personalities, too; that's why I hired you, but men like to flirt. They are going to be very playful and suggestive and try to talk to you all night long, but you will not have time for that if you are doing your job."

Ian came up and joined in the meeting. He made me a little nervous, but I continued, "I'm going to tell you, if I was in your position I would not be talking or letting anyone take my time up. Make these men that come in here pay. If you want to date one of them, that's fine, but don't do it on my time. What y'all do after the club closes is your business. Any questions?"

"If someone pays with a credit card and they give me a tip, how do I get my cash?" Shanice asked.

"That's a good question. At the end of the night, you'll bring me your receipts and I'll give you cash. If it gets to be too much, we'll do it at the end of the week. Oh, one last thing, when someone gets a bottle of champagne, I want y'all to lose your minds screaming and yelling, to show them a lot of attention. Get the sparklers. That is going to encourage others to buy more bottles and make them feel really special for just dropping five hundred dollars. So, let's get ready to make some money. And remember, if you are not someone, you have to know someone to get in Belize. Everyone say Belize on five." I counted up and everyone screamed it after me.

The next two hours went past in a whirlwind. People started trickling in, and then moments later the place was filled, the music was loud and full of bass, and the deejay was playing intense, dance-filled beats.

I spotted Angelique sitting in the upper-level blue section of the club with Shavone and Nytika, her two friends she said she didn't deal with anymore. I didn't care, I was just happy they were there. I walked over to her and greeted her.

"Adrienne, this place is amazing. I can't believe you got it done so fast." I thanked Angelique and spoke to the other ladies and asked them what they were drinking. I handed them drink menus and had appetizers brought to their table. Nytika scratched her head and asked if we had Cristal.

"No, we only have Ace of Spade and Moët."

"Um, yeah, I don't drink that it makes me belch?" I gave her a whatever-bitch glance. Angelique noticed and said, "We will take two bottles of Spade."

"Okay." I called Shanice over to the table to help them. Just as I was finished with them, I was called to the door by Keldrick.

"Hey, Adrienne, I need you to make a judgment call. This guy wants to get in and you said no sneakers. Him and three of his boys have on tennis shoes. He says he is a football player. I told him the dress code is for everyone. He asked to speak to the manager."

"Where is he?" I asked, looking around at the crowd.

"Outside." I walked out of the club with him, and he pointed to a burly guy with scruffy facial hair. His unkempt appearance was the exact opposite of what I preferred for my club. I didn't want to say no without at least speaking to him, though. I walked over to him and introduced myself. I extended my hand to the guy and separated him from his entourage. I immediately knew he wasn't a thug, judging by his clean manicured nails, twenty-five-thousand-dollar Audemars Piguet watch and clear asscher-cut diamond earrings.

"What's your name?" I asked.

"It's Khalif."

"Nice to meet you, Khalif. I'm glad you came out, but do you know we have a dress code?" I said, smiling but remaining firm.

"I didn't know that, but come on, sis, can't you just look out and let us in?"

"I could, but I'm not sure I want to. Look at you and your boys. Can't you just send one of them home to get you a change of clothes? I really don't want that look at my club." I turned around to point at all his friends in their tees and sneakers.

"What's that look? I'm a businessman. We just want to come into the club and have a good time. We may look a certain way, but we all are all good guys with jobs. My name is Khalif Hartwell and I play for the Minnesota Vikings. I just got in town, and a few of my friends told me it was a good party going on, so here I am." I knew I had him, and he really wanted to convince me that he wasn't a criminal. His boys kept looking over, trying to see if I was going to grant them entry or not. I purposely kept my face frowned as if I really wasn't sure yet.

"Okay, this is what I'm going to do. I'm going to let you guys in, but you have to come in through the side VIP door and you must buy four bottles at five a piece." He could take it or leave it, but I knew he wanted to show off for his friends.

"All right. That's cool." He walked over to his boys victorious, and they followed me to the side door. He thanked me and hugged me like I'd done him the biggest favor. I walked back over to Keldrick and let him know the stipulation. He called over to security and the side door swung open. They were escorted to their table, and I had just made two thousand dollars in ten minutes. Get money.

Back in the club everything was crazy in a good way. The music was turned up, and everyone was dancing, drinking, and partying. My dance floor was packed, and everywhere around me all I saw were classy, sophisticated, attractive people. Belize was everything I dreamed it would be. Shanice rushed over. "Um, this table is looking for you. A tall, skinny girl." She pointed to the table. I walked over to Zakiya, Jabril, and his teammate and wife to welcome them to Belize. Zakiya looked like a little couture model. She was still tall and lean, but now she had subtle curves. Something about her was more polished and womanly. She was not the nanny that I had met in the airport. I gave her the biggest hug. "Zakiya, you look great. I love your hair."

"Thank you. She did it. She is my hair and wardrobe stylist in one. This is Nichelle, and this is her husband, Lloyd. And you remember Jabril." Jabril stood up and greeted me. I was impressed. I'd asked Zakiya to make sure everyone came and she did.

"Your club is really nice. Will you be opening a restaurant?" her friend Nichelle asked.

"Maybe down the line after we are opened a little while." I was lying, but just the fact that she thought I could pull off a restaurant was great. While I had all these ballers around, I called over the photographer and found Ian. We had to take pictures for our club's website. I knew if people saw basketball players at the club, it would raise Belize's profile.

After the pictures, Zakiya and I caught up some and then I was pulled away by Tamara. She introduced me to more people, and I had to take more pictures and make more contacts.

"You know, you have a line outside of people who can't get in," Tamara informed me as we posed for the nineteen-hundredth picture.

"So, that's great, right?" I smiled.

"No, people who reserved that can't get in will feel duped and will just go somewhere else. I told you not to overbook."

"I don't see what the big deal is. It makes the club more exclusive. And they will return another night, just earlier so that they can get in. Right?" I said, smiling again as the cameras flashed.

"Okay, if that's what you say. I work for you."

"That's what I know."

Ian and I danced, mingled, and checked on the door twice. We were still turning people away. My girls were selling, and my guys were serving. I believed tonight was already a success, and it was only midnight.

Tamara came over and grabbed my arm. "I have someone I want to introduce you to," she said. Before I could object she said, "Adrienne Sheppard, this is Shelton James, an entertainment attorney. He's from Washington, D.C., but he practices here in Philadelphia and he is the head of the Northeast Chapter of the Black Attorneys Association."

"Nice to meet you," I said. Shelton James was an average-height man with above-average looks. His handsome face and bald head were a smooth toffee color. Just from looking at his suit and hands, I could tell he liked labels and the finer things in life.

"Nice to meet you, as well, Ms. Sheppard. You have a very nice place here. We are having our annual BAA event here in Philly in a few months, and we haven't secured our networking location yet. Tamara said you might be interested in hosting our event?"

"Thank you. And absolutely, we would be interested."

Tamara interjected, "We can definitely do something for you, Shelton, but hold that thought." Tamara excused herself. Shelton James continued, "Okay, I will have the committee reach out to you or Tamara early next week. And I will let them know that they can see their favorite celebrity or athlete here. That kind of thing impresses some people, you know. I'm impressed that I saw my favorite actress when I was coming in. I see you have a lot of famous and athletic friends." I raised my eyebrows at him. I wasn't sure what he was getting at and how exactly I should respond.

"Not really. I know a few people."

"You know a lot of people, Ms. Sheppard, that's obvious from all the people here. Yeah, I did my homework on you. You were married to an athlete yourself, right?" How did he know my business? People don't investigate me; I usually do the investigating. I was alarmed, to say the least.

Shelton snickered a little, like he had one-upped me, which he did, and then I said, "Mr. James, should I be impressed or scared that you took so much energy to research me?"

"Huh? That's funny. It's my job to know everything. No, I just used good ol' Google, and boom, you get someone's life history."

"You can't believe everything you read. You should know that, right, Mr. James? You are an attorney?"

"Yes, I am. Well, maybe I'll have the opportunity to sort out the truth from fiction. Here, take my card," he said as he touched my hand and an electrifying feeling took me over. However, it quickly dissipated when I looked down at his ring finger and realized he was married and that my own boyfriend was not that far away.

"You can take mine." Just as I reached in my pocket for a card, Ian came up from behind me and kissed my cheek. I introduced the men and said good-bye to Mr. Shelton as Ian ordered me to have a seat.

We sat at a table not too far from Zakiya and her friends. The moment she saw me seated, she came over to fill me in on her life in ten minutes. Although I was sitting down, I still needed to monitor everything I could. I was in and out of her conversation.

"So, what's new, Zakiya? I'm really happy you and Jabril are back together."

"Me too. We aren't doing too much. Um, we are thinking about starting a charity organization for at-risk kids."

"Okay, that's nice. At risk for what?"

"I don't know, you know, at risk for poverty, pregnancy, violence, that sort of thing."

"Zakiya, I don't know about that. Maybe you shouldn't rush into starting an organization so fast."

"Why not? I want to help people."

"Yeah, well, charity starts at home. You just got back together. Maybe just relax first, put your feet up this time and enjoy the life that you've been blessed with."

"Hmm, you might be right."

"I am. You don't have to save the world. Save yourself and concentrate on your man," I said as I stood and asked Shanice to grab the table another round of bottles right as she was about to wave her bosoms in Jabril's face. She was a little hustler that I didn't mind taking under my wing, but she had to use her tactics elsewhere. Zakiya was oblivious to someone trying to flirt with her man right in front of her face.

"Zakiya, did you see that woman just in your man's face with her breasts?"

"No, where?" she asked, looking around.

"Listen, Zakiya, be smart, don't be naïve. Keep your eyes open. Forget an organization and keep up with your man. I will call you sometime this week, and the next time you are here we will have lunch."

"Okay."

I reached out to her and gave her a hug. Seconds later Ian reached out to me with a microphone in his hand. Him having me sit down to relax was a setup. He spoke into the microphone, ordering the deejay to stop the music. I looked at him, confused. Everyone's eyes were fixed on me. I didn't know what he was about to do.

"I am very proud of you, Adrienne Sheppard, and of the woman that you are becoming. I think the only thing that would make me prouder was if you would be my wife. So I have a question for you: Will you marry me?" He dropped to one knee and opened a box containing a very miniscule chip of a diamond ring. Everyone in the club began to applaud. I was more shocked than excited. I loved Ian, but we had never really talked about growing old together. I didn't know what to say, so I just said yes. And then he tried to slide that crap on my ring finger, but I convinced him it didn't fit because I was so embarrassed. I thought I might have been overreacting until Angelique and her friends ran over and uttered, "Oh." And then they said to ask for a bigger ring as a wedding gift.

The club had emptied out, and I was helping everyone clean tables and pour bottles out. Other than my faux proposal, my night had been fabulous. I made some great contacts and potential business. It was a whirlwind, and I was exhausted. Light crept into the club when I realized that I had done it. Ian carried me to the car, and I remember him telling me he was so proud of me, that he didn't see my vision initially, but that Belize was going to work. He was glad that I was his woman and about to be his wife. At that moment I realized why I was with him, and maybe I could forgive him for having absolutely no taste or idea of what an engagement ring should look like.

We came into my house. Ian undressed me and placed my tired body in the shower. Feeling the warm water against my skin opened my senses. And it also prepared me for Ian joining me in the shower and pounding his long, hard body inside of me. I felt like I was having the perfect evening. A real grand opening, a loving man, and a beautiful lovemaking, until Ian marred everything by saying something very peculiar. He said that since the club was going to be such a success, I could now loan him the rest of the money that he needed to fund his movie. I acted like I was too out of it to comprehend what he was saying. The lucky thing was, I didn't have to answer him right away because he was leaving to go to Miami in the morning. It would be much easier to say "hell no" over the telephone.

Belize had had an awesome grand opening, and in less than twelve hours it was time to do it all over again. I was in my office at the club discussing with the ladies things they could improve on. I brought in sandwiches and energy drinks. I knew they were probably tired, too, but I decided that once a week we were going to have a meeting to make sure the club ran efficiently. Before the meeting began, I got an unexpected delivery. The girls all huddled around me as I opened the package.

"Your boyfriend is so sweet," Joi said.

"Yes, he is. He proposed last night and gifts today," cooed Darcel.

"Why aren't you wearing your ring?" Shanice asked.

"It doesn't fit. But what is inside of here?" I said as I curiously opened the box to see what was inside and at the same time change the subject. The box was filled with two dozen large, plump strawberries coated in chocolate. The card attached read: *Congratulations and lots of success! I want to know more about you without Google. Shelton James.*

"I thought your boyfriend's name was Ian, not Shelton?" Summer asked, reading the card over my shoulder.

"It is. Someone else sent this to congratulate me on opening the club."

"Chocolate and strawberries are very sensual. I think your admirer wants more than to say congrats," Joi joined in, eyeing my treats.

"Right, but I do have a man," I snapped.

"You mean a fiancé," Joi corrected me.

"A fiancé, right," I said, rolling my eyes at her. They were all becoming too comfortable, almost like I was their girlfriend.

"Girl, don't feel guilty, you're not married yet," Shanice said while reaching for one. I wanted to laugh with them, but I was struggling to maintain my composure and not smile.

"I suppose you're single until you are married." I was happy I was still on Shelton's mind. Evidently I wasn't the only one who'd felt the spark. I offered them all some, and then closed the box.

"Well, sometimes that don't matter if you have

the right connection and they are spending the right amount of money," Shanice added. I totally agreed with Shanice, but I couldn't agree with her in front of everyone. So I gave her a disapproving look and started our meeting back up.

Once our meeting was over, I called the number on the card and asked to speak to Shelton James.

"This is Shelton James. Whom do I have the pleasure of speaking with?"

"Mr. James, most married men do normal things like send flowers when they are sending a token of friendship and congratulating someone. With chocolate-covered strawberries, someone might get the wrong idea."

"So you see, I'm far from normal, Ms. Sheppard. I like to consider myself different. I make trends happen. I don't follow them."

"Ha, that was funny. I kind of set myself up for that one. Let's get together and have drinks soon, Mr. James."

"I would love to, but I have a busy week coming up. Let me check my schedule and I'll get back to you."

"You'll get back to me. Interesting. I'll wait to hear from you."

I never chased a man. Well, I've done some chasing, but never a married man. Shelton James had something very intriguing about him. I didn't know what it was, but I liked it.

Chapter 22

Zakiya

I was so excited to be coming home to Philly. We were in my town, so I had to make sure Nichelle had a good time tonight. I couldn't wait to see Adrienne's club, and I also wanted to make sure Miles and Kyle and even Mikey got to meet the team and have good seats at the game.

I called Nichelle while in front of Lisa's house. "Nichelle, I'm picking my sister up now, and we will meet you at your hotel. After our massages we can have lunch at a steakhouse downtown called Del Frisco's a few blocks away. I heard it is a really good place to go."

"I didn't say I wanted steak. I said I wanted a cheesesteak."

"Oh well, that's easy. I can get you a cheesesteak from anywhere. I'll be there in a little bit."

My nephews met me at the car with hugs and

kisses. They both appeared to be a little taller since the last time I saw them.

"Aunt Kiya, we have missed you," they both sang.

"I've missed you more. Look what your auntie was able to get for you." I gave them Kevin Durant jerseys and tickets to the game.

"Now, if you are really good, Jabril and his teammates might come out and sign your basketballs after the game."

"Good looking, Zakiya. Do you have any more tickets? My man and his son want to come, too," Mikey asked.

"No, sorry. I was only able to get these." That was rude. Here it was I was giving him good seats, and he wanted even more tickets. *Typical ungrateful shit,* I thought.

Lisa and I took off, and Lisa admired what Jabril called his old car. It was a BMW that was only two years old. Lisa played with all its features while we drove down the street listening to Rihanna.

"Wow, this car has everything in it. It is like something from a music video. How did you get it here when you flew in?"

"Jabril keeps this car in Jersey at the other house. He asked his uncle to bring it over for me to drive. I was just going to rent a car."

"Aren't you so happy? You and Jabril are back together."

"I am, I love him so much, Lisa. I mean, without all of this, I love him. All of this is just the extra blessing."

"I'm happy for you, Zakiya. You deserve this. And

I know you are not really a fan of Mikey, but he is doing really good now with the boys." I didn't really want to hear Lisa talk about Mikey. As far as I was concerned, he was still the same bum who didn't take care of his kids when they were apart. Plus, I was upset that he had the audacity to ask me for additional tickets, like someone owed him something. *Ingrate.*

The spa was relaxing, and Lisa kept thanking me for the massage, pedicure, and facial. She went on and on how everything was so nice. I told her to stop thanking me and it was no big deal, but she reminded me that I had just spent a month's worth of her bills on massages and facials. I didn't look at it that way, but I guess she was right.

After the spa we dined at a local soul-food eatery on South Street called Ms. Tootsies' and got Lisa's cheesesteak to go so we wouldn't be late for the game.

At the game my nephews were excited, and Mikey was acting like a clown. He was calling everyone he knew and taking pictures posting on his Twitter and Facebook pages. Like, look at me, look how close I'm sitting to the court, I'm doing it big. He was a certified dick eater. There wasn't any other way to describe it. Then, when the game was over, I could see he was making everyone uneasy by pushing my nephews out of the way to snap pictures and ask the team for autographs.

* * *

After the game, I asked Lisa if she wanted to join us at Adrienne's club. She said no because she had work in the morning, and I was happy because I couldn't take Mikey coming and acting like a fan all night.

Chapter 23

Shanice

Today was my first day of work at the club Belize. Last week I had to go and pick up and try on my uniform. Our uniforms were these cute black and purple corset-strapped dresses, and we wore black net stockings and purple heels. Our outfits are cute and look good without showing everything off.

The club was completed, and it was so pretty. It was lights everywhere and white curtains, tables, and chandeliers. I had never been to a club this fly ever, let alone worked at one.

I awoke this morning excited about going to work. This job could get me a new life and my own place, and I couldn't wait for them both to happen.

I hustled up some money and got a sewn-in twenty-inch Remi straight weave with a part in the middle. I got my lashes done and bought a bunch of makeup. I did my eye shadow and nails to match my uniform. I curled my hair and was going to pin-curl my hair up until I got to work. Once I get to the club, I was going to let it hang down. Courtney kept staring at me from her bed the entire time I got ready. I was ironing my dress when she said, "You are not going to wear that on the train, are you?"

"No, I'm going to change when I get there."

"Oh, your makeup look cute. Real cute, so does your hair. This club must be like that. I'm going to have to find someone to bring me down to this little club and buy some bottles from you and help you out some."

"Yeah, bring someone with a lot of money, because each drink is like twenty dollars."

"Wow, they are really trying to get it."

"Yes, they are. The cheapest bottle of liquor I can sell is two hundred dollars, and that's for a little bottle."

"Well, if you meet some ballers call me 'cause I'm there."

"I got you." I packed up my stuff and prepared to leave. I wanted to get to work early and check out my area and just be prepared to make sure I do a good job. We all have five tables each in our color-coded section, and then below the VIP area was for regular patrons and guests.

Right before I boarded the train, Tone called. "When am I going to see you?" he yelled at me. He had been hitting me up about seeing him for a couple of weeks. I never got a chance to return his call, and I wasn't really in the mood for his stubby dick.

"I don't know when. Look, Tone, I have a lot going on."

"What about right now?"

"I can't. Have to get to work now."

"So, I helped you out, got you the job, and now I can't get any love. What part of the game is that?"

"You didn't help me get the job. You took me to the interview and bought me a wig. I got me the job. I have to go and get down there before I get fired on the first day," I said with an attitude.

"I bet if I had some money for you, you would want to see me."

"No, that's not true. I'm going to hit you up. I promise."

"Whatever. You got what you wanted. You are about yourself, Shani."

"No, I'm not. I promise, I will call you after I get off." I finally got him off the phone and headed to my first day of work.

I arrived at Belize Lounge just in time for our big meeting. I thought Adrienne said to be at the club by nine, but she actually said eight. I was lucky I was on time and felt so excited to be a part of something so big. Adrienne had all these rules for us. She wanted us to check credit cards against the license; she wanted us to watch out for people spiking drinks, and people that had too much to drink. She did all the talking, and her boyfriend just stood by her nodding to everything she said. He seemed like he didn't know how to have any fun. He was cute but always so serious. I caught his eyes look at me a few times, but not like he wanted me but more like I was disgusting. I don't know, he seemed like the kind of guy that thought he was better than everyone else. On the other hand, his cousin Keldrick was annoying; he kept trying to have a conversation every time he saw me and I was not interested.

The doors opened to Belize at ten, and the people poured in. I saw some very famous people: actresses, actors, athletes. This girl from my favorite VH1 reality show and BET were covering the event. There were businesspeople, basketball players, football players, and so many rich-looking men. The women were nice, too, but I wasn't checking for them. Adrienne was my girl. She put me in the blue section, too, where the top ballers would be. Right in front of me was Darcel in the rose section. And Summer and Joi shared the yellow section and floor, which was unlucky for them.

We were going to do so well. I was so excited. The deejay was playing a mixture of current and old-school hip-hop songs as guests arrived. I started taking drink orders. No one wanted anything pricey yet. I took my tray and went to our bartender Terrance. He was becoming really busy. He asked me for my number. I didn't give it to him, but I flirted with him so he could make my drinks before Joi and Summer's. I gave my first table their drinks when I noticed Keldrick walking these two sexy six-foot-somethings to my section. I don't know what team they played for, but they both looked good. I was happy until I saw the women they were with trailing behind them. I walked over to the table excited, but they only ordered one bottle and a few drinks because Adrienne already had a bottle waiting for them.

I walked back to the bar and Darcel was standing, waiting for her order. Her rich chocolate skin was glimmering, and her new long, loose spiral curl weave and makeup were working for her.

"You look cute, lady."

"Thank you," she said, playfully flipping her hair up from side to side.

"So, are you doing good?" I asked.

"Yeah, my tables are loving me. Do you see how many bottles of Moët and Grey Goose they ordered?"

"I see. That's what's up, girl," I said.

"I got a feeling that tonight is going to be a good night," she sang. I couldn't agree with her more. "Wow, you might get that bonus tonight. What did you say to them?" I was amazed that she had almost three hundred dollars already. "What's your secret?"

"Nothing. I walked over to them and said, I know you guys came here to have fun, how many bottles do you want? I told them how much they cost and they said they would take four."

"That's what's up, go, Darcel." Waliq lit the sparklers on four bottles of champagne and I helped Darcel carry her bottles. I looked over at her table. They were a group of all guys, that was her secret. I was waiting on tables with men who were married and most had brought their girlfriends out, too. Boo.

But I wasn't going to let girlfriends or wives stop me. I came back to pick up my drinks from Terrance when I saw Joi and Summer come up with big drink orders, too. I needed to catch up. I got my drinks and sashayed over to one of the players, making sure I swiped my breasts on his shoulders. Then I leaned over and hypnotized them as cold smoke escaped the top of the gold bottle and I seductively tilted each glass over and slowly poured the ginger-colored, bubbly liquid into each glass for them.

"Anything else, fellas? Do you want to order some more bottles?" I asked, looking at this sexy young bull.

"Nope, you can take this for now," the one guy answered after he signed his check. His tip was good, and then I realized his number was on the back.

"Just let me know if you need anything else." I smiled at him and folded the receipt up. His wife was too busy talking to her friend to peep that her man was making moves. I was going to make sure I called him. He wasn't the one I wanted. I was on the young sexy one whose body and face were fine. But this one would have to do.

Chapter 24

Zakiya

Jabril and Lloyd have been to some of the fanciest places and they both said they really liked the service we received at Adrienne's club, Belize. We gave our names at the front door and a guy escorted us straight over to a section reserved for us that was a little higher than the rest of the club. There were bottles of champagne and these delicious trays of fruit and appetizers waiting for us. She might as well have had women fanning us and serving us grapes, because that was how they waited on us. My mouth was open from gawking at all the real celebrities and reality show wives who were there, too. And Adrienne's bottle girls were very nice and pretty. They kept coming over, being welcoming and friendly, asking if we needed anything.

Belize was a lot bigger than I expected. When

Adrienne said she was opening a club, I thought it was going to be a regular little place, not all of this.

When I first met Adrienne, I remember I thought her townhouse was so big and she was so rich. Of course, I know now she wasn't, but this club looked so extravagant.

Seeing Adrienne run her own club made me think more about what else I was going to do with my life. I told her about me and Jabril trying to start a charity and me starting a business one day. She said to focus on Jabril and our life, but I know I could do both.

Nichelle and I were dancing to a Pitbull song, bouncing together in front of our men. The guys were too tired from the game to dance, and they were ready to get back to the room, but still enjoying the atmosphere.

Back at the hotel room, I was ready to test out all I had learned from the Fellatio Queen on Jabril. The champagne I had all night was giving me a lot of courage. He lay down and turned on the television. I came out of my dress and drunkenly slid down his boxers.

"I love you, Jabril."

"I know you do." He patted my head and focused on the television, ignoring my speech.

"But I really love you, and I want to show you just how much." I took his large man and placed it all the way in my mouth.

"Whoa, what are you doing, Zakiya?" I ordered him to be quiet and then did to him every technique I remembered off of the video. I opened my mouth wide and relaxed my throat. I allowed him to go deep. I gagged a little and my eyes watered, but I recovered quickly without him noticing and kept giving him pleasure by dipping it back and forth in my mouth, letting it tap my tonsils. I licked and kissed it at the same time, giving it a warming massage. It was amazing how sweet he tasted now that I was into it, getting used to doing it. Instead of biting him and choking, I was devouring and savoring him. I did it so well that Jabril's manhood let out warm fluids in like three minutes. He was more surprised and sat back on the bed, speechless. In his trancelike state he tried to ask me how I became so good so fast. Once he recovered, he attacked every inch of my insides.

"Are you ready to have my baby, Zakiya?"

"Yes."

"My baby is going up in there, Zakiya. I'm serious, don't change your mind." I told him I wouldn't and said yes to everything he said. I didn't care, everything was a yes. He was going in hard sideways and up and down. I could barely take it, not because it was bad, but because it was feeling so good.

What seemed like hours, but was only a half hour later, Jabril was lying flat on top of me, out of breath. He had released inside of me, and I couldn't move if I wanted to. Not to get up, not to go to the bathroom, not to get any water from the minibar. I was done. Jabril had put it on me, and all I could do was fall asleep. I cracked my eyes long enough to see Jabril leave out. He said he was going down the hall to see what Lloyd was doing. I was satisfied. I'd satisfied him, and now I could rest peacefully.

Chapter 25

Shanice

"Adrienne said she was well connected, now I believe her." Darcel laughed as we both looked at all the VIPs in the club and repeated her motto, "If you are not someone, you have to know someone to get in Belize." The grand opening party was still in effect. I came back over to the bar area to talk to Darcel. She had just thrown back a shot and I had one myself.

"Right! This place is crazy." I hadn't made as much money as she did yet, but I was happy because so far the bull that was with his wife had signed for and tipped me two hundred dollars on his credit card receipt. I stored his number in my phone and texted him mine.

"So, why I got married ballers giving me their number right in front of their wife?"

"Stop. Really, girl? Well, I just need Adrienne's man to stop looking at me like he has a problem."

"Yeah, he is always staring at me, too! But not in a nice way."

Summer came over and joined the conversation. "I think he brushed up next to me the other day. I know he was staring all at my boobs the other day. I was like, hello, look up here."

"Hmm. He act like he hate women or something. Men usually like me. Not him, though. He looks at me like I'm trash." I laughed. "How is Joi doing with her tables?" I asked, being nosy.

"She doing okay, I guess. I think she likes Keldrick. She is all up on him, and she dropped drinks twice and he helped her clean up. Adrienne said she is going to take those drinks out of her check."

"Hmm, Adrienne is about her dollars. I fucks with her," I said, and they both, Darcel and Summer, said they did, too.

At the end of the night, I counted my tips and receipts. I had made five hundred dollars. I couldn't believe it. I made that much money for handing out drinks, having fun, and meeting men with money. Life was good and was about to get better. Belize had been closed thirty minutes, and Mr. NBA was already on my phone texting. *Hey sexy what's up with you tonight?*

I texted back: *I don't know. How long are you in town?*

I'm here until tomorrow. Maybe you need to come past my hotel and come and see me.

I was floored. Didn't he have a wife? I had to ask that question. I needed to know if his wife was with him, because I knew some couples were into that. I called his phone just to find out exactly what he was talking about.

"So, you want me to come past your hotel? But where is your wife?"

"Don't worry about her, she is resting. What's up with you and your friends from the club? The other girls that worked there? It's me and my boy, and we need some company. Won't y'all come out and check us out? Make sure you bring them all. We will make sure y'all are good."

"Okay, what's the address." I knew without saying he was going to look out and show us a good time. Me and Darcel were friends, but I didn't know if she was into what I was into. Joi was dumb and I didn't like her and I wasn't that cool with Summer yet.

"Hey, Darcel, you want to hang out with the ballplayers that were in my section, the tall dudes? I'm about to meet them at their hotel."

"No, girl, thanks. I'm going home. I have a class in the morning."

"Oh, okay." I saw Darcel wasn't with it, so I dialed Courtney to see if she could get down here so I could hook her up with the other guy. Courtney answered the phone sleepily.

"Courtney, how soon can you meet me downtown, and where is your mom?"

"I just took my clothes off and my mom not here. Why?"

"I'm about to meet up with these two guys I met from my job. They play in the NBA."

"Damn, okay, listen, get a number for me, please. I need that so bad in my life."

Shit, there was nothing I could do. I had to call him back and just tell him no one was available.

"Hey, my friend got class in the morning, and yeah, my other friends went home. What do you expect? It's the middle of the night. You should have called me earlier."

"Yeah, I know, but what am I supposed to tell my man now?"

"I don't know, but I'm not really worried about him. I'm trying to see what was up with you anyway."

"All right, come on then. Come to the Franklin House Hotel on Seventeenth and JFK Boulevard. Tell the desk to bring you to suite 1011."

It was after three thirty when I arrived to the lobby of the very nice hotel. I did what Lloyd instructed me to. I told the desk I needed to get to suite 1011. He made a call over his radio handset, and another man come from out of the back of the front desk and greeted me and I told him the room I wanted. He walked me to the elevator, entered a special code, and pressed the elevator for the tenth floor.

The elevator doors sprang open, and surprisingly Lloyd was sitting alone at a small empty bar overlooking the city. It was him and one bartender. He stood up and welcomed me with a hug. The older Asian man in a black and white uniform asked if he could get us anything. I was surprised they were still serving, but I ordered a shot of Patrón. He said they didn't have any, so I ordered Hennessey. I took the shot straight and he ordered me a second one. I was a little nervous the way Lloyd was fidgeting on his phone. It was none of my business, but I asked him where his wife was again.

"I told you, she is asleep. She is in a room all the way on the twenty-third floor."

"How you know she won't get up and start looking for you?"

He shook his head and said, "Listen, I know my wife. I've been married a long time. I'm not worried, so don't you be. I'm trying to get to know you. So, how long have you been working at the club?"

"That club just opened tonight, remember?"

"Oh yeah, that's right. So, hurry up and down that, because I want to get you upstairs. Do you smoke?"

"Yeah, I do."

"All right, come on."

I didn't know how to ask for my money, but I had to remind him that it was not free. From our conversation I thought we had an understanding. The suite three floors higher smelled like he'd already been smoking before I got there. I set my bag down on a desk across from the huge cream-colored bed. We smoked some and he told me to get naked, and he went right into tearing and eating my insides out like a starving man. I sat with my legs open, my body was trembling, and then his boy Jabril knocked on the door. I grabbed the top sheet to cover my body, but Lloyd snatched it away and said that his boy was going to watch.

Jabril had a seat across from the bed, and Lloyd returned to gobbling up my insides, and I didn't mind him watching. In fact, I liked it. Must be the hoe in me that had me winding my hips and acting extra whorish when I knew I had an audience.

After Lloyd tasted me, he flipped me over on all fours. He pulled out a condom and plunged in and out of me.

"Yo, your ass is perfect, big and round like I like 'em, girl," Lloyd said, forcefully slapping my ass, and it was feeling incredible on my end, too. I didn't think it could get any better until Jabril joined in. He came up behind me and started massaging on my butt, gently running his finger up and down the crack of my ass, sending chills up my spine. Having two muscular men doing me was making my entire body tingle. Shit, I wished someone was filming our ménage so I could watch it later to see how I was doing.

Lloyd busted his nut and I figured that was it. But then he pulled me to the edge of the bed and sat me on his face again. He worked me over with his talented tongue, and I sat twisting and winding all over his face when Jabril came over to me with his long-rod dick exposed. At first I began stroking it up and down, and then I placed it in my mouth and slurped on his thickness, making porn-star noises. I sucked one man's dick and rotated my coochie against the other one's face. My senses were on overload, and I suddenly felt a familiar warmth coursing through me. My legs started shaking. I was trying to pull away. I wanted Lloyd to stop before I went over the edge. But he kept licking and sucking, driving me insane.

Finally I gave up and let him suck me to a shuddering climax. It was amazing. So good, I couldn't concentrate on giving Jabril brain, so I let his dick slip out of my mouth while I gave in to the good feeling that Lloyd was giving me.

After I came, it took a minute for me to stop trembling and moaning, and when I opened my eyes, I could see Lloyd smiling as he licked my moisture from his lips. "You ready to take care of my boy now?" Lloyd asked.

All I could do was nod my head because I was out of breath and couldn't talk.

Jabril came over, and with my legs wrapped around his back, he thrust his thick, hard body inside of mine. He was groaning like I had the best pussy in the world. He lasted about ten minutes, cussing and growling until he came. After we were done, he fired up another blunt and started smoking. He passed it to Lloyd. Lloyd took a couple of puffs and then passed it to me. Next, we started doing shots of Hennessey that he brought up from downstairs. I was feeling nice when I got up to go to the bathroom.

After I peed, I was warming a washcloth, getting ready to wash my insides. There was a knock on the door. I asked who it was, and a voice said, "It's Jabril. I was seeing if you needed any help." Smiling, I readily opened it. He came in and immediately started grabbing my ass. I was happy because I'd wanted Jabril from the beginning. He already had a condom on when he lowered me down to the bathroom floor and got behind me, fucking me doggy-style. The bathroom door creaked open and Lloyd stood in the doorway, watching.

My juices were warm and bubbly as Jabril deep-stroked in and out. Switching our position, he pulled me up and bent me over the sink. Through the mirror, I could see Lloyd observing us, licking his lips as I screamed out in ecstasy.

Lloyd took another turn with me, and once again, he didn't last that long. Then me and Jabril fucked two more times. I thought I had met my match. Jabril had this long pipe that deflated and sprang right back up after a few minutes, and I was enjoying every minute of it.

After a while, Lloyd dozed off and Jabril rolled out. I got in bed with Lloyd and fell asleep lying next to him. In the morning, I tried to wake him, but he was in a deep sleep. I didn't know how much money I was going to be able to get out of him, but I knew that after all the work I'd put in, he'd better pay up. I fiddled around for another hour.

He woke up, startled. "Yo, what's up? What time is it?"

"Your boy left and I'm about to leave, too."

"Yeah, yeah. Okay, let me get myself together. You know how to make coffee?" he asked. I told him I did.

I made the coffee and gave him the warm mug. He sobered up and I started making movement toward the door again.

"So, well, I guess I see you next time," he said.

"Next time, hmm. We need to take care of this time."

"Right, here, take that. Give me your number again, and I'll call you every time I come to town. All right?" He placed ten one hundred dollar bills in my hand.

"Well, I'll see you." I left out the hotel room and called Courtney to come and get me.

I met up with Courtney a few blocks away from the hotel. I opened the car door, got in, and just threw the money I had made in the car and made it rain. She almost crashed, trying to catch and pick up some of the money, and yelled, "You all hype. Oh my God, how much money did you make?"

"I have to count, let me see, one hundred, two hundred, three hundred . . ." I laughed as I touched each bill quickly. I told her about my entire night. She couldn't believe it, and neither could I. I had made five hundred dollars at my job and a thousand when I got off. I loved being a working girl.

Chapter 26

Zakiya

Once we were back from Philly, Jabril and I spent a few days together, and then Nichelle invited me to Vegas for a girls' trip. Christie wanted to come, but it was too close to her due date for her to travel. She felt left out, because we had already had a good time without her at the club in Philly.

It was my first time in Sin City, and I wanted to enjoy myself. Nichelle and I were going to be out, and we didn't have time to babysit a pregnant woman. I packed lots of dresses and all my bags. I had even gone shopping yesterday and bought some more things. When I saw my Louis Vuitton bag, I immediately thought of Nichelle. I didn't know where we were going, but I had to make sure I looked up to par to keep up with the stylish Nichelle DeBurrows. She met me at the airport, and I was already dressed in case she wanted to go somewhere right away.

"Look at you, all dressed up, pretty girl. I saw that Louie bag last week. How do you have it before I do?"

"I don't know, I bought it yesterday. It goes with these silver *Balaenkaga* shoes I bought, too. I have to show them to you."

"Well, excuse me, Lil' Miss Diva and it is Bal-en-ciaga," she corrected me.

"You know what I meant. I'm trying to be like you." I laughed.

"I see. I'm so happy you are here. We are going to have a great time. We are going to go to a pool party after we check in, tonight a party, and tomorrow sunbathing and chilling by the pool. I want to stop at my favorite store to get something for tonight."

We walked into the luxury boutique and spent an ungodly amount of money. I had a dress to wear, but the sales girl in the store said that the dress she picked out for me was the last one. She told me she'd sold the second last to Kim Kardashian's stylist. I didn't know if she was telling the truth or not, but I felt like if Kim had it, I should, too. Once I bought the dress, Nichelle found an amazing bag and shoes for me that completed the outfit. Yes, they were five thousand, but I had more than enough in my account. Jabril gave me extra money this week and told me to enjoy myself.

From the boutique, Nichelle showed me to our room at the Palm's Penthouse at the Palms Hotel.

It was huge and furnished like a trendy lounge. The light fixtures and tables were modern, and the beds and sofas had multicolored decorative pillows.

I was surprised it was a deejay and a party in the daytime. The sun was beating on my back. The heat felt good. We made our way through the crowded pool area. Nichelle had a bungalow reserved for us as our own private area at the pool. She sat in the sun wearing a crimson, cute bikini and met up with some friends she'd gone to high school with. I changed into a cute two-piece navy and white marina tankini. We took pictures and I texted a few to Jabril. He texted back and said I looked good and I was about to have him jump on a plane to come and see me. Our server brought us over daiquiris, and we waited for one of her friends to meet up with us.

Nichelle screamed, "Oh my God!"

"What's wrong? Are your friends coming?"

"I have to go and see my parents. They are saying it is an emergency. I don't even know how they know I'm in town. Are you staying here or going with me?"

"I'll go."

Nichelle's parents' home was a twenty-minute cab ride from the strip. They lived in a small ranch home right off of Balazar Avenue. I don't know why, but I just assumed Nichelle came from money. She was so elegant and spoke so well and knew so much about everything. I assumed her life was always privileged.

Outside of the house was shocking enough, but inside I gasped. The sofa had dark dirt marks across the seats. It was hot, and there was no air-conditioning—just a bunch of box fans blowing around heat. They had an old television with the big back and antenna and converter box on the side, which meant they didn't even have cable.

Her sister Erica looked just like her with her long hair and complexion, but her body was flabby and her stomach was hanging outside the rim of her jeans. They both were a mixture of their black father and Mexican mother. However, it seemed Nichelle got all the good features and what was left over was given to her sister. She fed her baby daughter while her little son ran around with a saggy diaper. She looked me over and said, "Why don't you have a seat, Nita, and introduce us to your friend."

"I'm Zakiya. Nice to meet you," I responded for Nichelle while trying not to stare at their dilapidated home.

"Zakiya, I'm Erica. My sister is rude. Anyway, how you doing? You're pretty."

"Thank you."

"How's your husband, Nita?" Erica asked sarcastically.

"He's fine. I didn't come here for you to be asking about my life. I'm in town and checking in to see if Daddy or Mommy needed anything. Not you," Nichelle yelled.

"Then won't you take Daddy to the pharmacy? He needs his medication refilled. Take him to go get it. And get the central air fixed because, as you can feel, it is broke."

"I will take him, but I'm not getting the air fixed. Come on, Daddy, let's go." Nichelle looked at me and said she would be right back. I never saw that side of her and was surprised.

"So, how long have you known my bitchy sister?" Erica asked. I wasn't sure if I should answer or not, because by answering I was agreeing that she was a bitch.

"A little while. My boyfriend plays on the same team as Lloyd."

"Damn, y'all some lucky bitches. Your jewelry real and shit, ain't it? Let me see that necklace." She picked up my necklace off my neck, pursed her lips, and continued, "I been asking Nita to let me get at one of them basketball players for the longest and she refuse to hook me up. She said I was too fat."

"No, you're not fat."

"Aw, thanks, but you don't have to lie."

"So, why do you call Nichelle Nita?"

"Because that's her birth name. Fake bitch. Excuse me. All this Nichelle stuff came about when she left home. Ranita left one person and came back another. My sister is crazy."

"Oh, okay," was all I could say.

"Don't mind anything I say, I just tell the truth. I just don't understand how having things make you better than other people. It don't mean anything when you die. If your daddy and your mama ain't good, then you not winning. If I ever hit the lotto, we all going to be right." She was a little hood, but she was making sense.

* * *

Twenty minutes later, Nichelle and her dad came back. He seemed happy that he had spent some time with his daughter and filled his prescription.

"Daddy got his medicine enough for two months. So, I'll see you people later. Come on, Zakiya, let's go." I stood up and told everyone it was nice to meet them.

"When will I see you again?" her mother asked.

"I don't know, Momma, I will call you."

"It's nice you bought the medicine that he needs. Give Daddy some money. We need to get the air fixed," Erica yelled at Nichelle again.

"No, I'm not getting the air fixed. I don't have it. What would you have done if I didn't come here? I'm out."

"I don't know, that's why I asked. Well then, buy some of my jewelry I'm selling. Let me get the book." She brought the book out for some Traci Lynn jewelry.

"Erica, come on, you always trying to sell me something I don't need or have time for."

"Just look at the book," Erica begged her sister.

"I'll look." I didn't want any, but I felt like I had to buy a bunch. I flipped through the pages and said, "I'll buy some. Just pick out the sets that are nice and send them to Nichelle's house. I'll get them there." I dug in my bag and passed her some money. Nichelle looked at me like she was offended I was helping her sister.

"You sure you want five hundred dollars' worth of jewelry?" Erica asked.

"Yes, I'm sure."

Erica thanked me several times. I told her not to worry about it.

* * *

I almost felt guilty staying in our luxury Palms suite when I knew people like Nichelle's family were struggling. I was a little angry with her, because she could but wouldn't help them. I then started being angry with myself for beginning to become one of them. What did I need with a five-thousand-dollar bag when people couldn't pay their light bills? I felt horrible for having dozens of designer bags and buying things I couldn't pronounce just because it looked good and I wanted to impress my friends. What did it all mean at the end of the day when you die? Erica was right. It didn't mean anything, nothing at all!

I watched television, and sat in the room and sulked. Life was good, but only for some. I didn't know if I was blessed or cursed to have so much, but still be able to care about people who didn't.

A few hours later Nichelle returned to the room. She looked to have had a good time. Her hair was still wet and she had almost completed the cocktail in her hand.

"What's wrong with you? Why are we in Vegas and you're behaving like someone hurt your feelings?"

"Nothing. I don't know."

"Well, the pool was great, and I'm about to get ready to get dressed and go to my friend's party. By the way, I wanted to apologize for everything that happened at my parents' house earlier." I didn't want to be forward and say anything, but now that she had said something, I was going to speak up about it.

"How come you don't just send your parents money every month? I mean, you have a lot of it."

"Because I married money, they didn't. You don't know them, Zakiya. It's meds today, tomorrow the cable. I don't have time for them and their problems. That's why I moved away from the beggars. You'll see. People will always expect things from you. My family, they are lazy and always want you to give them something. My dad worked for thirty years and gambled all his pension and money away. My mother is silly for staying with him, and my sister could have got out of Vegas like I did if she wanted to. But all they do is sit around and complain, and I'm not helping anyone that doesn't help themselves. So that's why. So, are you going out tonight or what?"

I disagreed with her, but it was her life and her family. "Let me pull out what I am going to wear."

On the strip we gambled, and I won five thousand on the roulette table. I didn't know what I was doing, but I was lucky and every number I picked the ball landed on. I cashed in my chips and then we caught a cab over to Nichelle's DJ friend's party at a club called Pure in the Caesar's Palace. It was crowded but with mostly young college kids for some type of event. We still made the best of the club, ordering drinks, dancing, and having fun with Nichelle's friends. She kept buying rounds for everyone and making sure we all had a good time.

"You know what we should do?" she screamed over the music. "We should meet the guys in L.A. We can go back to the hotel, get our stuff, and catch a flight."

"How are we going to get a flight this late?"

"A private plane."

"We should. I miss my boo." That was a really good idea, the best thing Nichelle had said on the whole trip.

Last night we were partying on the Vegas strip and now we were on the tarmac of the airport, about to take off in a private plane, L.A. bound. I was exhausted. Right before we took off, Nichelle grabbed her phone and snapped a picture of us for her Instagram. She captioned it "No passengers on my plane." I had to laugh at her bragging, but I had to admit that the experience on a private plane was a lot different than a commercial flight. There were no babies crying, fat men sitting next to you, or strangers trying to strike up a conversation. The plush leather seats were large and comfy and our personal flight attendant attended to our every need. I didn't feel one bump or shake. The ride was relaxing. I fell right asleep and didn't awake until we landed.

In L.A. we stayed downtown at the Millennium Biltmore Hotel. We unpacked and had brunch at our hotel's beautiful restaurant.

"Cheers to Vegas nights and L.A. afternoons. To the life," Nichelle cheered as we tapped champagne flutes. I had to admit we were living the life; shopping, clubbing with celebrities, and having everything at our fingertips. Christie called me since Nichelle wasn't answering her phone.

"Put me on speaker phone? So I can talk to Nichelle. Are you guys having fun without me?"

"A great time," Nichelle said, amused.

"You are wrong. Just you wait until I have this baby. I'm going to be right there, having fun with you two. When you get to the game, make sure no chicks are all up on my Omar and have fun. Ooh, bring me back some Roscoe chicken and waffles. My daughter said she wants some."

"Greedy, we are not going there. Will talk to you later, good-bye, Christie." I disconnected the call. "We need to start planning her baby shower."

"Okay, I'll have Lloyd call Omar."

"And let's make it coed so all the guys can come. We can do like a basketball theme baby shower," I said, getting excited about my idea.

"And I think we should rent a suite somewhere so no one has to worry about kicking people out of their house."

The squeaking noise of sneakers pressing against the wood was loud as we arrived forty-five minutes before the game started at the Staples Center. They were playing against the Clippers. Jabril and a few other players were already suited up, doing a shoot around. I felt so funny walking down to the floor, screaming his name. Once Jabril finally realized it was me, he ran down the court and over to where we were. Nichelle spoke before I could. "Where is my husband?" she asked.

"He hasn't come out of the locker room yet. I thought y'all were in Vegas."

"We were, but we missed y'all so we flew down this morning to surprise y'all." I snatched a fast hug.

"I missed you, too, but you know we have to get right on the bus after this?"

"I know, but I wanted to see you in person to tell you. I'm ready now."

"Ready for what?"

"To do what you been asking me to do. To have our baby. Our son or daughter."

His face lit up and his entire disposition changed. "You are? Really, Zakiya? What made you change your mind?"

"I'm not afraid anymore. I'm going to get off of my pills."

"You just made my night, Kiya. When I'm up at the free throw line, I'm going to have something for you."

"Okay, have a good game, Bril."

I walked back up to where we were seated. I felt so proud that my man was playing on the same court as Blake Griffin and Chris Paul. I was a very lucky girl.

Our seats weren't that good, and we were seated near die-hard, annoying, corny Clippers fans, but I was so happy that my man was playing on the court.

"It would be nice if Westbrook would pass the ball to Jabril or Durant."

"Yeah, Jabril said he was a ball hog," I said, commenting on the game. Then I stood up when Bril made a basket. A rude Clippers fan told me to sit my ass down.

"These fans are kind of disrespectful," I said.

"The real L.A. team is not playing," Nichelle said loud enough for the man to hear. We both giggled hysterically, angering the man so much we decided to move at halftime.

"Hold up, girl, my phone is ringing." I answered, and it was Lisa. "Hey, Lisa, I'm in L.A."

"Okay, I didn't want anything. Just returning your call, Miss Hollywood."

"Oh yeah, I called y'all just to check up on you, and I'm going to come home soon to see you and the boys. What games do they want?"

"They are so busy with karate, they are too tired to come home to play the games. That karate instructor, Brian, asked about you. I told him you moved, but I would tell you he said hey."

"Tell him I said bye. All right, well, halftime is over. I'll call you back."

Jabril went to the free throw and he tapped his tattoo, then held up two fingers up and pointed up. I started bawling with tears. No one else but he and I knew what that meant. He was saying he loved our son who didn't make it. I startled Nichelle.

"What's wrong?" she asked.

"We are going to try to have a baby again. I'm going to stop taking my pills."

"I thought you wanted to go back to school?"

"I do, but he wants a baby real bad, and I don't want to deny him. He's said he has everything he ever wanted except for a child."

"That's nice, but whatever you do, make sure you are having the baby for all the right reasons. Having a baby is a lot. Christie and I will be leaving you next."

"Wow, no, you won't. I'm following y'all, big belly and all. I am ready, though. I want my boo to be happy."

"Aw, well, congratulations, new mommy."

"Not yet, but very soon."

In three days I had partied in Vegas, flown to L.A. for brunch and to see my man, and now I was headed back home to get some much-needed rest. Jabril had three more road games and then he would be joining me. It was good seeing him just for that little bit of time, and I couldn't wait until he was home so that we could work on our little one. This weekend I finally got to see that I'm so fortunate to have a great boyfriend and a family that loves me. To me that means the world.

CHAPTER 27

Adrienne

If you want to be seen and party at the most exclusive lounge in the tri-state area of Pennsylvania, New Jersey, and Delaware, then you might want to be at Belize Lounge. We have hosted so many celebrity birthday parties and industry events. I have people from New York and Washington, D.C., the club capitals, coming to party with us. Belize was so popular we were even taking advance reservations for tables. In order to secure their reservations, they had to leave a deposit of three hundred on a credit card, and if they don't show up, they forfeit their money.

Everyone noticed how well the club was doing. Keldrick asked me for a raise. He said he was one of the reasons Belize was popping. He did do an incredible job of getting the word out so I gave him a small raise per night, based on our drink sales.

Ian has been doing his thing in Miami. He's hustling, shooting videos for any and everyone seven days a week to get the rest of the money he needs.

With him being away, I have had a lot of time to think about our relationship. I wasn't wearing his ring even though he had it resized. I didn't want to marry him, either. I would really have preferred it if he'd bought me a cloudy big diamond. If he wasn't going to spend a lot of money, at least I could have worn it and pretended to be happy. Instead I hid that travesty of a ring at my mother's house. I was going to tell him I lost it. I don't know why, but I was slowly falling out of like with Ian. I think it had everything to do with him asking me for help with his movie. What did I look like, a bank? I'm not used to a begging man. It is not sexy. My money was not his. I would have a conversation with him when I picked him up from the airport this evening.

The other reason I was losing interest in Ian was all the successful men I was meeting each night. Men who take care of their women and who would never ask their women for money. And men like Shelton James, who is the biggest married flirt. He has been texting and been past the club a couple of times, but we still haven't gone out yet. I'm not sure what he wants with me. It is kind of confusing, but I will take him however I can get him.

I was in the back office at the club, looking at the numbers for the week. Belize cost a lot to operate. I never had been so overwhelmed with bills and writing checks, but I really loved my club. It also made me feel like the worst mom ever. I hadn't seen Asia in a week, and my mom wasn't going to let me get away with neglecting her grandchild. She left me a message saying, "Adrienne Sheppard, your daughter has been crying for you. It is nice you have a business and all, but your daughter should be your first priority." Then instead of just hanging up the call, she allowed Asia to say, "Mommy, mommy, come home, mommy. Asia say come."

It hurts me, but I have to strike while the iron is hot. I wake up, go to the club, come home, go back to sleep for less than four hours, and then do the same thing again. Right now I was solely concentrating on attending to my business. I missed my child, but having this club and the kind of money it could generate in one weekend, it could take care of her kids. I planned to go past my mother's to see her tonight.

Darcel tapped on my office door. I welcomed her in and asked her what was going on. She nervously took a seat and started fidgeting with her hands. I knew it was something serious from her facial expressions, so I got up and closed the door.

"What's wrong, Darcel?"

"Adrienne, I usually mind my own business, but I have to tell you about something that happened with Joi last night." I sat back down and waited for her to continue.

"So, last night, there was a table of guys in my section, and they kept asking me for the white girl. I thought it was strange, but I said okay. I brought over Summer. So they said no, the other white girl.

I still didn't understand what they were talking about, until I saw Joi come over to them and pass them something and they slipped her money."

"What did she pass them?"

"I'm almost certain she was selling them cocaine, and I know you own this club and I would hate to see anyone ruin it for you."

"Cocaine in my club? Darcel, thank you so much for bringing this to my attention."

"You're welcome, Adrienne," she said as she left my office and closed the door.

Joi was already on my radar, not because I thought she was selling drugs. She always was clumsy and didn't know how to count. On more than one occasion, she had slipped and fallen and given back the wrong change, but I didn't want to discriminate against the unintelligent.

I picked Ian up from the airport. He dumped all his equipment in the trunk, and I immediately began to tell him everything Darcel had told me about Joi. He was just as shocked as I was and told me I had to confront her and fire her immediately. That was what I had planned to do.

Joi came in to work, and I was so ready to fire her until she confessed that it wasn't her selling drugs, it was Summer. Joi said she did pass something to the guys the other night, but it was because Summer had asked her to. She started crying, telling me she didn't want to lose her job and how she was going to get Summer for playing her. I didn't know who was telling the truth. I brought Keldrick in and he vouched for Joi. "Adrienne, I can tell you she is not like that." I looked over to Ian to get his opinion. "I say we watch them both tonight and see who is lying."

"That's a good idea, but what if something happens in the meantime? Like a drug bust or something, while we are waiting to see if she sells to anyone?"

"We can just check her stuff when she gets here. Send Joi home so she won't let on that we know what's going on."

I agreed to send Joi home and the entire night I kept my eyes on Summer, but she wasn't doing anything abnormal. She, however, kept smiling in my face and speaking to everyone. I couldn't resist pulling her to the side. "Summer, are you selling drugs in my club?"

"Absolutely not. Drugs, please, that's not what I do. I don't even drink." She swore up and down, and then she started crying and becoming hysterical.

"Are you sure?" Keldrick asked as he sat next to her, intimidating her.

"Yes, I'm sure."

"She is lying," Ian whispered.

"I know she is, but I don't have any proof."

"She probably has the drugs somewhere in the club. We just have to find out where she is hiding them." While we were questioning her, Keldrick said, "I'll be back." Then he came back with Summer's bag. He opened her backpack and out fell a bunch of little bags full of white powder.

"That's not mine."

"Whose is it, then?"

"I don't know."

How dare this little bitch put everything in jeopardy and lie in my face? I went to slap her, but Ian blocked me. Once she missed my hit, she jumped out and shouted, "Fuck this setup club."

I came home ready to do nothing. I couldn't believe the events of the day, but I was glad it was over. I could just close my eyes, but Ian saw it as the perfect time to discuss *Falcon Hall Boys.*

"Adrienne, so when do you think you'll be able and how much you will be able to loan me for the movie?"

I sat up and said, "Yeah, I wanted to talk to you about that. I won't be able to loan you anything."

"I'm not understanding you, Adrienne?"

"Ian, I looked over everything, and I just don't have it."

"Wow, really? Now I have to postpone filming. I've scheduled everything and I can't move without another twenty thousand at least. I was already going to cut corners with everything else as far as my production staff goes. But I can't cut anywhere else."

"I can't do it, I'm sorry," I said, attempting to change the subject, but it was obvious Ian wasn't finished with his plea for money. He stood up and said, "No, I get it. You only have money for handbags, shoes, and bottles of champagne for your rich friends."

"Whatever. You sound very dumb, Ian. How about you try to make some sense."

"No, you sound greedy, but don't be mad because I'm stating the facts."

"Ian, you can state the facts to yourself, because I don't really care. All my money is tied up, sorry."

Chapter 28

Shanice

The last few weeks at the club have been off the chain. Bottle popping at Belize was an understatement. I was getting big tips, and I wasn't even naked swinging on a pole.

Last week this rapper named Trez from Atlanta was trying to get with me. He was all right, but I've been meeting so many dudes so I wasn't pressed on one. I've been too busy trying to stack my own funds. Anyway I should have been more aware, because last night I saw him on *Late Night with Jimmy Fallon* rapping with The Roots and I was like, damn.

And I'm really trying to get smarter and talk better. I be meeting so many high-powered people that I be concentrating on how to fit in. Adrienne introduced me to all these celebrities she knew. One night an entire cast from a play came in and tipped me three hundred dollars. Adrienne always looks out and she is cool and I can tell she likes me a lot. She took me and Darcel to lunch once and let me drive her car around the corner for her and parked it for her.

My wardrobe has come up, too. I love being able to go shopping whenever I want. I treated myself to three pairs of Christian Louboutin shoes and a Gucci purse and all these clothes, and I still have money left over. If I wanted to, I could move right now, but I'm going to wait a little while and just stack my dollars. I even paid the apartment rent this month by the first. I called up Mr. Woods and told him to come get his money. You would think Courtney and Aunt Rhonda would have been thankful and paid me back, but they weren't and they didn't.

Now that both of them see that I'm getting money, they just keep asking me for more. I got Courtney's hair done and her car fixed. Then she still asked me to give her money to go out with, like I was her dude. I told her no. She said I was fronting.

Another night at Belize Lounge, the music was loud and the club was extra crowded but after a while you get used to the noise and learn how to read lips. Since Summer got fired, we each got another table and our money went up. I walked around checking on all my tables, when I noticed guys sitting in my section who hadn't paid.

"Sorry, you can't sit there. This is a reserved VIP area."

"What? I want to know how you are going to have a VIP section in a supposedly all VIP club," the leader of the group said. I couldn't answer him, so I just hunched my shoulders.

"They sitting over there. You are not asking them any questions," his friend said.

"That's because that's a private party for the Eagles' wide receiver, Raul Canton."

"Oh, so, because they play ball, they can get better service than us."

"No, they paid for their tables. You can go in that section down there, but the minimum over here is two bottles. I can show you a drink menu." I handed him the menu and waited for his decision.

"Eight dollars for a bottle of water? This club is cheating, damn," he said while reviewing the menu.

"How much is it for a bottle of Rose?" Before I could answer him, Adrienne stepped in and said, "If you have to ask, then you can't afford it." His friends started laughing at how Adrienne was insulting his pockets.

"No, I can afford a lot of things, miss, but come on, you're telling me to order whatever and just wait and be surprised when I get my bill? That doesn't seem too smart."

I smiled at him and told him I didn't make the rules. He didn't seem to have enough money. I was waiting for him to get up and say he would just hang out at the bar, but he surprised me and said, "My boy is getting married tomorrow, and he is on his way, so I'll take three bottles." Unimpressed,

Adrienne asked for his credit card and license. She went over to the bar and ran his card. Moments later, she gave me the okay signal to serve him.

I walked to the bar and began placing ice in the buckets. Adrienne helped, placing sparklers on top of the cold containers. While we were preparing his order, Adrienne said, "You've really been doing a great job. I'm very proud of you."

"Thank you," I said, smiling on the inside. I really have been doing everything to get her to notice me and make her proud.

"You know, sometimes we have to put a little pressure on them and make them spend even what they didn't plan to."

"Yes, we do."

I walked back over to the table, happy that my boss had noticed how good of a job I was doing. Behind me, Joi had dropped drinks and Adrienne almost slipped on her mess. I would have helped her, but I saw Darcel helping her pick up the pieces of glasses, too. I returned with the drinks. And the team of men were still being very playful.

"Anybody need anything else?" I asked.

"Your name and number, and will you marry me? Never mind, we know you got a boyfriend." His friends requested more ice and cranberry juice, and his other friend wanted a Red Bull. I went to get everything they needed and then patted the leader of the table on his lap, letting him know I was there for him. He pulled me down to have a seat with him. He was loud, talking over the music. "You are so gorgeous. You should meet me for lunch tomorrow."

"Where?"

"In Maple Shade over in Jersey."

"I can't. I don't have a car and I live all the way in North Philly."

"No car. We are going to have to work on that. I sell cars. My dad owns a car dealership."

"He does?"

"Yeah, he does. Call me tomorrow because I'm not trying to see someone as fine as you on the bus stop." He handed me a business card and said his name was Kenny and to make sure I called. I took his card and smiled. I couldn't judge if he was serious or not, but I was relieved I didn't play him and miss out on possibly getting a free car.

The rush was slowing up. All of our tables were seated and waited on. Darcel was checking out the crowd and bobbing to the music.

"So, why was you helping your friend Joi pick up the glass she broke?"

"I felt sorry for that ditzy broad."

"Shh, here she come." I laughed nervously as Joi walked over to try to make conversation with us. Joi was cute, but everything about her was dumb. All she was was pretty. She had no common sense. One day she asked me to help her turn her cell phone on. There wasn't anything wrong with her phone, it was just dead. Yes, she is that stupid. I was talking to the bartender Waliq when Joi came up and said something to Darcel. She looked at me and then left to go take care of one of her tables.

"What was Dumbarella saying to you?"

"Girl, I don't know. I can't hardly understand

her baby voice. She was saying something about do we want to meet up with her and Keldrick after the club."

"What? I hope you told her no," I joked.

"I did. I said, hell no. Keldrick is a weirdo, and she is a dumb slut. Summer said she gave this guy a free dick suck in the bathroom, because he was cute and paid his tab at the end of the night."

"Stop it, and she is going to show us how to get some money?" We both laughed. "She better learn her left from her right."

"Yes, what's up with your table of guys? Are they giving you a hard time?" she asked.

"No, that light-skin dude just said someone as fine as me shouldn't be on the bus stop and he wants to buy me a car." We both laughed again as I walked from side to side, crossing my eyes and poking out my lips showing off how fine I really was.

"Well, you are kind of cute. Why don't you go to New York with me on Tuesday? I got a casting call for a video."

"A music video?"

"Yeah, by this rapper. I told you I model, too."

"Okay, I'll go."

I knew no one does anything for free or nothing in return. I knew it was a strong possibility that I was getting dressed and catching the train into New Jersey early for nothing. Why would Kenny help me? He didn't even know me.

I arrived at the train station, and Kenny said he

was on his way. *Maybe he was lying,* I thought when he pulled up in a Cadillac and was talking on his phone. He reached to open my door but did not stop talking on the phone. He was speaking in this professional voice and was trying to convince someone about meeting them and that he could get them the right interest rate they wanted. He went back and forth with the caller the entire ride to the dealership. I was expecting a little run-down used-car dealership, but it was a big, new, and pre-owned Honda and Subaru dealership called Stevens'. That was Kenny's last name. I tried to say something, but he put the one-minute sign up at me. I was fine. I just wanted to see how this whole car situation was going to work out. He finally ended his call, and we walked through the large car dealership into the service area.

"So, can you drive a stick?" he asked.

"No, I can't." I knew it had to be something like this. A damn stick. Then he walked over to another car. He looked over into the window, and said, "Oh, this not the one that was a stick, but it's got a lot of miles on it." It was a Honda and it was cute. I sat inside of it and became very excited.

"Now, listen, it's got a lot of miles. But you can have it. We aren't going to do anything but junk this car anyway. So you got a choice. Give me four hundred for it or a date."

"Hmm, let me think. I guess a date," I said aloud.

"All right, ma'am, you got yourself a car. And I want my date this weekend."

"I work every weekend, but my off days are Monday, Tuesday, and Wednesday."

"Then Wednesday. No more bus stop for you. That's bird shit, and you are a dime. You can have it. Let's do the paperwork."

"What do you mean, I can have it? Like, take it home right now?"

"Yes, right now. You got your license, right?"

"Yeah."

"All right, then, we will walk you over to my insurance man and we will get your paperwork done."

When I drove off the lot, I was still in shock. How did I have a car? It was running really good, I thought while flooring across the Walt Whitman Bridge back toward home. I didn't care how many miles were on the thing I was driving.

I beeped the horn in front of the door. I knew Courtney was going to be excited for me. She knew how badly I needed a car.

"Who let you hold they car?" she asked, coming to the window.

"It's mine. Come down and let's go for a ride."

Courtney got in the car, and I explained the whole story to her. Her response was, "Don't nobody buy you a car for nothing?"

"I'm telling you, he did. He didn't buy it for me. His dad owned the car lot, and he said it was a trade-in. At first I didn't think he was going to do it. He said, give me four hundred dollars or just go out on a date with him."

"Damn. That's what's up. Now, I don't have to drive to the club tonight."

"I can't go out tonight. I have to go to work.

Won't you come down to my job and get one of them dudes to bring you?"

"I've been trying, but every time I asked someone they say no, that it cost too much. Plus, they said the club was hot."

"Hot, how?"

"Like, cops be in there."

"No, dumbass, don't no cops be in our club. They meant hot, like popping."

"Oh. And I heard they play you at the door if your pockets ain't right and you got to look a certain way."

I laughed. "That's all true. Belize don't be playing. They do have some rules, but that's to keep all the thugs and crazy people out."

"Thugs. You're funny. Girl, please, since when do you have problems with thugs? Don't get with them people down there and get new, Shani."

"Whatever, I'm not."

Chapter 29

Shanice

I met Darcel at her college campus at four in the morning. We needed to be in New York in four hours. It only took two and half hours to get there, but she said we were going to get caught up in a lot of traffic.

"You're sure you don't want me to drive down there?" I questioned her. It seem more convenient to drive than to get on a bus.

"No, it is easier just to take the bus. It is cheap. We can just take the Mega Bus, talk and sleep, and I can type my paper up. There is Internet on the bus."

"All right. So, who is the artist?"

"I don't know exactly. The casting e-mail said video girls wanted for a hip-hop video. Usually, when you get there, they pick who they want. And if you are selected, you get like three to five hundred for the day."

"Did you ever get picked before?"

"Yeah, I was in a few videos, but the camera flashed past me so fast. I have to push PAUSE to see myself."

"Well, not today. We getting in a video."

We both fell asleep and awoke in the Holland Tunnel to the bus driver jerking on the brakes every few feet. I looked out the window to see cars moving slowly in every direction.

Once we finally made it to the bus station, we caught a cab to the casting call. It was early in the morning, and all the girls were already made up and ready. They were all beautiful and appeared to be flawless. Their legs and asses were perfect; they all had big, perky boobs, lots of makeup, and pounds of silky Brazilian weaves.

Eyeing my competition, I asked, "Are all of these girls auditioning for ten spots?"

"Yes. Don't worry, half these girls look too much alike. Me and you have a different look," Darcel answered.

An hour after waiting in line, a guy came out with a clipboard and said, "If your name is not on the list, you are not going to be seen today. I repeat, if you are a walk in and you don't have an actual invite, we don't have time to see you today. Thank you for coming." Hearing that news, I stepped out of the line and told Darcel I would wait outside for her.

"You don't have to. Don't worry, he will see you. Trust me." She pulled my arm toward the guy with the clipboard and said, "Joel, this is my girlfriend. Her name is Shanice, see if you can add her name."

"What's up, Darcel? You're looking good, girl. I don't know, it is so many girls today."

"Please, Joel, do it for me," she pleaded with him. He looked over at me and smiled and agreed to add my name. I was so happy Darcel knew people, because right after he spoke with us, he got rid of about a hundred girls who didn't have invites. They moved the rest of us to this big area with mirrored walls. A woman came out with a list and began calling off names. I noticed a few of the girls doing splits and ballerina squats, like they were preparing to break into serious dance moves.

"You ain't tell me we had to dance, Darcel."

"This is not dancing. Just follow what she does. You just have to look cute and swerve a little to the music."

I was becoming increasingly nervous and wasn't so sure I was cut out to be a video girl.

The women choreographers stood up and began showing us this side-to-side move, and they told us to put our own sexy spin on the dance and dip low like she had. We all had to line up and I thought of what I could do quickly. They started the music, and every girl began fighting for their position. I didn't know what to do, so I just did this twist-and-drop move I used to do when I worked at the strip club, called twerk without a pole. The music started, and I twerked my ass and dropped it to the ground a few times to the beat.

"Girl, you act like you did this before." Darcel laughed.

"She said be sexy, so I was just doing what I thought was sexy."

"Well, you sure got it."

By the afternoon, they had got us down to twenty-five girls. I felt proud of myself. This was my first audition, and I had made it this far. The director's assistants brought us some cold water and asked if we were hungry, but told us if we went out too long for food, we wouldn't be guaranteed to get back in. So Darcel and I stayed put.

We waited two more hours, and they informed us that the actual video was being shot today, because the rapper Wellzo was only available today. Everyone wanted to be in the video, so only two girls left to get food and they and another ten girls got the boot.

When they were sent out, we had to dance again in front of all these important-looking people sitting at a table. I felt like they were judges on a reality show. Darcel said that the video director was really famous. He did all these videos for Jay-Z, T.I., and Ludacris. I had never heard of him, and I was growing tired of dancing. They needed to come on. They started the music again, and the director got up and walked around us. He came over to me and said, let me see you do that again. I did my twerk without a pole for the five-hundredth time.

"What's your name?" he asked.

"Shanice."

"Is that all you, Shanice?" he asked as he tapped my ass. If he wasn't the video director, I might have punched him in his face.

"Yes, all natural."

"Hmm, what do your friends call you, Shanice?"

"Everybody calls me Shani."

"Where are you from?"

"Philly."

"Okay, Shani from Philly. Shani, I need more of that ass. Shani, love you more. Yeah, 'cause you got more ass than a lit bit. No, Shani, more, more." It became a joke, and we were all laughing. The director and casting guy were funny. Then he said lustfully, "Shani Amore."

"Shani Amore, I like it. I might use it," I joked.

"Shani Amore, thank me later for your name, and you are the lead girl, Shani Amore. I need you to do that dance all up on Wellzo when he gets out here."

So that was it. I had a new stage handle, Shani Amore, and Darcel and I, we had made it to the video. They finally brought us a sandwich. I wasn't even hungry, I was too excited that I was about to be in a music video and I didn't want my stomach puffing up.

The stylist brought out someone from wardrobe and makeup. They didn't ask us what our preference was, they just came over to us, telling us to squeeze ourselves in these small, silver sequin dresses that they promised would look better on camera.

We dressed and drove in a van to another studio. I couldn't believe the lights and the cameras were on us. We were against this bright green screen. All these people were around us directing us. I was a little nervous, but I didn't let it show. I was moving, and the attention was all on me. I got to stand next to the rapper, Wellzo. I never heard of him. He was from South Carolina and he was becoming popular for his remixes and mix tape downloads that he was putting out. The name of his song was called "Slide It Down." They had me dance up against his arms while he just stood there in this hard gangster pose. The director wanted me to do my twerk with no pole move nonstop when the chorus came on: *"Slide it down, girl. Slide it down. Slide it. Show me you want was in my pockets. Got them fifty. Got them hundreds. Slide it down, girl, show me that you worth it."* I was dancing as hard as I could, but the director positioned me closer to Wellzo and the ground and told me to bounce harder and pout my mouth out more. I was tired, but Darcel kept cheering me on every time we had a little break.

It was exhausting doing the same thing over and over again, but we were having fun. Between takes, the other girls were rolling eyes and being catty. I heard one girl say something like the bitches with the fake asses always get picked. Real bitches don't never get no recognition. I acted like I didn't hear what she said and kept it moving and waiting for the next scene. Until she repeatedly kept saying, "I hate fake bitches." And she was looking directly at me. That I wasn't about to let go.

"I'm ready to smack this shit out of this bitch," I shouted, standing up.

Darcel grabbed me and said, "No, you are not about to give this opportunity up. She is just mad she is in the back." Darcel was right. I couldn't be acting up and hitting people. I got calm and went back in position, waiting for the music to turn on again and the director to start filming.

When we left, they cut us checks for two hundred and fifty dollars. We had been there damn near twenty-four hours. The pay wasn't good, but I didn't care because I was the girl in the video.

Chapter 30

Zakiya

"Please ice that ankle and take something so the swelling can go down," I yelled at Jabril as he lay in his bed taking in a blunt. He coughed a little and said, "It's not swollen anymore. It doesn't feel like it is broke. I think it is just a sprain. I just wish I wouldn't have come down on it like that," Jabril said, inhaling some more smoke.

"You won't know exactly what's wrong until you see the specialist next week. Until then, the doctor told you to stay off of your leg, and you never listen. It might be broke, and you could aggravate it. Then smoking is not going to help it."

"I know what he said. And this helps to relax me. I told you that. He said it was okay to put a little weight on it if I felt like I could take it, but it doesn't feel like it is broke. I don't feel pain. I don't need ice or medicine."

"You're not taking the medicine because you think you are Superman, but you can't psych yourself out of an injury."

"No, Kiya, really, it doesn't hurt and it can't be broke because if it is, that's it for me for the rest of the season."

"Well, at least it happened at almost the end of the season."

"Yeah, I guess. But I don't want to miss the playoffs. But I tell you, it feels good to be in my bed. That's the one good thing that has come out of this. I hate being in hotels every night."

"I'm glad you are here, too!" I didn't want to express to Jabril how happy I really felt about him being stationary for once. I was secretly ecstatic about Jabril's injury. We hadn't spent this much continuous time together ever. I knew it was selfish to feel that way, but I couldn't help being happy that my man was home.

Claudette barged in our bedroom as usual and asked if we wanted anything else from the market.

"I'm okay, but can you make your son put ice on his leg and take his medicine?"

Jabril jumped up to show us both that he could walk, and he almost fell asking his mother not to forget his Fruity Pebbles cereal and chocolate milk.

"Sit your butt down before you be sitting on the bench," Claudette ordered Jabril.

"Never, I'm going to play regardless." He limped around the room acting like he was shooting an imaginary basket.

"Zakiya, babysit this fool. I have to go and get this long list of food he said he wants."

"Okay, I'll let her be my nurse as long as I'm the doctor and my nurse gives me an exam," Jabril said, cupping my boobs.

"Stop it in front of your mom," I said, smacking his hand off of me.

"She know we working on a little Bril. Right, Mom?"

Claudette turned her head away and said, "Do whatever you have to do to get the baby here, but not in front of me. I'll be back. I'm going to go get your stuff."

"Don't forget my Berry Cap'n Crunch, too, Ma."

I didn't have anything planned for the day but to love on my boo and plan for Christie's baby shower. I dialed Nichelle to go over the details while Jabril took a shower.

"Hey, lady, what are you doing?"

"I'm in the middle of doing Alana Clarke's hair. She's married to Dontae Clarke. You know her, right?"

"No, we haven't met."

"Oh, well, she nice and says hello. Put her on the list for the baby shower."

"What do you need from me? I'm kind of busy. I'll do the decorations, flowers, and cakes. Just tell her to register online for whatever she wants and we'll buy it. I'll pay half, but I'll call you later. Oh, and tell her to get her list together."

"Okay." I called Christie as I wrote my list out. "What's up, Mama?"

"Hey, Zakiya. I'm tired and feeling a little out of it. How is Jabril's ankle?"

"It's sore, but he goes to the specialist to see what's going on on Monday. I was calling you to tell you to get your list of friends and family for the shower."

"Okay, I will."

I hung up with Christie and began looking at the cute baby stuff on the Babies "R" Us website. Jabril came over my shoulder, snooping.

"What are you doing, looking at all this baby stuff?"

"It's for Christie's baby shower."

"She needs to be planning yours."

"Soon, very soon. When hers arrives it will be practice."

"Hmm, well, I hope she is around when the baby comes."

"What is that supposed to mean, Bril?"

"I don't know. Omar said she is really annoying. She rides and calls him all the time and just is in the way. I'm glad you not like that. No one wants a woman down they throat all the time. Especially because Omar be chilling. He's not that kind of guy."

Claudette came back from the market and cooked her baby boy, Jabril, a big feast. He barely enjoyed it because his two phones kept going off back to back like they were possessed.

"When you get another phone?" Claudette asked Jabril, and then looked over at me.

"I had this phone awhile. This the phone number I give all the party promoters and people I used to go to school with. They can't say I'm fronting because they have a number for me. I'm just never going to answer."

"I'm so tired of people thinking you owe them something. Please tell them to go get a job and find their own success." Just as Claudette spoke, the phone began ringing again. This time I said something about it.

"Turn off that phone, Jabril, it's annoying and disrespectful."

"All right, no problem." I didn't really care about his extra phone, but I didn't want it to prevent us from enjoying our meal and our family time.

Chapter 31

Adrienne

Sometimes you have to live in your own truth, and my truth is that I like my men rich, with swagger and lots of money. Since I've been in Philly and Ian's been back and forth in Miami, we have been falling apart. I'm grateful for his help with the club. I'm certain that without him and Keldrick, I wouldn't have been able to open it, but enough is enough. I'm going to have to break away from them, but not just yet. I want him to leave me so I won't have to deal with him saying that as soon as you came up you left me.

In the meantime I'm going to meet up with Shelton today. There is something so alluring about him, even though he is married. I hadn't been this excited in years about a man. We've been texting a lot and had a few conversations, and we've seen each other at the club, but this is the first time we are going to actually hang out. He has a very hectic work schedule and so do I.

The plan was to talk, enjoy the scenic river view on Kelly Drive, and then maybe go somewhere and have lunch. I knew it was so wrong to be doing any of this, but I'm grown up—and he is married, I'm not.

My eyes saw Shelton and immediately I got all type of urges. I wanted him bad. His navy suit fit his body perfectly, and he smelled amazing. He must have had a meticulous regime to keep everything so together. He was so handsome. I was glad I didn't dress down for the park. I'd kept on my stilettos instead of the flats sitting on the floor of the back of the car.

"Hey, beautiful. So, what are we doing?" he asked me as he leaned in for a quick hug.

"I don't know, you tell me. I thought I was just coming to meet you and walk and talk a little. You're so hard to catch up with."

We walked down to a small café at the end of the river's edge. It was pretty crowded for the afternoon, but we were able to find a table in the back. I noticed Shelton looking around to make sure he didn't see anyone he knew.

"Are you looking for your wife's friends?" I asked.

"No, I'm allowed to have business meetings."

"Business meetings, right." I winked at him and said, "So, you practice entertainment law."

"Yes, I do. I also do criminal cases here and there,

and I used to dabble in family law. Family law made me want to scream."

"Family law like custody court?"

"Yes, those type of cases. It was a lot. I saw so many broken families with angry moms and dads with child support and custody issues. Then their bratty kids would be screaming and crying, telling their parents not to argue. I just couldn't take the bickering anymore. I wanted to do something fun. I would rather read over contracts and help my clients make money than listen to parents complain."

"That's funny. That might be me one day. I hate that my daughter is back and forth with her dad and his fiancée in an entirely different state, but I deal with it."

"How about you? What did you do before becoming a club owner?"

"I used to work at a nursing home as a registered nurse."

"So, you know how to take care of people."

"I do."

"Where is your man and why aren't you wearing your ring?"

"Because I'm not sure if I want to be married to him, and he is in Florida. He is a film director and has a hectic schedule right now. Your wife?"

"The truth?"

I shook my head yes, that I wanted him to share the real reason he was attempting to engage in a romantic liaison with me.

"She is a doctor. She works in the emergency room at Jefferson."

"So, what's your issue with her?"

"I think we both have our issues. I wouldn't say *issues.* I would say we have circumstances that we need to find out how we are going to handle." He was speaking in code some, but then he addressed the obvious. "I like you and you like me, but I'm married and you're engaged, so now what?"

"It's up to you. We can be friends—or more." I wanted to let him know that I was interested in him in any and every capacity if he wanted me.

"More, huh? Well, I can tell you I don't really have a lot of time for a girlfriend. I have a wife and a full-time career. So, me, I'm interested in having fun, but not much else."

"How do you know I'm not interested in just fun also?" I asked him.

"Are you sure about that? You know how some women say they can handle certain situations, but then they get in it and they can't handle it?"

"I'm not like most women, and a good friend is all I really need," I said.

"And what do you require of your friends?"

"You're Mr. Google. I think friendship is easily defined and self-explanatory."

Once we established that we were going to be friends, we then took our friendship outside and to the next level. I don't know who convinced whom to fuck in the backseat of his car, but that's where we ended up. I felt like a slut. Like a truck-stop whore, but that didn't stop me from pulling down my thong and straddling him. The idea that we might get caught by joggers passing by intensified the sexual energy between us. Impatiently, I tugged on the front of his pants, urging him to hurry up and give his dick some freedom. I didn't have to waste time getting him ready because he was already as hard as granite, and he was having a hard time getting it out of his pants.

Once it was out and standing ready in his hand, I eased down on it, and let out a soft sigh as he filled me with all of him. His hands cinched my waist, bouncing me up and down on his stiffness. "Fuck me," I cried out as he delivered a hard pounding. "Harder," I demanded, and he obliged. He covered my mouth with his, tasting my tongue as he mixed tenderness with the hard pounding he was putting me through. I rode him, matching his frantic pace. Moments later, we released together, and together we took deep breaths until our heartbeats finally slowed down.

I cracked my eyes open and was surprised that I couldn't see anything outside. The windows were so steamed up, it was apparent that we'd had complete privacy; no one could have seen a thing through those foggy windows.

My rendezvous with Shelton gave me just what I needed: a distraction from the club and all the goings-on. His friendship was welcome, whether it was full- or part-time. I was sitting in my office reminiscing about our last encounter.

I had already fired Summer, and now I was about to get rid of Joi's ass. The other night she had this group of Hispanic and white guys who were ordering drinks and asking for everything. They looked nice and clean-cut, but when I was not looking she let the transaction go through without checking their identification. So today, I learned by way of the Bank of America fraud department, that the unauthorized charges would not be processed. I was so frustrated and angry. I'd just left a message on her answering machine demanding for her to come and speak with me. Once I was done with her, Ian called and detected my negative energy.

"What's going on with you?" he asked.

"Nothing, I'm just having a bad day. This club is driving me crazy. I'm tired and I have dumb people working for me."

"What happened now?"

"I'm about to fire Joi, because she accepted a bad credit card with a tab of fifteen hundred dollars. Which means I have to hire and train someone else."

"Why are you going to let her go?"

I took the phone away from my ear and stared at it as if he could see me. "Why? Because she just cost me fifteen hundred dollars, Ian."

"Give her another chance. I'm sure she didn't mean to. You know how crowded it is, and you want them to hurry up, get drinks, run credit cards, and then she probably just forgot."

"So, I'm supposed to just eat fifteen hundred dollars. I can't do that."

"Take it out of her paycheck or her tips until she pays you back. She made an honest mistake. That's Keldrick's girl, and he says she is a good person. She just comes from a rough background," Ian said.

"Don't we all? I'm going to give her one more chance because of Keldrick. She should thank him because she doesn't know how close she was to being gone."

"All right, Adrienne, that's done. Listen. I have some good news."

"What's that?"

"I have all the money for the movie. We start shooting next week. I'm calling the crew and cast, and we are finally going to do this. *Falcon Boys* is finally going to happen."

"That's great, babe. I'm so proud of you."

"I know you are. So, come home. I need you to fly down and celebrate with me."

"I will as soon as I get a moment to breathe."

"Adrienne, I need you here."

"Okay, let me see what day I can get away." I looked up at my door and saw Joi nervously standing there. "I'll call you back. Joi just got here." I hung up the phone.

"Have a seat, Joi." She looked very scared as I closed my office door and said, "I want to talk to you about something."

"Yes, I already know. Can I can explain what happened?"

"You can explain what? Just because someone looks nice doesn't mean they are not a thief. You cost me over a thousand dollars."

"I'm so sorry, Adrienne. It was a mistake. Please don't fire me. I really need this job. I love working here."

"All I have to say is, please don't accept any

more cards without I.D. You can keep your job this time. But next time I'm going to let you go."

"Thank you. It won't happen again. I promise."

"Oh, and it will be deducted out of your tips until it is paid back."

CHAPTER 32

Shanice

The music video I shot was on YouTube and got a few hits. The majority of them were probably from me and Courtney. As soon as it was posted, we texted the link to everyone and kept watching it over and over again ourselves. I followed Wellzo on Twitter and he followed me back and thanked me for being in the video. Courtney and I were talking about Shani Amore the video girl for like a week straight, but that was it. No one else really saw it, but I was still grateful for the chance to go to New York and be in a video.

Today I was taking my daughter out to the mall and Valerie couldn't say anything, because I had my own car now and a booster seat. She had to give me my child without any excuses. I called her and said, "Valerie, I'm coming to get Raven."

"How are you coming to get her? She can't be on the bus."

"Valerie, I'm driving."

"I don't want her driving around with just any strange man. Plus, you don't have a booster seat."

"It's my car and I have a booster seat for her." Something told me she was going to try to give me a hard time with my picking up Raven. I thought about all of the excuses she could possibly give me and came up with a solution for every one.

"Well, you can come and get her, but you must have her back before dinner."

"Fine."

I pulled up in the driveway in front of their big house with lots of grass and big windows, to see my daughter's father, Ray, the college man. He still was handsome, but he had gained some weight. Initially he didn't realize it was me, and when he did, he opened my car door and said, "Nice car, Shanice." I got out and he surprised me with a quick hug.

"Thanks."

"So, what have you been doing with yourself lately?"

"Working, how about you?"

"The same. I get my master's degree at the end of the year. I'm a little behind. But what's an extra year or two?"

"Yeah, must be nice to take as long as you want in school," I said. "Well, I have to go. I'm picking up Raven, and your mom wants her back by dinner. Let me knock on the door." Before I could get up the driveway, I saw Valerie stomping toward me with Raven in tow. She didn't want me anywhere near her precious son. What did she think? I was going to get pregnant by him again by talking? Ray looked over at Raven and said that she was getting big.

"You live here. When was the last time you saw her?" I asked him, confused.

"I don't know. I don't be here like that."

I shook my head and then said, "Raven, say hi to your daddy." She gave him a quick smile, then took my hand and said good-bye to her grandmother. Valerie watched as I strapped Raven in, and I pulled off before she could make any more excuses about why I couldn't spend time with my daughter.

I brought Raven to the apartment to see Aunt Rhonda and Courtney. They hadn't seen her in almost a year. They both commented on how big and pretty she was getting. Raven was being shy at first, but then she got on the floor and started playing with Ayana with her toys. While I had Raven I wanted to spend quality time with her and take her somewhere special.

"Courtney, let's take them to the movies or something."

"You treating, working girl?" Courtney asked, turning her lips up.

"Yeah, I'm treating. Hurry up and get dressed because I only have her for a few hours."

We took the kids to the mall and I bought them a few outfits apiece from The Gap and The Children's Place. There weren't any kid-friendly movies playing, so we just settled with going to the Chinese Buffet and then the playground. The girls were happy just to run around the park with each other. They licked on their ice cream cones, and we sat on the bench watching them and talking.

"They are having fun. We have to do this more often," Courtney suggested.

"Yeah, I know. Do you know how long it's been since I was able to get Raven on my own? Valerie be really acting like she hers. That shit makes me so angry."

"She had her for such a long time, she probably forgot that she didn't actually give birth to her. But you are still a good mom, though, Shani. You go get her and buy her stuff. But I do think when you try to take her back, Valerie is going to fight you for her."

"Yeah, well, as long as she don't have full custody paperwork, she has to let me see her, and I'm her mom so I always can take her back when I want to."

"You got it made. I wish Ayana knew her other family. Antwan don't even be bothered with her."

"I know I'm lucky, that's why I don't really make a big deal about anything. I just don't want her to forget that I'm her mom. She already don't call me mommy." My phone started chiming.

"Hey, Shanice, where y'all at? I just wanted to spend some time with y'all."

"Who is this?" I asked, not recognizing the number.

"It's Ray."

"Ray?" I repeated and looked at the phone. What the hell did he want? He hadn't called me since I'd told him I was pregnant six years ago.

"What's up, Ray?"

"I just wanted to say you looked real nice and maybe we can go out or something and talk."

"I don't know about that. I be working all the time, so I don't think so. But I'm sure our daughter would love to hang out with you." I hung up the call in disbelief. I'm not sure why Ray thought I still wanted him.

"Tell me that wasn't your baby dad, Ray?" Courtney asked.

"It was. He wants to go out and talk."

"People can smell when you up, huh? Shaking my head. He seen you looking cute and you got a car now and he trying to get at you. He really need to go somewhere and have a seat. You don't want him. Do you?"

"Hell no. He don't have shit I want."

"Yeah, he was just like, look at my BM in her new car. By the way, what happened to that guy that gave you the car?"

"I don't know. I called him to keep my end of the deal and go out on a date with him, but he is always busy."

"Well, forget him. You got the car already."

"Yup, and Ray can go somewhere too." I looked over at Raven and Ayana. They were taking turns chasing each other on the slide. Raven ran over to me and gave me a kiss and then went off playing again. Courtney stood up and said, "So, cousin, I wasn't feeling what you was saying about the job before. But now I get it. You think you can hook me up if I come down there to the club? Do they need anyone else?"

"Yeah, I think I can. This girl supposed to be

getting fired for accepting a stolen credit card. These guys ran this huge bill up. She was bragging, talking about she made all this money and they gave her a two hundred tip, and that shit didn't even go through."

"I know she was played."

"Yes, she was. I'll ask my boss, Adrienne. She's real cool. I'll just bring you to my job tomorrow and see if she can interview you on the spot."

Courtney was definitely cute. She pulled way more dudes than I did, but she didn't know how to turn her hood on and off like I did or I was learning to. Like that bitch on that video set, I would have handed her her hair and eyeballs, but Darcel reminded me why I didn't need to fight. Courtney was hood twenty-four/seven, and my boss, Adrienne, is kind of bougie and I don't know if it will work, but it was at least worth a try.

When we dropped my baby girl off, she started crying, "Shani, I want to go with you." I had to pull her out of my car. She was crying so hard I was beginning to cry myself. I calmed her down and gave her a hug and promised I would come and get her the next week. Ms. Valerie grabbed her hand and snatched her away from me. She looked so aggravated, like I did something wrong to my daughter. At that moment, I decided it was time to start making plans to get my daughter back.

On the ride home Courtney was asking me what I thought she should wear to impress my boss, Adrienne. I knew she should try to pin her hair up and talk as little as possible. My phone began ringing, and I couldn't reach it, so I asked Courtney to answer it. She handed it to me, placing it against my ear. I said hello, and the caller on the other end said, "So, just wanted to let you know I'm a fan, Shani Amore."

"Shani Amore? Who is this?" I asked, shocked.

"Jabril. Remember, you, me, and my boy, Lloyd, was all hanging out after that club opened in Philly."

"Oh yeah, I do. How did you get my number?"

"I know people that know people."

"Is that so? So how are you a fan?" I asked, surprised.

"I saw you in that Wellzo video. My man sent me the video yesterday. He said you got to check out this jawn, she bad, she from Philly. And so I looked at the video a few times. And I was like, that's my girl. I know her. You were looking sexy as hell. The way you was moving those hips had me thinking all kinds of things."

"Did it? Thank you. So that's what you called to tell me. You like the way I move my hips."

"Yeah, pretty much. But more importantly, I wanted to link up with you next time I come to town. This is my number, so lock it in and get with me."

"All right. I will. I'm going to call you." I added his number to my contacts.

"Matter fact, I'm coming to town tomorrow. You want to come to my game?"

"Yeah, I want to come." I gave him my full name and he said he was leaving me tickets at the will-call window. Courtney was right, people can smell when you up. I had my daughter's father all up on me, and now I had a basketball player, too! What a day.

"Who was that?"

"You're never going to guess! All I'm going to say is, we going to a basketball game tomorrow. The dude I was trying to get you to come down and meet. Well, he coming to town tomorrow, and he said he is going to have two tickets waiting for me. He said he saw me in the video."

"Shut the fuck up. Cousin, oh my God. Oh shit, I need two outfits. One for the game, the other for the job interview."

"Remember my first night working at the club, and I came home with all that money."

"Yeah, I remember that."

"This is crazy, because I was on him from the beginning. But I fucked his teammate because he came at me first. He was supposed to call me, but he never did."

"Right. So, how you wound up fucking his bull, too?"

"The first dude, Lloyd, let him in and he was just watching, and then when he finished, me and the bull, Jabril, started going at it."

"Damn, well, he must not care and he must have liked the way you worked it, because he calling."

"Right, we there."

"Yes, we are. We going to your job and then to the game."

I took Courtney past my job to meet Adrienne, and I think she is going to get the job. Courtney was very mannerly, using big words and being extra-polite to Adrienne. I could tell Courtney was nervous, but she did a good job answering all of Adrienne's questions.

Once we left Belize, we went to the Wells Fargo Center to pick up the tickets. I forgot where he said to go to get them from. I tried calling his number, but his voice mail kept answering. I asked someone where we picked up tickets on hold. They directed us to this window; there were a few people in line. Once we reached the window, I gave my name and the man kept saying he didn't see anything. He asked me how to spell my name a bunch of times and still wasn't coming up with anything. By the fifth time I spelled and sounded it out for him, I was becoming concerned. He looked around some more in the office and in the computer and then said he still didn't see anything.

"Oh my God, he probably ain't leave no tickets for you," Courtney sighed, pouting.

I waited calmly, ignoring Courtney and wishing that she would shut up. Then the man said, "Oh, here they go. I got them right here. I just need your ID." I handed him my license and he said he couldn't find the tickets at first because my name was spelled wrong. It didn't matter. I just wanted to hurry and get to our seats and watch the game.

Our seats were so close to the floor, we were stopped by these men in black, Secret Service–looking type men. They checked our tickets with a scanner and then ushered us to our seats on the third row right by the team. The game had already begun, and I didn't see Jabril anywhere.

Then I looked over at the bench and there he was with a towel over his head. He didn't see us, though. He looked better than I remembered, and when I pointed him out to Courtney she couldn't believe it.

"So, that's really him. He looking too fucking good. I might have to help you out with that. If that's what be coming in that club, I can't wait to be working at your job, too. I need to meet me someone like that." I didn't know how to tell Courtney I already got a text from Adrienne that she was not what Belize was looking for. I felt sad for my cousin because she was really trying to get it together now. I don't know. Maybe I could help her find something at another club.

We left the game and Jabril texted he wanted me to meet him at his hotel. I wanted to bring Courtney with me, but I was a little afraid she might try to be up on him, so I dropped her ass off.

When I got to Jabril's hotel room, he answered looking more than good. He said what's up and then stretched out on his bed. I could barely concentrate when he asked me to have a seat at the edge of the bed. His muscles were showing off the tattoos peeking out from under his green T-shirt.

"So, what's up with you besides looking good in videos, Miss Shani Amore?" he said, sliding over to me and touching my cheek.

I responded, "You look good yourself. I saw you in the game scoring. You were doing your thing even though y'all lost."

"Yeah, but I was a little slow on the court tonight.

This is my first game back since I sprained my ankle. But I don't want to talk about that. I want to discuss how that thing was looking right in the video. Stand up and let me see. You going to do that 'Slide It Down' for me?"

"Maybe."

"Why maybe? Say definitely. I'm going to make sure it is worth your while." Jabril pulled out a stack of twenties from the nightstand and told me they was for me. It looked like a couple of thousand. I could dance for that. I started seductively removing my clothes down to my pink bra and G-string, and began performing like there was music playing. Jabril bit his lip, came up behind me, and started palming my ass like it was a ball. "Girl, how you got an ass this big and a waist this small?"

"I don't know. It's real, though," I said as I backed it up on him some more.

"I know it is. I can tell, and so are these." He squeezed my breasts together roughly and then kissed on my neck and said, "I'm going to go get in the shower. Here's the remote." While he showered, I counted my money. It was four thousand dollars. I put it in my purse.

Jabril came out of the shower and I was ready for him. I dropped his towel and got on my knees. He looked down at me then pulled the towel back up and said, "We don't have to get right into it. We can chill first."

"Oh, okay." I got off my knees, feeling a little silly. "I thought that's what you wanted."

"I do, but we got all night. And I told you I want

that dance, too. But first, are you hungry? Let's order some room service."

He handed me the hotel menu. "Pick whatever you want," he said and slipped on some boxers.

I ordered the most expensive thing on the menu—king crab legs. Hell, no telling when I'd get the royal treatment like this again. While we were waiting for our food, we started talking, and he pulled out a bag with a blunt and lit it. He inhaled and puffed a few times then placed it in my hands. I took a couple of tokes and mellowed out some more.

"This is some good weed," I said, smiling and already feeling the effects.

"I demand the best of everything . . . cars, weed . . . and women." His eyes roved over my body. He reached for me and I melted into his arms, lifting up my chin and accepting his kiss. His lips were so soft and sweet.

"How did I luck out and get a bad bitch like you, starring in music videos and whatnot?"

"Stop playing, Jabril. You know you meet gorgeous girls all over the country, all the time."

"True. But ain't none of 'em fine as you."

While I was grinning from ear to ear, he leaned close and began inhaling my perfume. "You smell good, too," he complimented.

"Thanks," I said in a whispery voice.

His lips trailed down to my breasts. As he caressed my lower region with one hand, he magically unsnapped the back of my bra with the other hand. With my boobs free, Jabril softly sucked one nipple and then the other, making my toes curl.

"I can't get enough of you," he muttered, his voice cracking with yearning. Sexual tension rippled through the air.

My eyes lingered on his hard-muscled thighs with heavy veins traveling toward his groin. His body was a work of art. And when his dick peeked out through the opening of his briefs, I reached for it, tightening my fist around it and rolling up and down like an expert. By the way he was flinching up and biting down on his lip, I knew he was enjoying it.

Taking it up a notch, I replaced my palm with my mouth, licking his balls soft and leisurely. I had him moaning and groaning.

"Damn, that shit feels good," Jabril said as I gave him a hand job while licking and nibbling on him at the same time. "I ain't never letting you go nowhere," he mumbled while in the heat of the moment, and I couldn't help but wonder if he actually meant what he was saying.

Then Jabril climbed on top of me, fitting his dick inside my pussy as he stared down at my face telling me a bunch of shit he couldn't mean. He told me I was with him now and my pussy belong to him. My mind was racing, trying to figure out something to say back to him. He kept repeating, do you hear me, and I was saved by the knock on the door. It was our room service. He wrapped a towel around his waist and strolled over to the door.

I pulled the covers up to my chest as Jabril opened the door and signed for the food. I had a feeling that me and Jabril were heading for something a little more serious than hooking up when he came to town. The way he was fucking me, I knew it meant a little bit more.

Jabril was out in the morning to the next city, but I had a good time with him. He had a big dick and could fuck. I would have done that shit for free, but luckily I didn't have to.

CHAPTER 33

Adrienne

The club is making money, but with success comes no rest. I had bags under my eyes from not getting any rest. On top of the bags, I know I gained a little weight also, probably from drinking and stressing out too much. I haven't had much time to work out, because every time I turn around there is an issue that needed to be resolved. Last week we had a rodent problem, this week it was the water pressure in the bathroom.

It seems like the more money that came in, the more I spent. It cost so much to keep everything running. And the credit card fees were killing me at eight percent. I wish I could put up a sign that said CASH ONLY like a corner store. But even with all the pressure and bills it was great to be my own boss.

* * *

Shelton texted asking my location. I texted him that I was at the club and he responded he was on his way to meet me. I couldn't wait to see him again. We'd been talking here and there but nothing consistent. He had been working on a big murder trial case and was always picking up new clients and I was busy with work and my daughter.

He walked into Belize looking distinguished and clean-cut as usual. He was wearing a black suit with a blue tie and navy shoes. I couldn't hold back from smiling at him. He came over to me and gave me a polite, friendly kiss. I wondered how we appeared talking and laughing to my employees, even Keldrick. But if they hadn't actually seen us do anything, they couldn't say something was going on between us. I hoped no one caught me licking the rim of my martini glass. Teasingly, I licked the rim again. Slowly. Working the tip of my tongue around the rim of the glass while watching his expression.

Shelton murmured, "I can't wait to be with you again."

I had a buzz from the martini and was feeling sexy as hell. "Maybe we can get together sooner than later."

Shelton glanced around the club. Frowning in confusion, he said, "What are you saying?"

I leaned forward. "We can find somewhere," I whispered. I told him to follow me. Feeling like a powerful seductress, I couldn't help swinging my hips as I led Shelton to the ladies' room.

"Whoa." He hesitated outside the door. "I'm not going in there."

"Why not? Scared?" I asked, challengingly.

"No, but . . ."

"Then come on. This is for my employees, no one comes back here. They are all out there making money." I pulled him in and checked all the stalls, no one was inside. Shelton relaxed when he realized we had complete privacy. I backed Shelton onto the counter and started unbuckling his belt.

"Damn, this is like the ultimate fantasy," he said, breathing heavily as I worked him out of his boxers.

"I thought having two women at the same time was every man's ultimate fantasy."

"Yeah, that, too, but this is the second ultimate fantasy." Shelton laughed nervously and kept his eyes fixed on the door. "Suppose somebody comes in—"

"Shh. You're talking too much." I hopped up on the counter and spread my legs.

It wasn't like this was the first time Shelton had given me oral sex, but for some reason tonight my pussy was super-sensitive, and I was jerking and squealing with every tongue stroke. Apparently Shelton had finally forgotten about watching the bathroom door because with his face buried between my thighs while his tongue gave me pleasure, he no longer seemed concerned about who might catch us.

He leaned me against the sink, separated my lining, and began delightfully encircling my clit and probing my inner region with his fingertips while suckling on my breasts at the same time.

"Take a look in the mirror and see who is doing this to you," he demanded, pulling my hair, yanking my body into obedience.

I looked over my shoulder. "Yes, I see who is doing this to me."

"Do you like it?"

"Yes, I do." He kept slapping my ass, sending a tantalizing sting throughout my entire body. I was totally into it—until Shanice walked in the restroom.

Once she spotted us, she said, "Oh, I'm sorry," and ran out of the bathroom. Embarrassed, I hurried and fixed my clothes and ran back out to the club floor. I was trying my best to look inconspicuous and find her. I caught her in the back talking to Darcel.

I pulled her to the side and said, "What just happened? Let's keep that between us, okay?"

"No, absolutely, Adrienne. I understand and I would never say anything. I look up to you like a big sister, and what you do is your business." I felt relieved that she wouldn't spread my business around the club.

After I talked to Shanice, I searched around for Shelton, but he had already left out and texted me that he would see me another time.

I had a crazy night last night, and I should have told my mom that she could keep Asia. I was exhausted and she wanted to play. Asia was at the foot of bed pulling clothes out of my dresser, dumping them on the ground and ignoring the Nick Jr. channel that I'd turned on for her. At this moment, I could have won the Worst Mom of the Year award. It felt like first thing in the morning, but it was already three and I had to go down to the club to do payroll and a bunch of other things. I lugged out of the bed only to almost trip over a pile of clothes.

"Asia, you made a mess, but it is okay. Mommy fell asleep. Come on, let's get up and do what we need to do."

"You not sleepy no more, Mommy?"

"No, I'm not sleepy."

I managed to get myself and Asia ready and down to Belize. Sitting in front of the club were Darcel and Shanice. They were talking and both spoke to me as Asia and I got out of the car.

"Hey, what are you doing here so early?"

"I had to meet up with Darcel. She had to look over my contracts for me. I'm about to have a manager and everything for my modeling, and then me and my daughter are going to the mall and to get some lunch," Shanice said.

"That's good. I didn't know you had a daughter." I yawned and tried to stay focused.

"You look like you need to go take a nap, Adrienne," Darcel said, noticing how tired I appeared.

"I do, but I only have my daughter for a week and I didn't want to put her in any daycare for a few days. So I'm trying to rough it."

"Well, how about this? I can help you. She can go with me and my daughter," Shanice said, pointing to her little girl sitting in the car.

"You sure you wouldn't mind?" I really needed

to get some work done and rest, and I knew Shanice was a good person. She wouldn't harm my child.

"No, not at all." Shanice was helping me for the second time in two days.

"Okay, she can go. Thanks."

With Asia gone, I completed the majority of my work. I ordered all of the alcohol, did payroll, and returned phone calls. After I was done, I put my head on the desk and took another nap. I didn't awake until Shanice was in the club dressed for work with Asia holding her hand.

"Oh my God, what time is it?" I exclaimed.

"Ten fifteen. Sorry I'm late. They had a lot of fun today. She can come with me anytime."

"Thank you, Shanice. Ask Keldrick to come here."

Keldrick came in my office. "Are you okay, Adrienne?"

"Yeah, I'm just a little tired. I'm going to go home. Can you watch the club tonight? Anybody that has tips on credit cards I'll cash them out tomorrow."

"No problem. I can drive you home. You probably shouldn't be driving. Just meet me in front of the club."

I locked up my office and accepted Keldrick's kind offer. Holding Asia's hand, I waited for Keldrick to pull up. He took us home in his silver Range

Rover. It was brand-new; the plastic was still on the seat. If I hadn't been so out of it, I would have complimented him on his nice ride. He watched and made sure me and Asia got in the house safely. I opened the door, laid Asia down, and then fell asleep on the sofa.

Chapter 34

Shanice

This woman named April Fox of Eye Candy Queen Entertainment hit my e-mail saying that she wanted to be my manager if I didn't have one already. The video, "Slide It Down", had started doing numbers. The rapper Wellzo was on a bunch of remixes and was about to sign to Rick Ross' Maybach Music Group, so any video he did everyone was searching for. She had gotten my info from the video director. I called her back and she began telling me where she wanted to see my career go and what I needed to be doing. She had so much "G" she almost sounded like a pimp.

"So, like I was saying, if you don't have any management yet, you should sign with me. I can get you some more videos. Girls get messed up when they out there without any representation."

"So, how much do I have to give you up front?" I asked.

"No, you don't give me anything. When I get you a job, I get twenty percent. Most of the jobs are going to be in New York. Do you know how to get up here?"

"Yeah, I can catch the bus up there. My friend comes up all the time."

"All right, well, I'm going to send you a contract. Print it out, fill it out, and then drop it in the mail."

Five minutes later, my phone sent me an alert that I had an e-mail. I was going to print the contract out and have Darcel read it when I got to work. I liked what April was saying and I wanted to be with her.

Darcel read the contract and said that it was fair and that April was a real agent. She herself had never signed with her because she booked herself on jobs. I sent the contract back, and April booked me work immediately.

On my first assignment I didn't want to take that ride to go back to New York City on my own and Darcel had classes so I asked Courtney to go with me.

She needed to get out of Philly. Without me she was not really making any moves meeting anyone new. Courtney really did try to start looking for a job, but she was fighting this girl a few years ago and they both were locked up and it was still on her record. She was going to need a lawyer to get her record expunged. It was a shame that Joi didn't get fired, because Courtney would be so much better to work with than that dumb chick. Courtney was so thankful I was letting her come to New York with me. I told her they might need another girl, so she should get dressed up and be prepared just in case.

"So, what if it is like for a Drake video or something? If I see Drake or Lil Wayne, yo, I'm going to pass out."

I was trying on different lipsticks and eye shadows in the mirror. I always wore pink lip gloss and I was trying to change it up some.

"Yes, I hope it is a Drake video, too. So, what do you think about this makeup?"

"I wouldn't put all that eyeliner on if I was you. Your eyes are already far apart. You don't need to bring any more attention to them."

"Right," I said, looking back in the mirror and wiping off some of my liner.

April met us at the train station. I was expecting someone big and gangster, but April was a little petite, only about four eleven. It was so funny that she was talking and negotiating real tough and big for such a small, nonviolent-looking woman.

"Is this your assistant?" she asked when I introduced her to Courtney.

"No, I'm her cousin and I model, too," Courtney answered.

Hardly turning around, April said okay. While in the car, April went over how she was in the process of getting my website done and that she wanted me to do a calendar.

"Wellzo is hot right now, and everyone is feeling him, and you are associated with him as the 'Slide It Down' girl. So, Shanice, you have to take advantage of everything while it is in front of you. There is always a prettier girl with a better shape coming out. But I know what it takes to have longevity. I just ask that my models respect themselves and not sleep with the rappers because this industry is so small. And you're not setting yourself up for the next video when you sleep with them—you are making sure you are not in the next video. You understand that?"

"I do."

"In addition to the website, we are setting you up a Twitter page and a fan page on Facebook. Make sure you interact with your fans, and let them know where you are and what you are doing. It is very important. If they feel like they know you, they will support everything that you do. Most importantly, when you start doing club appearances, be sure to take pictures when they ask."

"Okay, that's cool. I can do that."

"I have a guy coming to interview you during the photo shoot. Just be sweet and nice and shout out your site, Shani Amore dot com. We are going to take a lot of shots and I'm sending your stuff over to XXL for model of the month, King, *Black Men's Magazine*, and you will definitely be included in the ladies of *Chrome and Platinum* group pictures."

"Okay," I said as I looked over at Courtney. All I could think was that this was really happening.

* * *

We arrived at a studio with a full cast of makeup and hair people. There were huge lights with black umbrellas attached. I immediately noticed the other model who got smart at the last casting call.

"Oh, you manage her, too."

"Yeah, that's my daughter. I was watching her video and that's how I saw you." It was a real small world. I was so glad I hadn't smacked the mess out of the girl at the last shoot. April then led me to hair and makeup. Everyone was making a big deal over me. They thought I was too hairy on my arms so they waxed me all over, ripping hair off everywhere. They said that even the smallest of hair would show up on film. I trusted them because they were making me look hot. They had me looking like a prettier version of me.

Courtney sat around just watching everything. I wanted her to be a part of all of this, she was just as cute as I was. I wanted to ask April did she need anyone else, but I didn't want to ruin my opportunity.

"April, do you need any other models?"

"I guess I could use another one."

"Because my cousin does modeling, too."

"All right, tell her to get in the chair."

Excitedly I ran over to Courtney. "She is going to put you in the shoot." Courtney was speechless and happily sat down in the stylist's chair.

"Shani, so what do you think my new name should be?"

"I was thinking about Court and then N-A-Y. Like, Court-Nay."

"But it sounds the same."

"I know, but I like the different spelling."

"Maybe. We will think of something."

I left Courtney because it was time for me to get in front of the cameras and go to work.

My first shoot was in the shower with a neon-green bikini, and it was untied from the back. It didn't cover much, but I felt so beautiful and sexy every time the camera flashed. After the shower shoot, I changed into a gold swimsuit that had silver perforated cutouts on the sides. They had me modeling on and against a blue Kawasaki motorcycle. After that, I wore a fur bikini and sat in a tiny white chair next to an all-white background. I crossed my legs and was trying out different poses, but the photographer instructed me to turn around in the chair so that my rump would hang off. He told me to look over my shoulder toward him and hold my mouth open. His camera was capturing my every movement like he couldn't get enough of me. Between takes I texted and talked to Jabril. I told him I was working on a photo shoot, and he asked me when he could have another private session with me. He kept saying he needed my mouth because it was something special.

"Really, you need me, so when the next time you coming out here?"

"Not for a few weeks." *So why is he calling me now, teasing me?* I thought.

"But you can come out here. I can send you a ticket today."

"I can, when? Right now I'm in New York at my photo shoot. I have to work through the weekend, but I'm off Monday through Wednesday. Don't your chick live with you? Where am I going to stay?"

"That's why they have hotels."

"Okay, I'll come."

"I'm going to get you a ticket for Monday."

"All right then, I'm there."

I hung up the phone with the biggest smile on my face. If I wasn't all made up and done, I would have gotten up and started dancing. Courtney started asking who it was.

"Who was that?"

"Jabril, that guy we went to the game and saw."

"You for real? He keep calling?"

"He does. He wants me to come out there where he's at, in Oklahoma."

"Damn, girl, everything is happening for you. I'm jealous. So he going to buy you a plane ticket and everything."

"Everything is happening for *us*. You are a part of the everything, too, now."

April pulled me over to come do an interview with Mike, who had his own YouTube show called The Street Report. The man had on a safari hat and a towel wrapped around his neck. He was short and didn't look like an official interviewer, but I was very nice even when his camera guy almost blinded me with his light. He did his intro for his show and then he began asking me questions.

"So I saw you in the Wellzo 'Slide It Down' video. How you feeling? The streets are talking, they saying you the next, you know, the next 'it' girl."

"Really, the streets are saying that? That's nice." I giggled.

"Yeah, Shani Amore, I mean, how you feeling? You're beautiful as hell, and everyone is talking about you and you just got in the game. How can your fans see more of you?"

"I feel good. I feel honored, and my fans can check out my website for Shani Amore and be on the lookout for my calendar coming soon."

After my interview wrapped up, I watched Courtney's shoot. She was killing it, and I was so happy she came with me. I think we both are going to make the magazine, and we can party and make money together.

CHAPTER 35

Zakiya

Christie was so blessed to have me and Nichelle as friends. Well, really, she should be so happy to have me as her friend, because I paid for the majority of the baby shower. Nichelle didn't do half of the things she promised to. I had to go and buy the cake and the flowers. I was going to just hire a party planner for the coed event. However, the guy I interviewed thought it was totally preposterous that I wasn't interested in any of his traditional pink or blue themes.

He couldn't decorate the shower the way I wanted, so I found everything I needed at the party store. I felt at home planning and decorating everything. I might have finally found my calling.

I decorated the suite in the Thunder colors of navel orange and electric blue, with a splash of hot pink. On each table there were pompoms and basketballs. Christie had a long registry and I bought almost everything off of the list. I bought her every receiving blanket, sleeper, stroller, bouncy seat, bassinet, and pacifier. I had been running around everywhere, and I was exhausted and feeling a bit under the weather myself. I felt like I was about to pass out.

I couldn't believe Christie and Omar had the nerve to be late to their own baby shower. I told her to be there by two and it was now three. She knew everyone on the team was leaving for an away game tomorrow; The majority of the people who were in attendance were just people from the franchise that knew Omar and not her. His family didn't like her and wasn't coming. Her mother said she didn't fly after I offered to buy her a ticket to attend.

At three fifteen, Omar and Christie arrived. Christie was wearing a cute pink wrap maternity dress and pink and white heels. Omar looked like he was fresh off the block. He was wearing dirty-looking jeans and a gray hoodie. They came and spoke to everyone, and once everyone was seated, Nichelle took over the shower like she had planned it, starting the baby games and directing the caterers. She could take all the credit because all I wanted to do was sit down. I felt so nauseous myself. I ran to the bathroom and let everything up that I had eaten in the last two days. I kept flushing the toilet, hoping it was over and that I was finally done. I heard someone enter the bathroom. The person was checking each stall. Then I heard Christie's voice asking, "Are you okay, Zakiya?"

"Yeah, I'm fine," I said, finally feeling a little better. I came out of my stall. I rinsed my mouth and grabbed a towel to wipe my face.

"I wanted to thank you. No one has ever done anything like this for me in my life. Everything is so pretty, and this means so much," Christie said, hugging me. "I got everything off my registry."

"That's great. By the way, why were you guys late?"

"Omar was arguing with me again. He has been so moody now, like he is pregnant. Can you believe he asked me for a paternity test?"

"He did?"

"I'll give him one. I just think he is acting so weird. I don't know, after this is all over, I may just go home. I don't want to, but I can't have him keep finding reasons to be mad at me."

"You can't go home. He is probably just nervous about becoming a dad." I ran back in the stall to throw up.

"I hope so. What's wrong with you? You don't look so good."

"Yeah, I'm just not feeling that well."

"Are you pregnant?"

"Yeah. I took a test this morning." I wiped my face with water from the sink and washed my hands. "I didn't tell Jabril yet," I confessed.

"Oh my God, really? You have to tell him."

"I will. We were trying. So I knew it was going to happen—just not this soon. I'll tell him when we get home."

"Okay, well, come and have a piece of cake with me. The babies are hungry." She laughed.

"I'll be out there."

I came out and took a seat next to Jabril. I just wanted to go to sleep. I lay on his shoulder and waited for them to figure out how many pieces of toilet tissue it took to wrap around Christie's big waist. I just wanted the baby shower to be over.

Christie had opened all her gifts, and people were beginning to leave. She thanked everyone for coming and tried to get Omar to say something, but he just shook his head. He was an ass.

"Thank you all for coming out and celebrating our baby. Me and Omar appreciate it, and I'm sure if we need a babysitter we can count on all of you to come over. Right?" She looked around at a few people, laughing. "Well, I really want to thank my girls, Nichelle and Zakiya, for throwing this great shower, and I also want to make an announcement. I know you said not to say anything, Zakiya, but Omar is not the only one about to be a daddy on the team." Everyone looked at each other. "Jabril, Zakiya has something she wants to tell you."

Jabril looked over at me with a surprised look on his face. I nodded my head and he was so happy. Everyone came over and started congratulating him. It wasn't the way I had wanted to tell him, but the secret was out.

CHAPTER 36

Adrienne

An artist named Nerv Trap had reserved the entire club for his birthday party, and it was twelve thirty and he hadn't even shown up. He was a gangster rapper from Baltimore with hardcore fans. He was in Philly for a music conference and wanted to celebrate his birthday with us. Just for the night, I had to relax the dress code to accommodate him and his fans.

Ian came to town just to help out and get some footage, and we brought in some extra security for the night. Ian came gave me a peck and brought over a Red Bull. I thanked him. Although at times Ian was irritating, I appreciated that he had come up for a few days while he had a break in filming to help me. I still had mixed feelings about Ian. I wanted to make a clean break from him, but he was still trying, so I was going to hang in there a little while longer.

"So what time is this guy coming?"

I looked down at my cell phone and said, "He was supposed to be here by now."

"Adrienne, just be patient. This is a good connection to have. He's hot right now, so any footage of him is going to pop and give the club so much more exposure. Whatever I film tonight, I'm going to have it posted to your site by next week."

Everyone was still waiting for Nerv Trap to arrive. I dialed his manager so many times and he finally got on the line and said, "We're pulling up in front of the club now."

"They are out front."

Ian, Keldrick, and Mack followed me to the door to usher him into the club. People noticed, and as soon as he came into the club the atmosphere changed. He was dressed in jeans and a black T-shirt surrounded by an entourage of bodyguards. He got on the microphone immediately.

"Thanks, everyone, for coming out to my party. I want y'all to enjoy yourselves, and just for showing me love, I want to buy you the next round. Y'all heard me right—the next round is on me." My radar went up. I grabbed Nerv Trap's manager as he strolled to his seat.

"Excuse me. How is that going to work?" I asked him.

"We gave you a ten-thousand dollar deposit. That should cover it."

"That was the for the club rental fee. Not for liquor and buying the entire club a round." He huffed at me, then handed me his American Express card. I wasn't giving any free drinks out until the card had been charged. I got approval for another ten thousand. I did my math: at fifteen dollars times five hundred, that should cover his drinks and then some.

APPROVED came up on the receipt. His manager signed, and Waliq and Terrance began serving everyone. I could rest easy. My girls were taking care of Nerv Trap, and Ian was filming everything. I finally was able to take a break—until I was called to an emergency coming from the bathroom.

"Someone call an ambulance!" Darcel yelled out when I reached the doors of the restroom. A young Puerto Rican girl was lying on the bathroom floor having a frantic seizure with foam bubbling out of her mouth. Then she stopped moving altogether. I was so scared she was dead. Mack stepped near her, and I ordered him not to touch her.

"I know CPR." It was a genuine gesture, but we didn't know what was going on with her.

"Anything can be wrong with her. Just wait until the paramedics get here. They are close by. I can hear the sirens."

The paramedics and fire department rushed into the bathroom, ordered everyone out, and tried to revive her. They pressed on her chest, but she was not responding, and I wasn't sure if they could successfully bring her back. Thankfully they knew exactly what to do. They gave her a shot in the arm and she sprang up and started coughing. The paramedics then carried her away on a stretcher through the back door. I asked them what was wrong with her, and they said they weren't authorized to say, but the last guy leaving said she had overdosed.

The girl in the bathroom didn't die, but the night from hell wouldn't let go; it just kept going. There was a big uproar in the back of the club. The only thing visible was a huge free-for-all. Mack and all my security guys were trying to pull people apart, but people were fighting, running in every direction, smashing tables, and throwing chairs. It was like a war zone. Ian grabbed my arm and pulled me into the men's bathroom. He didn't let me go until we got the okay from Keldrick that everyone had evacuated the club and the police were outside.

"Is everyone okay? Where are the girls?" One by one they were accounted for. I didn't want to talk to anyone until I knew exactly what was going on. I pulled my security team together and asked Mack what exactly had happened.

"One of Nerv Trap's boys kept pushing up on this dude's wife. So the guy was like, that's my wife, don't disrespect me. So then Nerv Trap said, fuck you and her, and he grabbed his nuts and poured liquor on them. So Bull snatched a bottle from another table and cracked it upside Nerv Trap's head. Then everyone began warring after that."

"So, Nerv Trap started all of this?"

"Yeah, he started it all. You want us to start cleaning up?"

"No, just make sure no one was injured please." God, I sighed. I wasn't sure if my insurance covered rappers fighting like this.

I glanced outside the club doors and saw that the police already had a bunch of people in handcuffs and sitting on the curb. Then the news vans started pulling up. I wanted press for the club, but not this kind. I didn't want to cry, but I was on the verge of it. Then, to add insult to injury, Nerv Trap's manager started calling me, screaming, "Your club needs better security! My client is sitting in the emergency room with glass cuts and a black eye. He is supposed to leave for his European tour next week! How can he do that? You are responsible for all of this!"

"What? Your client *started* all of this."

"You will get our bill, and we are reversing the charges on the credit card. We are not paying for shit."

"Try it and see how fast I sue you."

I was done. I just walked out. I couldn't take any more. The girl almost OD'ing, the fight, and now he was trying to take his payment back. How much more could happen?

The day after, I awoke to the nightmare of Belize being associated with five arrests. We had had a drug overdose and we were on the front of the Philadelphia daily newspaper. I immediately got up and headed over to the club.

The devastation in the daylight was almost unbearable. My mirrors were broken, my white curtains were pulled down, and dirty track marks and spills were all over the white furniture.

Ian was more hype than I was. He wanted to get the club repaired quickly and he began pricing everything. I didn't know if I wanted to call the insurance adjuster. I didn't even know if it was safe to open the club back up. Hopefully we would be able to be back in business by the weekend.

CHAPTER 37

Zakiya

The phone rang in the middle of the night. Jabril and I both jumped up, but surprisingly it was my phone. Sleepily I picked it up and heard Christie tearfully say, "Zakiya, have you seen Omar?"

"No, why? Is everything okay?"

"No, it is not. He hasn't been home in two weeks. I have no idea where he is. I didn't want to say anything at first, you know, but now I'm getting concerned."

"I'll ask Jabril." I muted the call and then asked Jabril if he had heard from Omar. He turned his head in the other direction and said, "I don't know anything. I'm asleep."

"Christie is on the telephone. What should I tell her?"

"Tell her that he is fine. I talked to him earlier

today. Then you hang up." I told her what Jabril said and that I would call her in the morning.

Jabril turned over and said, "Zakiya, they are going through something, and you need to stay out of it. We have our own baby and family to worry about it."

The next morning I didn't listen to Jabril. I called Nichelle to ask her if she knew anything about the Omar/Christie drama.

"Nichelle, did you know that Omar hasn't been home in two weeks?"

"Maybe he is getting scared since her due date is any day. Reality is probably setting in. Lloyd said that Omar didn't really want the baby. He's been telling her to go home, but she won't leave. He said they had breakup sex and she became pregnant. He didn't want to be a deadbeat dad, so he has been forcing his self to stay and be with her, but he doesn't love her anymore. He was complaining that she keeps the house dirty and never cooks. We know that's true."

"Why can't he just work it out with her and hire a full-time housekeeper? He was acting like an ass at the baby shower."

"I don't know, and I can't worry about them. Christie knows how he is. This is not the first time he's been shady to her. He'll be back, but in the meantime just stay out of it."

* * *

I didn't have a cold heart, so I couldn't just mind my own business. I had to go check on Christie. I knocked on the door, and she answered, looking extremely disheveled. I entered the house and it was filthy again. Dishes were everywhere, and the dogs were barking from the garage and hitting the door like they were trying to escape. Christie looked at me and started whimpering.

"It's going to be okay. You are not alone," I consoled her.

"He didn't leave me with any money, Zakiya. There is nothing in the refrigerator, nothing in my bank account. Why would he do me like this?"

"I don't know, but I'll take you to the market and give you some money. How about your doctor appointments? Are you good? Do you need a ride?"

"No, I've been to my appointments. There is a little gas left in the car. That's the only place I've been."

"Well, if you need anything, I can help you."

"Thank you, Zakiya, you really are a friend. Nichelle didn't answer the phone for me. This is all crazy. I just never thought this would happen: me pregnant, broke, and alone. I'm the one who freaked my man out. I made sure he eats. I don't cook, but I ordered him whatever he wanted. I'm not the cleanest, but I took care of him and hired someone to clean up and I really love him."

"I know you do. Don't worry about anything. And he'll be back."

"I think he has already moved on. He has a new girlfriend already."

"Don't worry about any of that. Let's just focus on you and the baby."

I drove Christie to the market and stocked her refrigerator. We fed the dogs through the slit underneath the door, and before I left I helped her straighten up some. She asked me if she could borrow some money, and I gave her what I had on me, which was nine hundred dollars. I then promised I would be over to give her more later.

Jabril hadn't done anything to Christie but I came home mad, and I was heated with him, too. How could he be friends with someone who didn't take care of his responsibilities?

"Where have you been all day?" he asked, taking his eyes away from his PlayStation game.

"Helping Christie."

"Helping her do what?"

"Your friend left her with nothing, and she needed to get groceries and things. I mean, she didn't have *anything*. It was horrible. I couldn't imagine being pregnant and helpless like that." I started crying. I had been strong for Christie all day, and now I was in the comfort of my own house and I could let it out. Jabril jumped up and comforted me. He said that Omar had said Christie was crazy and being with her was driving him mad.

"But does that make it right for him to walk away from his responsibilities?"

"No, but I'm sure he has his reasons. And whatever they are, I don't need you stressing over them. I want you relaxing so that *our* baby can get here healthy and worry free this time. Listen, I want you to go away. You, my mom, and Nichelle should take a trip somewhere exotic and I'll pay for everything. "

"That sounds good, but can you at least talk to Omar about going home and trying to work it out with Christie?"

"I'll talk to him."

CHAPTER 38

Shanice

I was praying the entire flight to Oklahoma City, Oklahoma. I had to look on a map to even find out where it was. It was by Texas and Kansas in the middle of nowhere. I wouldn't have gotten on the plane if I didn't really like Jabril.

I told Adrienne I needed time off to take care of some modeling stuff. I was really going to see my boy. I don't think she will miss me that much. The club has got so much bad press that it hasn't been real crowded like it used to be.

I landed in Oklahoma and then took a twenty-minute cab ride downtown to a hotel called the Colcord. It was a really nice place. The gentleman at the door insisted on carrying my luggage even though I said no several times. I didn't have to sign anything at the front desk because they were expecting me. The clerk handed me the room key and told me to have a good day. The man carrying my luggage showed me to the elevator and my room. I thanked him, he slipped the key into the slot, and the key lock kept turning yellow. He knocked on the door and Jabril answered.

"Hey, you made it. I didn't think you would be here already," he said.

I walked in the room to see that Jabril had this Asian chick in short red booty shorts already lying on the bed. From her facial expression I could tell she wasn't happy to see me, either. I know I'm a freak, I always will be. I'll even fuck two dudes together, but bitches, that's just not my thing. I had flown all these miles to see Jabril, and I needed all of him to myself.

I was a little mad at him for having this other girl here. She got off the bed swishing all around the room like she owned it and wanted me to see her little perfect shape. I took a seat on the bed and sighed really loud.

"I'm hungry, Jabril. What are we going to eat?" she complained.

"All right, chill, yo. We can all go get something to eat." He finally noticed I had an attitude.

"What's up, Shanice, are you okay?" He looked over at me, trying to check my temperature.

"I'm fine," I lied. I wanted to leave, but I didn't know what time the next flight was. I really had thought Jabril was different. He just saw me as a freak, too. Did he think I was going to fuck him and her together? Why else would he bring me here when he already had a girl with him? Jabril kept looking over at me. It was obvious I wasn't with this whole situation. He came over to me and pulled me over near the bathroom.

"Are you sure you are okay, Shani? I feel like something is bothering you."

"Not really, but I'm here to see you, not her."

"So, should I make her leave?" I wanted to scream, "hell, fucking yeah," but I just remained quiet. He then answered his own question and said, "Okay, no problem. It's done. I'll make her leave." He walked back over to where she was sitting and said, "Hey, sweetheart, I'm going to call you." She looked at me, rolled her eyes, and then packed up and left.

I couldn't control my anger. I was so upset with Jabril that I blurted out, "Next time don't have anyone else here when I come to see you."

"I'm sorry. I didn't mean anything by it. That's just a chick I'm cool with that wanted to stop by and check me out. Sorry about that." He held me down on the bed and snuck a hug so I would no longer be mad.

"So, what's up? What do you want to do?"

"You brought me out here. You tell me."

"We can go get something to eat or something."

"I'm not hungry."

"What we should do is go to my house and chill. No one is there."

"I am not going to your house."

"No, my house is empty. My mom and my girl are on vacation. I sent them to the islands. My chick is pregnant, and I don't want her to do anything stressful, because our last baby died."

"That's a shame."

"It was. I was messed up about it for a long time. But we getting a second chance at it. Where is your family? What's your story? I know you are Shani Amore, but what did you do before the club and the videos?"

"I don't have a story."

"Everybody has a story, like, where is your parents and sisters and brothers?"

"I never met my dad, and my mom is in jail. I'm the only child."

"Oh."

"Yup, my aunt raised me and my cousin, and I was just figuring out life before all of this."

"So your mom is in jail. What did she do?"

"She killed her boyfriend, and she is not getting out any time soon. I haven't seen her in over ten years. She doesn't write me or allow visits. That's why I want to do better for my daughter."

"You got a kid?"

"Yeah, she is five. Her name is Raven."

The conversation was getting too personal, so I asked him about himself. "So, you are from Camden."

"Yup, and it is real rough. So, I know about hard times and people going to jail, so don't feel no type of way."

"I don't. I just don't want to talk too much."

His phone rang and he jumped up and said,

"Hold up, that's my girl." He spoke to her for a little while, then came back to the bed with me.

He took his T-shirt and hat off, and I was all over him, ready to take off my panties, but I couldn't get his full concentration because his phone kept ringing. She was getting on my nerves. He needed to relax with all the phone calls. She was annoying as fuck. He put her on the speakerphone and she would be rambling about the dumbest shit.

"So, what's up with your girl? Why does she keep calling you like that?"

"We had some issues before, and now we got back together and she feel like she got to call me all the time to make sure I'm not doing anything. Her friends are probably in her ear. She is a little insecure right now." He showed me a picture of her and I was not impressed. I guess he could tell because he said, "She's not all fancy, but she is mine and she loves me for me. But that doesn't mean we can't have fun, you know, but she is the one who has my back. I'm supposed to have a ride or die in my corner."

"So, you always cheat on her?" I questioned him.

"No, I love my girl, but honestly, she not nasty like you."

"So, I'm nasty?"

"Yes, you are very nasty and I like it. Come back over here." He playfully grabbed my waist.

We talked more about his uncle, his mom, and his family, and he asked me why I let Raven live with her grandmother.

"Because I was young and I didn't have my life

together yet. I miss my daughter sometimes. Her grandmother doesn't have full custody. I do, but she makes it hard for me. It's just a lot." I felt myself getting kind of emotional so I paused.

"We talking, Shani. Like I said, I understand. My dad died when I was young, and my uncle helped raise me."

I felt tears streaming down my face. "I don't know. I just feel like my mom not being there was so crazy. I missed her. I know if my mom was around, I wouldn't have made all the mistakes I did. Like having a baby early. My aunt let us do whatever we wanted. She should have been the one who said, no, it's too late to go out, or no, you have to go to school, but she was always like our friend. My mom would have made sure I went to college and did something with my life." I started crying. "I wish she would let me come up and see her. You probably think I'm crazy. Sorry for crying."

"It's okay, Shanice. I mean, I don't judge you for anything that you do. You kept it real with me from the beginning. So, when are you going to get your daughter and move?"

"My goal is that by the time she is in the first grade, me and her are going to get our own house."

"That's what's up, but listen to this. You seem cool. You know I have a situation, and if you play your part, then we can do us and I can make sure you and your daughter get a place now."

"You will?"

"Yeah, the season over anyway. I'm coming back home, and I'll set you up somewhere in Philly."

"Okay."

The entire weekend he showed me a great time. We went shopping, and I went with him to the car dealership and helped him pick out a new car. He wasn't just all about busting all night. He held me and we talked. We made love—we didn't fuck.

Chapter 39

Zakiya

Turks and Caicos with Nichelle was a peaceful, well-deserved trip. My first trimester was over, and I felt like I had energy and could do things again. Claudette didn't even really bother me too much. She had her own room and made friends with other singles on the island. While we were away, I talked to Jabril five times a day. He acted like he couldn't function without us being home. He was so bored without us that he even went and bought a new car—a Bentley GT. I can't hate. It is a nice car, but then he said no one could drive but him. He is having it shipped, and we were going to fly home to Philly next week.

I am so glad the season is over. I'm going to spend time with my family and Jabril. We had a lot of packing to do before we left.

While we were gone, Omar decided to go home.

He was suffering from the jitters. Christie sent me a long text thanking me for being there for her. She said Omar was acting like nothing ever happened and they were good again.

Omar went home just in time because a few days later Christie went into labor. We rushed down to the hospital to be by their side.

"Congratulations, man," Jabril said as Omar gave us both a hug. He had a cigar in his mouth and let it hang out like an old-time gangster would. Whatever jitters he had, apparently he was over them. He walked us to a small waiting room on the Labor and Delivery floor. His friends and parents were all enthusiastic and waiting for the birth of his daughter. This was how all children should come into the world.

"Omar, how did you know it was time?" I asked.

"We were sitting watching television. Then she jumped up and said she thought her water broke. I was so scared. I just grabbed her bag and we came down."

"Well, congrats. I'm happy for you."

"Thanks. Let me get back there to see what's going on. They might need me to cut the cord or something." We laughed with him and had a seat.

Ten minutes later, Omar came down the hall crying, his mother running after him. I looked at Jabril. I didn't know what to think. Jabril ran to catch up with him. My immediate thought was that something was wrong with their baby. Did her baby die like mine? Was she cheating on him and the baby was obviously not his? All these scenarios popped in my head. I just bust out crying because I knew whatever it was it couldn't be good.

"What's going on? What happened?"

Jabril came back, grabbed my arm, and said, "I told you that bitch was crazy and that we all needed to stay away from her."

"What did she do? What's wrong with the baby? I don't want to leave her like this."

Jabril yanked me down the hall toward the elevator. He pushed the DOWN button on the elevator and I think what whatever was going on affected him, too.

"Zakiya, she wasn't ever pregnant."

"What do you mean, she wasn't ever pregnant?"

"She lied. There is no baby, she made it up! That sick, psycho chick made it up."

"I don't understand. We saw her stomach and everything. She looked pregnant."

"But she wasn't. The doctors said it. There's a name for that shit."

In front of the hospital Omar was on his cell phone with tears falling from his eyes. I felt sorry for him. I couldn't believe she had gone through all of this and did not have a child. I began tearing up, seeing him so hurt and also knowing she had fooled me. Jabril approached Omar to try to talk to him, but he kept venting.

"She in the room smiling, saying she sorry. She sorry! I tried to leave that bitch. I tried! I wanted to do the right thing, but I knew I should have left her ass. I gave up everything for that crazy bitch. The doctor tried to explain the condition she had, a hysterical pregnancy some shit. But I can't listen to that mess right now. I don't want any counseling. I don't want anyone. I need to get out of here because the way I'm feeling, I might kill her. Tell my family I'm out." Omar got in his car and sped off. I stood confused.

"But I don't get it. I saw her stomach! She was huge and I felt it," I said, trying to make sense of it all.

"I told you, Zakiya. You have to stay out of other people's problems." There was nothing I could say to Jabril. He was right and I was wrong. Christie had played us all.

Chapter 40

Adrienne

Just when it seemed like all hope was lost, Ian performed his own miracle. He knew one of Nerv Trap's producers. He'd worked with them before, and they were able to talk to Nerv Trap and his manager about everything.

"Okay, they are not going to sue the club."

"How do you know that?"

"Because I called his manager, and well, we talked. I told him he didn't want the bad press from us countersuing his client. So, here." He handed me five bundles of money.

"How much is this, Ian?"

"Fifty thousand dollars. For their alcohol and some of the damages."

"Thank you. Wow. I can't believe you were able to pull this off."

"I bluffed, Adrienne. I told them, look, we know

Nerv Trap hit that guy over the head, and if you don't fix the damages in the club I will send the tape to his probation officer in Baltimore and to all of the media."

"Thank you, Ian, you don't know how worried I was about all of this." I felt a little relieved. It had just been one thing after another. First Joi quit. I should have fired her a long time ago. She didn't even call, she just stopped showing up and then Shanice quit, too! But she was modeling or something. So now all I have is a new girl I hired, Ebony, and Darcel, and it's been so slow that's all the help I really need.

"Adrienne, you are going to have to revamp the place some." Ian was addressing the obvious. I was going over my invoices and looking at my receipts, attempting to figure out why sales were down and business was dwindling. Most nightclubs eventually fall off a little after a year, but I didn't think it would happen to us just four months after opening.

"What can I do?"

"You can have after-work parties and maybe a reggae night or old school night. You can have all new clientele while you build your old ones back up."

"I don't know, Ian, that's really not what I want. That's what every club does, and I wanted Belize to be special."

I didn't want to let the after-work crowd in, but Ian was telling me that they had money and bought drinks, too, but people living from paycheck to paycheck was not exactly the crowd I was shooting for—but I had to do something.

Chapter 41

Shanice

I never thought I would be famous. I think when I was little, I dreamed of being a movie star. I'm not in any movies, but just from being in music videos, people are beginning to recognize me. I think it is because most people watch the videos they like a lot of times. Then while watching, they keep seeing your face, and then they begin to believe you are bigger than life.

April sent me on three auditions, and I booked two out of the three. The one I didn't get, they said they weren't going for my type. I didn't know exactly what that meant. One of my videos was for this female rap group, Eqaiye, and their video, "Give Me Love," has been playing on MTV and BET. For that video I did a little acting, I was acting like I was mad at my boyfriend and then meeting a new guy who I was in love with.

Then last week, this club paid for me to fly out to Houston to host a party. I made twenty-five hundred dollars in two hours. Getting paid to just show up at parties? I didn't think it could get any better than Belize, but it has. And now, instead of being one of the girls included in the ladies of *Chrome and Platinum* magazine, I'm on the cover and they are throwing me a cover party next month. Courtney made it into the magazine, too, but only in the group shots. She was happy about it, though, and thanked me and said she was going to buy a hundred copies.

I'm just thanking God daily for moving my life in another direction. I don't know what Jabril's girlfriend's life is like or how she is living, but he is making my life a dream. He started giving me money every week just because. So much so that I left Belize. It was slow there anyway. Then he also made good on his promise of getting me a place.

I met him one afternoon downtown, and he was like, go somewhere with me. So I go and then he hands me keys and tells me to open the door. I thought it was a new house for him and maybe his friends, but he said it was mine. He put it in my name, and the rent was paid up for the year. The loft was in this really nice neighborhood not far from the art museum and already furnished when I moved in. All the appliances were new, and there was a room for Raven. That made me the happiest—he didn't even know her and he was kind enough to think about her.

Jabril is the best I ever had. I knew he had a chick and she was pregnant, but he was so good to me that I really didn't care. Not in a mean way, I just could care less about her. I know my position, and I'm happy to be in it. Plus, we hang out at all the clubs together and now he is staying with me a couple nights out of the week.

I was going to get Raven today and keep her for the weekend. I wanted to buy her a dog and finally introduce her to Jabril. Valerie couldn't believe I had my own place and she asked me to bring her a copy of my lease. When I came, she really read it and looked at the signatures to make sure it was for real.

"How can you afford something so nice?"

"My modeling, Valerie."

"Back in my day, models used to have to be skinny and in shape."

"Well, nowadays it is a different type of modeling. So, I'll bring Raven back on Sunday." I was tired of her questioning me and I was ready to get out of there.

"Okay, well make sure she eats and brushes her teeth."

"I will."

Once Raven was in the car, I started telling her about what we were about to do. "Remember when Shani said she was going to buy you a dog? Well, we are going to get one today."

"We are getting the puppy! Oh yes," she chimed excitedly.

"Shani is going to let you pick out any puppy you want, okay?"

"Yay, I'm getting a puppy!" she shouted and started

going on and on about what she was going to name her dog.

In the pet store Raven ran all around so excited. It was the biggest decision of her five-year-old life—to pick which puppy she wanted. She settled on a cute little brown and black Maltese. She picked him up and wouldn't let him go.

Aunt Rhonda called me and asked me to stop by. I hadn't really seen her or Ayana since I moved. Aunt Rhonda was watching the news, and Ayana was playing with her toys.

"Hey, Aunt Rhonda, what's up?"

"Can you let Courtney come and stay with you and help her get in a video? I need her to do something like you, Shani, because right now she isn't doing anything but fighting with Antwan and his wife. They came here the other day. Both of them banging on the door. Then when she finally came to the door with a knife, they called the cops and she was about to get arrested."

"She didn't even call and tell me. All right, she can come with me for a couple of days. But she can't move in. I'll help her get herself together, though."

"I appreciate it. I know with Courtney being around you, good things will rub off on her, too. You are just like your mom, Shanice. When you were young, she kept you so cute, and she would always make sure Courtney had the same things, too. You are more like her than you realize. She just fell for the wrong man. Everything she did wasn't bad, and I know she would be proud of you."

"I know she would be. Thanks, Aunt Rhonda."

I was going to let Courtney come and visit with me, but I would let her know that when Jabril came over she had to be gone. I didn't plan to tell her about my conversation with her mother. I just came over a few days later to get her.

"Oh my God, you have another new car. What kind of car is this?"

"It is a Bentley, and no, this is his car, but wait until I show you the apartment I'm staying at, girl."

We pulled into my designated space and took the elevator up to my loft. A swarm of bees could have flown into Courtney's mouth. She couldn't believe I lived in a place like this. She ran around the apartment admiring my bedroom set, my clothes, and the kitchen. "This is banging, Shani. Jabril is nice as hell, you better be good to him."

"Yeah, he is nice, but he has it like that. Plus, he has a pregnant girlfriend. So he better have his shit straight."

"I wouldn't give two fucks. I would call that bitch up and be like, yo, we sharing your man, do you need me to help you with your baby when it's born?"

"You're crazy, Courtney. So, we are going to meet up with Jabril tonight in Atlantic City at this club, HQ Nightclub, inside Revel. Him and a bunch of his friends are going to be there."

"Wow, I didn't think we were going out so I didn't bring anything to wear."

"You can just wear something of mine. It is going to be a little looser on you, but it will still be cute and we wear the same shoe size."

I let Courtney play dress-up in my closet. She picked out my favorite black bandage dress and a pair of my Alexander McQueen sandals. I hadn't worn either yet, but it look so nice on her I let her rock it. Once we were at the party I didn't see Jabril, but Courtney had a few eyes on her, looking in her direction. I wanted her to meet someone with some real money, too.

We sat in VIP and began ordering shots and dancing with one another. The club was crowded, and I was just enjoying being out with my cousin. An hour into our partying, Jabril came over and showed us love by sending two bottles over to the table. Courtney tried to open the bottles herself, but I told her she had to wait for the bottle girl to do that and pour it for us. She did, and then we had glass after glass. We were having a good time until I spotted Jabril's boy Lloyd. Damn, I didn't know how to react. He came over to me and spoke. I said hey and then he kept trying to dance with me. He asked what was up and told me what hotel room he was staying in. I didn't know how to say I was no longer interested, but luckily, Jabril came over and rescued me. He gave Lloyd a shake and then said, "So, what you saying to my girl?"

"I asked her what was up for the night."

"She is busy tonight with me now. Only me." Lloyd looked over at me and said all right, and then he found another chick to dance on.

Everything was going right, people were taking pictures, we were laughing and having a fabulous time. Courtney was drinking a whole lot, but she was still looking cute. One of Jabril's friends introduced himself to her. He came over to her and extended his hand and said, "I'm Aleeq." Then he asked her to dance. I knew she had a winner. He played for the Sixers. Courtney got up to dance with him, almost falling, and looked him over a few times between drunk dancing. She said, "Aleeq, so who is you?"

"Excuse me," he said, trying to make sure he heard her right.

"You heard me. If you going to be hanging with me and my cousin, we need to know who is you? Like, what you do? 'Cause we only mess with them ballers." My eyes popped out of my head. I had to shut her up.

Aleeq looked over in Jabril's and my direction. He stopped dancing and said, "Damn," and started laughing as Courtney tried to continue to dance with him. I didn't want to be noticeable, but I was about to snatch her up. I could only mutter, "You're so crazy, girl." I pulled her in the bathroom. "Girl, you are making a scene. Get it together."

"What did I do wrong?" she questioned me drunkenly.

"You can't be saying that we want some ballers. You sound thirsty as fuck."

"Oh, so now you are the authority on getting

dudes with money. I'm the one who showed you the way. Get off of me." She snatched herself away from me. I yanked her back.

"Courtney, chill. You are embarrassing yourself and me."

"Whatever—embarrassing you? Please listen. Take me home. I can't even say anything without you talking. I want to go the fuck home."

"You don't have to leave, Courtney. I'm just sayin' to chill, relax, and act regular. Don't drink anything else. You've had enough."

"Whatever. I'm leaving. I'm tired of your fake ass trying to front on me." She stumbled out of the bathroom and out of the club.

I found Jabril and told him I was taking her home. I pulled up to drive her home as she stood on the corner waiting for a cab. Once in my car, she passed out for the forty-five minute drive back to Philly. Jabril said he would meet me at the apartment so I drove Courtney's ass home. I placed two hundred dollars in her pocket and left her on the doorstep. I knocked on the door hard and Aunt Rhonda came down.

The next morning I got a call from Courtney yelling at me. "Bitch, you getting brand-new. You acting like you better than me. You can keep your little money, too. Nobody don't want your money."

"I'm not acting like anything or any way."

"Yeah, whatever, all this fly girl shit. Bitch, please, you from North Philly and you a hood bitch just like me."

"Whatever, look, Courtney, you can't be ghetto and sloppy drunk all the time. It's fans around, and somebody might see you."

"Bitch, please, you ain't got no fans. You took your clothes off in a magazine; that ain't no big deal. I did that shit, too! If you was a real woman, you would have your daughter living with you and handle your business like I do every day. You fronted on me, your cousin. Bitch, I knew you your whole life. You think you on just because you fucking somebody with some paper. He ain't really feeling your smut ass. He got a girlfriend already, which mean you just his side hoe. You ain't shit, Shanice, or should I say, Shani Amore. Fronting ass bitch."

"It's not like that, bitch, are you tripping? You need to go somewhere and get some help, because the world don't revolve around you. I'm tired of your shit, Courtney. I've been trying to help you and help you, and now I am done." I disconnected the call. I was so tired of Courtney and her drama. Good-bye and good riddance.

CHAPTER 42

Zakiya

I was starting to show, and I have been doing everything precisely: taking my prenatal vitamins, not stressing out, and eating healthy. Since we've been back to Philly, I found a new doctor and learned I'm having a girl. My due date is October, right around preseason. I hope Jabril will be able to be there when I go into labor.

This pregnancy has been fine. I'm not getting sick, and I'm taking care of myself. I also have my sister and nephews to take care of me. Claudette, too, but her and Jabril leave me in the house alone all of the time. I see less of Jabril now than I did when we were in Oklahoma. He's out all the time with everyone he grew up with from his neighborhood and other players he knows in Philly. It seems like every week he is partying at a club or gambling in Atlantic City. Some nights he doesn't even come home. He told me he gets a room so he won't get a DUI. And most of the time, when he does come home, he just sleeps all day. I didn't really like his friends from Camden, they all seem like users and want to go out with Jabril just because he pays for everything. Eric and LJ had been his friends since third grade, and they were cool. He gave them money and even let them drive his cars. Everybody wanted something from him, it was all sickening. And something in my gut has been telling me that something is not right with him. I thought that if I called him and called him and always checked on him, he wouldn't have enough time to cheat. I thought that he would know that because of what we've been through and now that I was pregnant, he would be on his best behavior. I didn't want to go through his stuff, but I had to know what he was up to.

I found his phone while he was downstairs and scrolled through his text messages—and it was clean. The only text messages were from me and his mom, his uncle Wendell, Lloyd, and his friends.

I knew he had that other phone, but I didn't know where he kept it. I was so frustrated, because he would be coming back upstairs soon. My phone vibrated, and it was Christie. She had been calling and calling, and I had told her to leave me alone. She had me stick my neck out for her for nothing. Jabril was so mad at me for being in the middle of that mess. Omar isn't talking to anyone; he is really depressed. I was even depressed for a few days, because I was really getting close to her and believed in her and she'd played me. She'd played us all. How she could live with herself I don't know. I scrolled through Jabril's phone some more and was not coming up with any information. I placed the phone back in his pocket and then a blocked number appeared on my phone. I answered to hear someone say, "Hey, Zakiya." I knew who the unsteady voice belonged to. It was Christie again. Why was she still calling me?

"Christie. What you did was so awful and insane, and I never have anything to say to you again in life. Please stop calling my phone."

"Zakiya, I didn't know. Me and you were friends. You know me. I'm not crazy. It was a mistake. I didn't know I wasn't pregnant."

"Christie, I don't know you, and I'm not your friend. We are never going to be friends. I was loyal to you. Now I look crazy right with you. You had me convince Jabril to talk Omar into coming back to you, so you wouldn't have to be pregnant alone—and you weren't even pregnant. You were faking, so that makes you crazy."

"I didn't know, I swear I didn't know. My stomach was huge—you saw it."

"Women know when they are pregnant and when they are not. And you knew you weren't. I'm pregnant now and I know I am. And if you did or didn't know, you are highly delusional. You had me and Nichelle buy your baby all that stuff." I was becoming angry. She was still talking and I didn't want to hear any more.

"That's why I was calling. I wanted to send you all the baby stuff for your baby," she muttered into the phone.

"I don't want that shit. I don't want to ever see you again. Listen, Christie, this is the last time I'm going to tell you. Don't call me anymore, ever, for anything in your crazy life, bitch. Okay?" I didn't even sound like myself, but I meant it.

"You'll see one day no one is perfect. Not even your Jabril, Zakiya."

"Don't talk about Jabril, he has nothing to do with this. He had your back, too."

I was so aggravated from Christie, so imagine how upset I was when she said, "You don't know what Omar was doing to me. You don't know how he talked to me. He cheated on me all the time, and Jabril is cheating on you, too." Christie had yelled a bunch of nonsense, and most of it I didn't bother to listen to, but when she said the words *Jabril* and *cheating* it got my attention.

"What do you mean, Jabril is cheating on me?" I snapped.

"Jabril is seeing this video chick, Shani More somebody."

I didn't say any more. I just hung up and began doing my research. I knew Christie was deranged, but I also knew she might have been telling the truth. Jabril had promised me everything, that if I came back he wouldn't cheat on me. I was such a fool because I believed him and now he was dealing with this big booty video girl. I Googled her name and all this stuff came up. Now all my suspicions were true. He was parading around everywhere with her. I looked at these modeling pictures of her on my phone screen. She was okay looking, but her Nicki Minaj body, huge butt, and little waist were disgusting. I researched her some more and found a picture of her online working at Adrienne's club.

I dialed Adrienne to find out who this girl was.

"Adrienne, Jabril is cheating with a girl that was working at your club, a girl named Shani More. He has been staying out and now I know why. It is all these pictures of them together at all these clubs. Call her and tell her to leave him alone."

"Zakiya, Shanice doesn't work here anymore, but I'll have a conversation with her. She is reasonable. I told you to watch him. I'll call her and see what she says. "

"Okay, please do."

I confronted him as soon as he came up the steps. "Who is the hell is Shani More, Jabril?"

"Who? Shani More?" he asked like he had no idea what I was talking about.

"Jabril, you know her. It's all over everywhere that you are dealing with her. Come on, you promised me you wouldn't cheat on me anymore."

"I thought you were going to stay off those gossip sites. I told you before that they are filled with lies. I think I know who you are talking about, and she is just cool with me. She hosted a party with me before. I don't know her like that."

"Stop lying, Jabril. We got back together and now you are making me look like a fool again. Jabril, really? You did all of this to get me here to do wrong by me again. Huh? Why? Why would you want to play me? I love you. But you keep hurting me. I'm carrying our baby, the child you begged me to have, and you do this?"

"Kiya, listen to me, no one will ever be in your shoes, no one. I don't know what you heard or saw, but it is not true. I take care of you and buy you everything because I love you. You have to trust me I would never hurt you. So don't come to me with these rumors." He walked out of the room leaving me with my thoughts. I was so angry but I couldn't go after him. I knew he was lying, but I could not prove it. I almost went crazy last time seeing and worrying about all the rumors. But this chick wasn't a rumor. She was a real person and I was going to find out what was going on.

Chapter 43

Adrienne

I don't know what happened to my beloved Belize. One day the line was around the corner to get in and then the next day it was the club that no one wanted to come to. I've tried everything to get this club back on track. I reached out to a bunch of players and D-list reality show people and even offered them free parties and money to come and host events, and everyone has been turning me down. Nerv Trap getting into that fight was really the beginning of the end of my club.

So, I had to do what I had to do. We needed business. And I could no longer be selective with who could come in. I had to open my doors to everyone.

Belize now hosted an "International Night" on Wednesdays. Oh God, my club was like the United Nations. I didn't have anything against the badly-dressed people. I just hated the music they played.

It was a type of techno music. The beat went *boom boom boom boom* in every damn song.

And worse than the International Night were the old-school, after-work parties we hosted on Fridays. We had drink specials and contests for the grown and sexy. You no longer had to be someone or know someone to get in Belize. Anybody could just stroll on in, and I hated it. I grabbed a glass of wine and went to my back office.

The one thing that was taking my mind off the club and everything that was going on was Shelton. But even he had suddenly been missing in action too. I hoped his wife didn't find out about us. I don't know. I suppose he will call me when he gets some time.

From my office I called Shanice. I was in a very awkward position with her. I liked her. I saw her transformation, but she couldn't fuck with Zakiya's man. After a few rings she answered.

"Shanice. It's Adrienne. I need to talk to you."

"Hey, Adrienne. What's going on, girl? How's the club doing? How are you and Malaysia?"

"Well, good, the club is good, but I'm calling you about something else. Shanice, I'm calling you about Jabril Smith."

"What about Jabril?" she asked rudely.

"Listen, I'm really proud of your success with your videos and modeling. But I know you have been dealing with Jabril, and I know his girlfriend. She is a really good friend of mine, like a little sister, and whatever is going on between you two has to end. I need you to leave him alone."

"Adrienne, me and you are cool, and you did a lot for me, but you can't tell me who to date. I date whoever I want to. Remember, you're single until you are married. Well, Jabril is not married, either. And how come it is okay for you to be engaged and be sleeping with a married man and it is so wrong for me to be friends with a dude that's not?" If I was near her, I would have smacked her. She was so right, but so wrong.

"I asked you nicely, Shanice. I thought we were friends. I guess not. So consider me done with you." I disconnected the call and felt like Shanice was now my enemy.

Entering the house, I thought of ways to get back at Shanice. I didn't like how the call had ended, but I was still going to call Zakiya back and tell her I'd handled it. The last thing I wanted was fragile Zakiya worrying about someone like Shanice.

Chapter 44

Shanice

Tomorrow was my cover release party for *Chrome and Platinum* magazine. Me, Shanice Whitaker, aka Shani Amore, was on the cover of a magazine. I was so excited when April sent me the email, but then when I got the hard copy by FedEx this morning, I jumped up and down. It was my night, and a few of the other Eye Candy Queen girls were coming down from New York to support me. I really wished Courtney was here with me to help me celebrate, but she just doesn't know how to act. I missed my aunt and my cousin, but if every time Courtney does something Aunt Rhonda is just going to take up for her, then I don't have anything to say to her, either.

Life is good. I have a good guy in my corner, my career is taking off, and I'm on the cover of a magazine. It does not get any better than this. Jabril is coming to my party tomorrow night at Rapid, and he is letting me drive his car to the club.

I had a hair appointment at ten and I intended on being my stylist Daphane's first client. I thought that was the way it was going to happen, but judging by all her clients who arrived before me, that might not take place. I still needed to get to the nail salon and I wanted to go to King of Prussia Mall to make my final selection of what I'm wearing. Then after that I wanted to relax until tomorrow, when it was time for my party.

The shampoo girl finally came, washed and set my hair, and put me under the dryer. She said she was going to start braiding my hair and sewing my tracks in once she washed a few more heads. Out of boredom, I picked up a hair magazine and completed the entire issue front to back. I was waiting for my stylist to rescue me from underneath the dryer, but she was still curling the same woman's hair. I sighed and checked my cell phone screen for the time, and I saw I had nine missed calls and five text messages.

I scrolled down to see that most of them were from Darcel. I hoped she would be able to make it to the party tomorrow.

I called her phone and as it rang I checked the text messages. I couldn't believe what I was reading: YOUR COUSIN IS GIVING INTERVIEWS ABOUT YOU CALL ME ASAP.

Interviews to who and about what? I thought. I knew we weren't speaking, but I knew she would not go and tell anyone my business. I read through the texts and saw a link, and I clicked on it. It went to a gossip website called BallerAlert.com, and the headline read, "Wannabe Video Vixen Is the NBA's Jumpoff." I wanted to cry and scream. There were all these pictures of me online. I saw a picture of my old bed, all my old clothes stacked high in the closet, and a picture of me and Courtney when we worked at the strip club that she had conveniently cropped herself out of. I got up from under the dryer and ran out the door. The stylist assistant came out and asked me if I was okay and said not to go too far because I was next. I read the paragraph in horror:

Video girl groupie Shani Amore is the NBA # 1 jumpoff according to her cousin, model and actress Court-NAY. Shani Amore is a former stripper, escort, and bottle girl at Philadelphia nightclub Belize. But now she is making her money through videos and ballers. Her latest financer is Oklahoma Thunder forward Jabril Smith. We hear Shani Amore doesn't care that Smith has a girlfriend and a baby on the way. "I hate to say it, but my cousin is a whole whore that fucks for money and she even fucked teammates on the same team, now that's just trifling," says her cousin Court-NAY. Damn, when your family go in on you it must be a problem. If you don't know who Shani Amore is, check her out in the following videos below and on the cover of this month's Chrome & Platinum *magazine.*

Underneath that horrible story there were

YouTube clips of my videos, pictures of me with Jabril stolen off my Instagram and Twitter, and then next to that was a picture of Jabril and his girlfriend. This had to be the saddest day of my life. Who does their family like this? Not a regular person. Even when you mad, you don't do this. I went out of my way for my cousin and she still stabbed me. The assistant stylist came outside and said it was my turn to go in the chair. At this point I didn't even care about getting my hair done anymore. I waved that she could take the next person.

I couldn't do anything but cry. All I kept thinking about was, *Who is reading this and what are they thinking about me?* If April reads this, I know she is not going to represent me any longer, and I know Jabril and I are over. And just when I didn't think it could get any worse, there was another text with a link to a website. Courtney gave an interview with a radio show on 103.8 The Heat with a girl named Milo Gossip. I cringed as more tears poured from my eyes while I listened to the interview and heard Courtney laughing and telling the radio hosts how I didn't take care of my daughter and had given her away. I fucked old men for money and she gave me all the money that had gotten me started. She was telling every secret I ever told her in my life and even making some things up. Courtney said that I'd forgotten about my family and would do whatever for money. I couldn't listen to any more. My fucking cousin had accomplished her goal to end my career. When everyone saw and heard all of this, my name would be mud in the industry. Then my day got worse. Courtney started texting me naked pictures of myself, and under each one she texted: *If you sexy and you know it clap your hands.* She said I could pay her or she would send them everywhere. I got myself together and realized I was going to have to kill Courtney or die trying.

Chapter 45

Adrienne

I took off my shoes and was resting on my sofa when someone knocked on my door like they were the police. I opened the curtain and saw an older white guy in a suit and a young black woman. He was looking up at the second floor and she was looking directly at me. She opened her light blue jacket and revealed a gold badge. I guess that meant that she saw me and I needed to open the door. I had no idea what they wanted, but I wasn't opening the door without finding out first who they were. I looked over at the tags at a car in front of my door. They were blue and municipal. I closed the curtain and searched for my phone as the knocks grew louder. I wanted to call my mom and Ian and let someone know what was going on. I dialed Ian. I needed him to answer, but his assistant answered and said he was on set and was not available. She hung up on me before I could say it was an emergency. The knocks persisted; they knew I was in here so I had to answer. I dialed my mom.

"Mom, the cops are at the door. I don't know what they want, but I'm going to put the telephone down and you just listen, okay?"

"What do they want? What did you do?"

"I didn't do anything, but if anything happens, I have money in the bank. Write yourself a check for whatever you need and sign my name and get me out."

I set the phone down and went to answer the door. They flashed their badges again. It wasn't the cops; it was the FBI. I was having a what-the-fuck moment. My heart hit my feet.

"Yes?"

"We are looking for Ian McKinley."

"He is not here."

"Do you know where we can find him?"

"What is this in reference to?"

The woman officer looked over at the older male officer.

"Ms. Sheppard, is it possible that we can come in?" They came in and introduced themselves, the lady officer as Agent Montgomery and the male officer as Agent Lewis.

"It depends, and how do you know my name?"

"Ms. Sheppard, we need to speak with your boyfriend about an ongoing investigation into the business practices of yourself and Ian and Keldrick McKinley at the Belize nightclub."

"What type of business practices?" I was feeling uneasy, like maybe I needed to consult an attorney. Before I said anything else, I let them in my home. I knew I hadn't done anything wrong, but I still felt nervous.

"We are here because your boyfriend is being investigated for distributing drugs, extortion, and attempted murder."

"Huh? Whose boyfriend? Ian? Never."

"Do you know a Joi Anderson?"

"Yes, she used to work at the club. She quit."

"She did quit, because she got a better job running drugs from Florida to the Washington, D.C., area. Ian's associate and cousin, Keldrick, also is involved."

"Okay, you're discussing drugs, but what about this extortion thing?"

"It is our understanding that you have cameras in your nightclub."

"No, I don't have any cameras in my club," I stated confidently.

"Well, you do have cameras that you may not know anything about. Mr. McKinley has captured images of some of your clientele in compromising situations. Keldrick McKinley provides your clientele with drugs and girls. And then Ian McKinley films them with the cameras that are everywhere in your club and in hotel rooms. Once they have the victim on tape, they contact them by text messages with pictures and demand a specific amount of money," Agent Lewis said.

"I didn't know anything about this. I need to speak to an attorney, because this isn't making any sense. I need to call my friend. He is an attorney. His name is Shelton James."

Agent Lewis continued, "Ms. Sheppard, Mr. James is a part of our investigation, as well. He was recently sent pictures of you two, engaged in sexual activity, with a note attached that he needed to pay twenty-five thousand dollars or his wife and colleagues would see it. Do you know anything about that?"

"What? No." I thought I might pass out. I couldn't think. The agents began showing me pictures to back up their story. I couldn't believe what I was seeing—they showed me pictures of Ian and Keldrick picking up and meeting people, but the picture of Ian and Joi holding hands stood out the most.

"When was this picture taken?"

"This picture was taken two weekends ago. In Miami, Florida, in front of the Gladwyn Condominiums. Where Ian and Joi live."

"Hold up—they are living in my house?"

"Yes, the condo unit registered to you, number 2317, is where they have been residing."

"Yes, that's my place. You have to be kidding me. They can't be. I know Ian would never disrespect me like that." Even with the proof right in front of my face, I was having a hard time comprehending everything. "This is all so hard to believe."

"Has your club seen a steady decline in business, Ms. Sheppard?" Agent Montgomery asked.

"Yes, but all clubs go up and then go down and then they just level out."

"Yes, that probably does happen, but it happens even quicker when people are spreading the word not to go to a certain establishment because they might get set up. This same blackmail/extortion thing has happened to over a dozen of your patrons and has made somewhere in the neighborhood of six hundred thousand dollars." *Six hundred thousand,* I repeated to myself.

"So, you know who is doing it, and you know the cameras are in the club, and obviously you know I don't have anything to do with it, so why are you here?" I still couldn't believe I was just trying to keep the club doors open and Ian and Keldrick were nailing them shut. But it made sense that Ian had magically got his investors and Keldrick suddenly had a new car. And that bastard knew I was cheating on him and didn't even say anything.

"So again," I asked, "why are you here? What do you want from me?"

"We need you to get a confession out of Ian and link him and Keldrick to the cameras and cell phones that they are sending the text messages from."

"I thought you guys don't come until you have a solid case."

"Correct. We haven't arrested them yet. We need help getting the last pieces of evidence."

I had so many unanswered questions. I had given Ian everything and this was how he repaid me. He wanted to make that damn movie so bad that he was willing to risk everything I'd worked for? Now I knew why Shelton wasn't being bothered with me. He thought I had something to do with all of this. He was a distinguished attorney, and he didn't need this. And Keldrick—I knew there was something I didn't like about him. How was I going to save my club and myself?

CHAPTER 46

Zakiya

Jabril said he didn't know this girl, but I just listened to an interview with Shani whatever-her-name-is' cousin. I found so much on her once I began Googling her some more. I found interviews she did and even her Twitter and Instagram pages. She had the audacity to Tweet: DRIVIN' THIS TO THE PARTY TONIGHT. THANKS #41. YOU THE BEST. It was a picture of Jabril's car. Jabril insisted he didn't know her. Well, maybe he doesn't know her, but she knows him well enough to drive his car. She had pictures in front of the new Bentley, and she had a flyer for a party she was hosting—some magazine cover release party tonight at a club called Rapid over in Philly. He was getting the car detailed, I guess, so this girl could shine. I don't think so. I walked in on him in the garage and the guys detailing it.

"Jabril, what's going on tonight? Where are you going?" I asked as he walked back into the house. I followed behind him.

"I'm stopping in to a party right quick. LJ is going to be my chauffeur, that's why I got the car clean. You know him and Eric like to stunt. You can come, too, if you want." He was lying, and he really must have liked this chick enough to lie to me in my face.

"Why would I want to go to a party when I'm pregnant and I'm supposed to rest?"

"I'm just saying, if you wanted to come you could."

"I can't and I'm not, but you have fun."

I ran up the steps to the bedroom, locked the door, and called Nichelle all upset. I didn't know how much more I could take.

"Nichelle, I have a big problem. Jabril is cheating with this girl and letting her drive his car to a party tonight."

"Okay, so what's the problem?" she replied.

"Did you hear what I just said? Jabril is dealing with this girl. He didn't just fuck with her. He's been dealing with her and her cousin is putting on blast saying that she was fucking his teammates, too!"

"What? Did she say which one? You know what—I don't even care. Zakiya, if he is seeing her, fine, but he is living with you so she doesn't matter. Until she is trying to come for your position, you are not even supposed to worry about her. Don't stress yourself out. She is probably not the first nor is she going to be the last. Girl, go shopping and buy some stuff for your baby because that is the only person that matters." I was truly disappointed in the advice I was receiving from Nichelle. I was not going to quietly deal with Jabril's cheating and let him have a pass. I wasn't living my life like that, but I still didn't know how to handle the situation.

Jabril was done having the car detailed and he was downstairs watching a Kevin Hart comedy DVD with Claudette. They were busy laughing, and I was upset. I looked down the steps and knew I wasn't having any of this. I went into his drawer and found his extra phone hidden in between his boxers and under his bags of weed. I searched for her number, then I dialed her. Before she could say anything I was going to ask her how she knew Jabril. Then I was going to tell her she had better stay away from him. The call connected and she answered, and I said, "This is Jabril's girlfriend. What is going on between y'all?" I waited for her to pop off so I could have a reason to cuss her out.

"Uhm, me and Jabril are just cool. I see him at parties, but I don't deal with him like that." She sounded like she was lying.

"And so y'all not together? Because that's not what I'm hearing," I said.

"Nope. I know you are pregnant. He talks about the baby and you all the time. Jabril is just my homeboy. We are just cool."

I couldn't think of anything else to ask her, so I hung up on her. She must have thought I was the dumbest woman walking the earth. I knew she was fucking my man, and I still had to stop her.

So woman-to-woman talking did not work. What

Nichelle said was crazy, and I needed some real advice. I called Adrienne and told her about this girl denying that she was having a relationship with Jabril, but saying that she was driving his car to the club on Instagram. I asked her what she thought I should do. At first she gasped, then she said, "Zakiya, you're not me. I would do a lot of things."

"Like what Adrienne? I need your help. I don't know what to do. I don't want to fight her. I just want to get rid of her."

"Then handle her, Zakiya, before you and your baby will be back in Philly and she will be there living your life. I have a lot of things going on, and I can't steer your life right now, but you had better take the wheel and figure out a way to eliminate her. Do whatever you have to do. Think of something, but if she is driving his car and taking pictures with it, she feels like she can do whatever she wants and she thinks you don't even matter."

"But I do matter!" I screamed to Adrienne.

"Well, you had better make sure she knows that."

Talking to Adrienne made me furious. I had to think of something to do to this girl—and quickly. I didn't know where she lived, and if I called her back she would never tell the truth. I had to do something. I walked back past him and his mom.

"Jabril, I need to talk to you."

"Man, come on with the dumb stuff. I'm watching TV, leave me alone, Zakiya," he said, halfway ignoring me. I had to get him alone, away from Claudette. She couldn't hear me cuss her son out. That was the disadvantage of having his mother always in the same house.

"Jabril!" I screamed at the top of my voice so he could get that I was serious. I had had enough. He wasn't going out and no one was driving his car. I waited at the top of the staircase, and I heard Claudette say, "Go see what she wants. I'll pause it."

He came up the steps, and I said as calmly as I could, "Jabril, I don't want you to go out tonight."

"Huh? I already told you I was going out with LJ."

"Jabril, I know about Shani Amore, the little bitch you been talking to."

"What about her? That's my friend."

"That's not what she said."

"She didn't tell you anything, Zakiya, because there isn't anything to tell. I'm going to go out for a little while, have some fun, and come back."

I started crying. "I don't want you to go, Jabril. I want you to stay home tonight."

"You are really on some shit tonight, Zakiya."

"Jabril, why would you bring me back, get me pregnant, just to play me?"

"I'm not playing you. I love you. You are just tripping. I'm going out with my friends. I'll be back." His phone rang and then I heard him tell someone he would be ready in an hour. Jabril said he was done, and then he left me and my feelings in the hallway.

I was so angry. I felt like walking to that driveway and slashing the tires of that car and then no one would be driving anywhere, but I couldn't do that. I had to do something. Adrienne saying that Shani thought I didn't matter infuriated me. If Jabril ever left me like Omar did when he thought Christie was pregnant, I would die. Anything could happen, because these men switched on you easily, but it wasn't going to happen to me.

Ten minutes later, I sat on the bed. My mind was racing and trying to come up with a solution. I thought of a few things I could do, and then it came to me. If she wanted to drive his car, she could, but it might be the last car she would ever drive. I flicked the light on in Jabril's walk-in closet and picked up two of his extra big bags of weed that he had stashed under his socks and boxers.

I took the bags, put them in my purse, and walked to the driveway. The GT was on display. The cream paint was shining, and the gold-colored rims were sparkling. I looked around to see if anyone was watching. What I was about to do was for my unborn child; it was for Jabril's and my future. I took the bags of weed out and tucked them under the driver's seat. He was out of control, and Adrienne was right. I had to get rid of her because she was the worst kind of female—a female who would cheat with your man, lie to your face, and then help him cover his tracks.

I came back in the house a little elated. I sat on the sofa and laughed with Claudette at the last of the DVD. Tonight Shani Amore was going to have the time of her life. She really was going to wish she'd never met Jabril.

CHAPTER 47

Shanice

My phone rang all night. People I hadn't heard from were texting me and calling me asking if what Courtney was saying about me was true. I wasn't taking anyone's calls and was saying the hell with everything. Darcel called me a bunch of times and I finally had enough courage to talk to her.

"Why is she trying to ruin me, Darcel? I worked hard at all of this, and she is just coming and fucking it all up."

"Isn't this the same cousin you tried to get a job for at the club?"

"Yes, I tried to get her in at Belize. I got her in the magazine. I always was helping her. But she still wants to hurt me. I don't know what to do. I need someone to help me."

"What you need is someone to contact all those blogs and the radio station on your behalf and demand that they take those pictures and interviews down. Call Adrienne, she will know what to do."

"I don't think she will help me, Darcel. Jabril is her friend's boyfriend, and she asked me to leave him alone and I kind of told her off the other day."

"I don't think she will hold that against you. Adrienne is a good person. Just try her and call me right back."

"Okay. I'll call her and see what she thinks I should do." I inhaled deeply and tried Adrienne. She answered right on the second ring. She still must have had my number saved in her phone because she answered, "What's up, Shanice? I'm busy. What do you need?"

"Um, Adrienne, I really need your help. My cousin is on the radio and the blogs telling all my business, talking about me and Jabril and telling all these lies, and it is about to ruin my career. Should I call in to the radio station and defend myself or just let it blow over?" I sobbed.

"Sorry to hear about all of this, Shanice, but that's the consequences of living a dirty life. Things happen. When I tried to talk to you before you didn't want to hear what I had to say. So now you are on your own."

"I'm sorry. I didn't listen, but I really need your help."

"Again, maybe I could have helped you if you would have had some respect when I called you, but you didn't, so I can't. Good luck."

Adrienne was really cold and callous, and I felt all alone. I just wanted to crawl somewhere and disappear. Everything I had worked for and relationships I had built were all down the drain. Why would Courtney do this shit? The only explanation had to be because she was a fucking jealous ass hater.

Darcel called me back. We talked and she convinced me to go get my hair done and go to my party.

Out of the shop, my hair looked nice and I was ready to step to Courtney. I blocked my number and dialed her phone as soon as I got in my car. She was dumb enough to answer.

"Courtney, so it is like that, bitch?" I screamed into my phone.

"You motherfucking right it is. You thinking your ass is something that you not. And I hope that dude leave you when he find out who you really is. Bitch, you will learn never to play and change on me."

"Bitch, I ain't change on you. You are just a stupid hoe that ain't going nowhere. I hope it is worth it, because you was acting crazy, embarrassing me, and I'm supposed to keep taking up for you and let you fuck up my situation. Hell no. Whatever he do, stay or leave, I'm still good. I'm still on magazine covers, boo. I'm still in videos. What you doing with your life? Huh? What you got, broke ass? You still with your mom in that room I left you in. Is that why you mad—because I'm up and you not?"

"You not up, bitch. Go get your daughter, how about that? Go get your mom out of that jail. You ain't shit, bitch. I'm going to keep talking, bitch, and sending pictures. After I'm done, no one will ever want to talk to you." She hung on up me, and I called her back.

"Courtney, you can do whatever you want, but you are not going to win. You're broke and you're mad. I'm at the mall every day. You want to talk about me, fine. But talk about all this money I'm getting and this rich-ass nigga I fuck with." This time I hung up on her and then I called her mother. I had to let Aunt Rhonda know what her daughter was doing.

"Aunt Rhonda, Courtney calling in to radio stations giving interviews hating and spreading rumors about me everywhere. It is not right, Aunt Rhonda. Talk to her, please, and tell her to stop," I said all in one breath.

"Slow down. What are you talking about?"

"Courtney is talking about me and our family business to strangers on the radio and on the Internet."

"She did what? I don't know what all this is about, but I'll talk to her."

"Aunt Rhonda, there is no reason for her to do this. She is lying. Make her stop. You have to make her stop."

"I will. I'll call her now."

After talking to Aunt Rhonda, I calmed down some. April's number came up. I didn't want to answer, but I needed to speak with her.

"April, what's up?"

"I don't know, you tell me. Why is this chick talking reckless like this? "

"I don't know. It is my cousin. She is crazy and is mad at me because I'm coming up."

"Well, Shanice, you are calling in to that radio show this afternoon to promote your party and deny all rumors associated with your brand. I don't care what's true and what's not, but make sure you get people to like you and pick up some magazines."

"All right. Shit happens but this is not stopping anything. Just know family are usually the first people to fuck you every time."

By the time my conversation was over with April, I felt like the world was not ending after all. I was so happy that April was my manager and on my team. I was going to my party and I was going to fight all of this hatred head-on.

I called in to the radio station. I was about to go toe-to-toe with this scandal. I was waiting to speak to Milo Gossip. Her producer said she would be on the call in the next ten minutes. I was practicing what I was going to say and how I was going to combat everything Courtney had said about me. She got on the call and I heard her introduce me.

"We have the beautiful Shani Amore representing Philly in the Wellzo video and that *Chrome and Platinum* magazine cover. She is on the line and ready to let us know what's real and what's not. Tell the people what's going on, Ms. Amore. Yesterday we spoke to your cousin and she had a lot to say about you."

"Hey, Philly, hey, Milo Gossip. Everything she said was pure lies. She is a hater, and if haters can't be you they have to make up things to say about you."

"So, there is no truth to the prostitution and having sex with old men for money and stripping rumors."

"Hell, no. Well, I did strip for a week, but she was with me, and I never was a prostitute. That's just crazy."

"Now, she also said you are dating Camden's own NBA baller Jabril Smith and some of his teammates, even though his girlfriend is another Philly girl, is that true?"

"No, that is not true at all. Me and him are only cool, and I don't know any of his teammates. I don't know where she is getting this stuff. My cousin is on some ish and she crazy. She must have forgot to take her medication."

"Okay, well, glad to hear your side of the story. So, you are going to be at Rapid tonight for your cover of *Chrome and Platinum* magazine?"

"I am, and I want everyone to come out and help me celebrate."

"Well, that's what it is. Shani Amore is reppin' Philly, and might I add, doing it beautifully. Check out her videos and see her tonight at Rapid. I'll be there to support her, and all haters, shut up and let this lady do her thing."

The interview was over and I was so relieved. Now I had one last person to talk to and that was Jabril. I should have called him yesterday, before he heard it from anyone else. I called his phone, and then I drove around while waiting for him to pick up.

"Jabril, I need to talk to you."

"What's up?" He must not have heard the rumors yet. I thought about not saying anything, but I had to.

"Jabril, remember my cousin, the one that was out with us in Atlantic City?"

"Yeah. What's up with her?"

"Well, she did an interview and it has made it onto a few websites, talking about us. She sees that my modeling is taking off and she is mad. Basically, she is just making up a bunch of shit about me, you, and my past."

"Really? What radio station?"

I was surprised he hadn't heard about it yet. "Um, 103.8 with Milo Gossip. My manager had me call in to the station and tell them none of it was true. I don't want you to get in any trouble with your girlfriend."

"All right, let me call you back, Shanice. Let me see what's going on."

"Okay, and Jabril, she is lying."

"Yeah, all right," he said, and I knew that was the last time I was ever going to talk to him. At least Darcel was going with me tonight, and April said she was thinking about driving down from New York to support me. I had real friends, so fuck a fake cousin.

In my apartment I decided exactly what I was going to wear. No matter what, I had to show that bitch that she couldn't hold me down. I showered, took my time, and perfected my makeup. Then I curled my weave, making sure every curl was in place. Once my hair and makeup were done, I slipped on my black short dress that ended right at my butt cheeks. Completing the look, I wore black high tie up boots and diamond accessory bangles and earrings.

Just as I was done getting dressed, Jabril called me back and shocked the shit out of me when he said, "Shanice, whatever you did or didn't do before me, that's your business. You know what we have and how I feel about you. I'm with you no matter what."

"But, Jabril, I didn't do anything she said, and it is just fucked up." I began crying and could barely talk.

"Shanice, all right, I believe you. I'm telling you it don't matter. I'm still going to the party tonight, and you hold your head up. Nothing has changed."

Jabril dropped the car off to me and said he would see me at the club. I drove to pick up Darcel and pulled up in front of Rapid in Bril's GT on chrome. It was so crowded outside, it reminded me of working at Belize.

In the club they had my magazine cover on display all over and treated me like I was the biggest star. Darcel and I were sitting in the front of the club near the stage, and people were asking me to sign their magazine covers. I thought everyone would be against me because of the rumors. But that was not happening. So many people were coming over to me giving me support. The *Chrome and Platinum* magazine editor had even come over to me, telling me he wanted me to do some other work with him and that he would call April tomorrow. Then, in the middle of the partying, I saw

Jabril and a few of his friends come into the club. The majority of the crowd was following him all around. Right in front of everyone, he came up and showered me with love. He kissed my cheek and hugged me and then sat at the table with Darcel and me. "Thank you for coming out, Jabril. I know you didn't have to."

"I told you I had you and you didn't have to worry about anything." He kissed me again on the lips and hugged around my waist, letting everyone know I was his girl.

At the end of the night, we were going back to my place and I was feeling good. Instead of breaking me and Jabril up, Courtney had actually made us stronger. I couldn't wait to reciprocate the love he'd shown me all night. The valet brought us his car, he said good-bye to his friends, and we drove off.

A few lights away from the club down Broad Street, for no apparent reason at all, a cop just came up behind us flashing his blue and red lights.

"Are you drunk? Were you just swerving?" Jabril asked.

"No, not at all. I didn't even drink that much." Jabril looked back in the mirror and said they were drawn, but for me to just pull over to see what they wanted. I pulled over and once they reached my window, I already had my license and the paperwork in hand ready for them. "Miss, where are you coming from?" the officer asked. That was an odd question to ask, but I told him I was coming from Rapid, right down the street. He called in the license plate on the radio hanging from his blue-collared shirt and then asked me to step out of the car. I looked over at Jabril. Neither of us knew what was going on.

"Have you been drinking, miss?"

"Earlier, a little bit." I didn't have to lie because I wasn't drunk. He listened to the radio again and then said, "I'm going to ask you both to step out of the car."

"Why?" I asked, confused.

"Because I asked you to."

Jabril whispered, "He needs a warrant to search this car. And he can't just pull us over for nothing and ask us to get out of the car. Let me call my uncle." The cop saw Jabril on his phone and told him to hang up. Jabril began telling him that he knew his rights. I didn't want anything bad to happen, and so I just told Jabril to stop arguing with the cops and for us just to get out.

Once we were out of the car, the cop sat us on the curb and told us not to move. Then he took his flashlight and began poking around, checking the glove box and under the seats like he was looking for something. We sat on the curb and watched as he called another cop over to the car and they came back with a big Ziploc clear freezer bag of weed. I looked over at Jabril, and he looked at me. His eyes were as big as mine.

"Did they plant that there?" I asked him under my breath.

"No, that is mine, but I don't how that shit got in the car."

"Maybe you forgot and brought it out."

"I didn't, unless one of my boys forgot it. I'm

sure I didn't. I don't know what the hell is going on, but I can't go to jail. This will mess up my life. Shanice, it's my car, so they are going to look at me. You have to take this for me. Just say it was yours and I didn't know it was in the car. I'll call my uncle and he will bail us out."

The officer came over to us and asked Jabril to stand, then they leaned him against the car and handcuffed him. He looked over at me and said to say it was mine. I lip-synced "okay" to him. Moments later, a woman officer came and frisked me then placed me under arrest.

Without him asking, I knew I would take the case for him. I would never want him to hurt his reputation or see him in jail, but I also know he had to look out for me.

Chapter 48

Adrienne

Sometimes you have to see things with your own eyes, and I had to see if everything the agents had told me was true for myself. They needed evidence that I was not involved in any of the extortion business, and I planned to cooperate with them and give them whatever they needed. I bought a spy voice-recorder pen and I planned to get a confession out of Ian's ass.

I flew into Miami under the radar. I thought about driving down, but I knew driving would make me too tired to kick their ass. I also didn't want to tempt myself with stopping in Georgia and buying a gun. I'd heard Georgia had a really lax gun law. I don't want to lose it, but I'm not sure what my reaction is going to be when I see the two of them together. If I see that airhead-bitch-who-probably-couldn't-count-to-twelve Joi chick in my condo, using my stuff, sleeping in my bed, I might just lose it and kill him and her with my own two hands.

The entire flight I pondered why all of this was happening to me. In my past, I wasn't the best person, but I thought I'd fixed and made up for all of my bad choices. I was a business owner now, and I worked hard every day. I took care of my mother and daughter.

This all was not fair at all. Why would Ian bring drugs in my club, set up my customers, and fuck one of my employees in my damn house? If I did decide to kill them, it would be justified.

My flight landed in Miami, and I rented a car and began my drive home. Home didn't feel the same. Crossing the bridge into South Beach, which I had traveled so many times before, just didn't feel right. The blue sky and water weren't as inviting, because my mind was gray with clever thoughts and ways to surprise my houseguests. I laughed in the car by myself at the audacity and stupidity of both of them. Did they really think they were going to get over on me? They should have known better.

I parked around the corner from my condo. I said hello to the doormen and waited for the elevator to arrive. I made it to the door and tried my key. It didn't work. This motherfucker had changed my locks. He had truly lost his mind. I was really mad now. How was it possible that I couldn't gain access to my own place? I got so enraged I banged on the door and received no answer. I was tempted to kick the door in, but I didn't know what was on the other side. I gathered my luggage and went back downstairs to the building's front desk.

"Excuse me, I am locked out of number 2317." I showed them my identification. "Did my fiancé happen to leave a copy of our key down here?" He looked over at my file and said, "No, but we can call you a locksmith?" I knew a locksmith would take too long and I needed to get inside before they came home. "Never mind, I'll just call him," I said as I saw the maintenance man, Philip. I flashed a hundred-dollar bill at him and told him my dilemma. He helped me in my apartment without a fuss in minutes.

"Gracias, *señor.*" I thanked him once more, then smiled and stepped into my condo.

Two feet in, I could see they were really living in my damn house. What was going to be his excuse for all of this? This really goes to show that men aren't worth shit. Every single last one of them, even the artistic, romantic, fight-the-power, save-the-planet types. I became so angry I ran into his office and began taking his camera and computer equipment and slamming it to the floor. I then dumped water on all of it. He'll never make another movie! After I destroyed all his equipment, I found everything that belonged to her inside my daughter's room. Her clothes and shoes. I snatched it all out of my Asia's closet. Anything that touched her filthy body shouldn't be anywhere near my child's stuff. I took all her belongings and sat it at the door. I placed the pen in the living room on the table and waited for them to arrive.

* * *

I waited for less than twenty minutes before Joi and Ian came in. They walked in, giggling and happy, until they saw me. I stood up and Joi ran behind him. He put his plastic bag full of takeout from his favorite vegetarian restaurant on the counter. Ghost, aliens, a leprechaun—all of these were probably more believable than seeing me in the condo.

"Where did you get that food from, Ian? Pull out some plates, I'm hungry, too. Joi, how are you doing? Next time you quit a job, give two weeks' notice. It is called consideration." They both were in shock and still silent. My calm crazy was freaking them out, they had no idea what I was about to do.

"How did my stuff get out here?" Joi asked, suddenly realizing she was being evicted. Her stack of belongings lay haphazardly at the door.

"Bitch, because you're moving. You're very lucky I don't whoop your ass right now. Then call the cops and tell them you've been living in my apartment without my permission with my man. I'm sure they are going to tell you, you should be grateful to still have your life. Get your stuff and get the fuck out my house before I kill you." She chose to be smart and began to move her things out the door.

Ian didn't bother following her. He sat at the table and began eating his food like nothing had just happened. I stood across from him, still angry. I wanted to hurt him, but I couldn't. I needed him to talk.

"Ian, I need to know what is going on. What the hell are you doing with Joi? And tell me, why aren't my customers coming back? Why am I hearing all these rumors about you, your cousin, and my club, drugs, and cameras?"

"I don't know about anything like that," he lied.

"Ian, I know about everything. How could you do this to me?"

I stood over him. I was ready to hurt him, but instead I remembered to grab the pen and sit at the table with him.

"Are you going to tell me the truth or continue to lie to me?"

"All right. I did place cameras in the club, Adrienne. The cameras were for just in case anything happened. I did it to help you out. That's why I was able to know that Nerv Trap started the fight. I did it for you."

"You did it for you, not me. If you did it for me, why not just tell me. Huh? You didn't do shit for me, you fucking liar." I couldn't control my rage anymore, so I took my hand and slapped the food from in front of him. I missed and he didn't budge. He sighed and just started talking.

"Adrienne, you know I'm an artist. I'm the guy that makes films and movies. I never was your type. I always knew in the back of my mind that maybe I wasn't good enough. That I would never make enough money for you. That was my fear—what if I never become a successful filmmaker? How would I be able to provide a good life for you? I didn't deal with Asia, not because I didn't want to, but because I was scared of getting my heart broken twice. I didn't want to come into the stepfather role until I could take care of her and her mother. Adrienne, I didn't want to be just that guy with a dream. I was so proud of you when we opened the club. One day you were saying that's a good idea, and then the next thing I knew, we were at the grand opening in another city. But the hotter the club was becoming, the more we grew apart. I asked you to come to see me. I asked you to help me with the movie, and you refused. I had this same dream of making a movie for years and years, and it never came true. I wanted it to work. I wanted to be on so bad. Remember what you said when we were in L.A.? You said, let's open the club, then film the movie. But when the club started being successful, you forgot about me. Then that same night you said, what if my movie doesn't sell? At that moment, I knew you didn't have any confidence in me and that you didn't believe in me and we wouldn't work."

"I wasn't saying it like that." I rubbed my temple. He was telling me so much. I just couldn't bear hearing it all.

"Then I gave you that ring because I knew I could lose you at any moment, and I said let me hold on to her. Let me show her I'm real, but it was too small for you. How do you think that made me feel? I knew you was dealing with that attorney guy, and I couldn't get mad because Joi had already come on to me and told me everything you were doing from the beginning. And I had the proof right in front of me. But I still loved you and somehow I wanted us to still work."

"So, that made you set everyone up and extort my clients."

"No, I didn't extort anyone. Keldrick did everything. Initially, Keldrick asked me could him and his friends hustle a little coke out the club, I said no. I knew you wouldn't want that in Belize, but he didn't listen and he did it anyway and gave me a cut, and one thing led to another. I installed the cameras, and we set the first person up, and then the second person, and it was so easy. We made one phone call or sent one text with a picture of them snorting or with a girl at the hotel and they gave us money for it all to go away."

Tears were coming down, and I wanted to turn off the tape recorder. I hated looking at him. He'd hurt me. I wanted to forgive him, and I wanted to help him. I think in my entire life he was the only man I'd really loved and I knew without any doubt that he loved me. And the sad thing is, I was just realizing it right now. He didn't deserve to go to jail, he was a good guy. I wanted to give him a heads-up and maybe we could both blame everything on Keldrick.

Chapter 49

Zakiya

When I put the weed bag underneath the driver's seat, I wasn't thinking that Jabril could possibly get in trouble. Yes. I knew it was his car, but I didn't think he would be in the car with her. I thought she would be alone. I called the police around 2 A.M. and told them I wanted to make an anonymous tip about a drug deal about to go down. I gave them the car's license plate number and a description of the seller, and I told them exactly what that whore looked like.

Adrienne had told me to get rid of her, and I knew that was a surefire way to do that, but now I might have just ruined Jabril's NBA career in the process.

I feel so sick, like this baby is going to come up through my throat. I know for sure that Jabril is going to test positive for marijuana. He smoked right before he left, and he was probably still high now. Oh God, I wish I could talk to someone, but I couldn't admit any of this to anyone. I didn't know what to do.

Oh God, what if they fingerprint the bag of weed? I thought. *Then my fingerprints will be all over the bag.* I was so terrible at being bad. I paced back and forth and tried Wendell's phone again, no answer, then Claudette. Neither one of them answered. I felt trapped and sick. I had fucked up really bad. I just wanted to get her away from my man. I didn't want my man to go to jail.

By 5 A.M., the morning news was on, and they kept repeating the same four stories every twenty minutes. The news anchor's voice was irritating. The way he said, "Camden, New Jersey, native Jabril Smith, who plays for the NBA's Oklahoma Thunder, was arrested overnight by the Philadelphia police for marijuana possession. He was pulled over in a vehicle driven by an unknown female."

I turned the television off. I couldn't take hearing any more. *Didn't anyone else do anything this morning? I'm sure someone was robbed. Please stop saying his name, and God, please help Jabril. Please forgive me.*

I called Wendell again. He answered, but rushed off the phone. He said he was down at the police station trying to get Jabril out of there. I started crying hysterically, and he passed the phone to Claudette.

"Zakiya, don't worry about Jabril. He is going to be okay. I don't know who the little hoe was in the car with him, but she should not have been smoking weed around my baby."

"Claudette, I don't want him to go to jail," I cried.

"He is not going to. The attorneys are here, and they are advising us of the next move."

"I really messed up," I said aloud.

"You didn't mess up, Zakiya. This is not your fault. This is my dumb-ass son's fault, don't you dare blame yourself." I couldn't believe I'd slipped up and said that. If Claudette had known it was me who set up her precious baby, she would have strangled me.

I paced and prayed that my baby was balling up, too. She knew what her dumb mommy had done. I fell asleep on the sofa when Claudette ran into the living room shouting, "Jabril is getting out." We drove over to Philly to meet him and Wendell at the police station.

We arrived to see news crews positioned in the front and the back of the building. The police showed Bril kindness and let us leave through a side entrance. Jabril leaped in the waiting SUV led by Wendell and his attorney. He was released because the girl he was with had confessed to the drugs, and I sighed in relief because he was out and safe and no charges were being brought against him.

CHAPTER 50

Shanice

Who knew I would get locked up after my own party? Jabril's friends had to have forgotten that weed was in his car. Why else would he be riding around dirty? I automatically knew I would take the case for him. He didn't even have to ask. I was down for him and wouldn't let him give up his career or get caught on any petty drug charges. But for my loyalty, he better hurry up and get a lawyer here ASAP. I'm not facing anything without any representation. Especially when these cops kept badgering me every few hours. They wanted to know everything about me and Jabril. They wanted to know where we were coming from, what I did, why I had all that weed, where I got it from. They even asked me did I know Jabril had a girlfriend. I guess that was supposed to make me mad, so that I would start snitching, but I kept my mouth closed.

I was waiting to be seen by the judge and spent my first seventy-two hours in a tiny cell in the Eighth Police District. I was told the process was that I would get arraigned and then go before a judge and my bail would be set. But that never happened.

The cops who arrested me came and took me out of my cell in the middle of the night and questioned me more about the drugs. I think they believed that after a few days I would be too tired to lie and change my story. It seemed like they wanted the big case of their careers—to bust an NBA basketball player. Instead I kept confessing and claiming the drugs as my own. My lack of cooperation must have angered them, because the next thing I knew, they handcuffed me, put me in a wagon, and took me to another jail. They said I would be arraigned over closed-circuit television and that they were moving me to the county for a little while. I walked into the county jail, and I knew I had arrived with the big girls. I felt like I had to watch my back and that I was naked. They made me take my weave out and all my eyelashes and nails off.

I wasn't there half the day before the women began testing me. They kept saying I looked like a stripper bitch and I probably was a dirty prostitute. I ignored their comments because I couldn't beat the entire jail.

I was a loner until I ran into a few girls from my neighborhood. I talked to them about my case, and they said the cops were definitely trying to play me and for me to just wait it out until I was arraigned. They also made sure no one else said anything to me.

After almost two weeks of sitting with no charges or information on my case, I was told I had a visitor. The guard walked me into the meeting room where a black older woman wearing glasses was waiting for me. The woman introduced herself as Elizabeth Riley and my attorney. She was definitely not a public defender. I knew she had been hired by Jabril. She didn't even look at me. She just started speaking about my case without waiting for my response.

"You have a hearing on the ninth, and I will be representing you. If they take the case, this trial, I will be requesting information on how things were handled from the onset. But I don't believe that will be necessary. I'm going to be talking to the district attorney and see if we can get this case thrown out altogether. Do you have any questions?"

"Yes, can you tell Jabril to get in touch with me?"

She turned and looked at me like I wasn't making any sense and said, "I don't know a Jabril."

"I know Jabril Smith is paying you, and I need to talk to him."

Ms. Riley lowered her glasses, stared down at me, and said, "Young lady, I was hired by a private company. Let's just say they are doing you a favor by handling your legal expenses. If I were you, I wouldn't be concerned with anything but getting out of here."

She spent the next half hour going over my case and telling me the worst-case scenario: I was facing six months to a year in jail. I didn't want to do any time. She said that it was good that I didn't have a record and she might be able to get me house arrest or probation.

When she left, I felt alone. I was in jail by myself. I wasn't on good terms with my aunt or my cousin. I couldn't let Ms. Valerie know I was in jail. She would never let me see my daughter again.

I had a lot of time to think, and I realized that all I wanted to do was become something more than what I was. There was nothing wrong with that, but my only mistake was in thinking that I could. Who was I kidding?

CHAPTER 51

Zakiya

Six Months Later

In the Bible Gabriel was an angel, and "Jabril" is Arabic for Gabriel. My Jabril has become a changed man; almost angelic. When Jabrilah Zaki Smith was born, healthy and blessed, Jabril held her and cried. He was relieved, like I was this time, that our baby had made it.

I had such an easy delivery. I pushed a few times and she popped her little body right out and into this world. I wasn't in any pain afterward. I was able to get right up and walk around. I could not ask for a better fiancé or father for our daughter.

Yes, we are engaged now. He proposed to me right after I gave birth to her in the delivery room. He just blurted it out: "Will you marry me?" in the middle of the cleanup and while holding Jabrilah.

Of course I said yes. The nurse and doctors were happy for us, but also confused because we had just had a baby. Everything has been out of order with us, but I don't care. I'm just happy he wants to spend the rest of his life with me and our child.

Jabril has been cleaning up his act on and off the court, too. He said he asked God the night he got locked up for one more chance when he was arrested. He promised himself if he was given another chance, he would not waste it. And so far he hasn't. Jabril apologized to me, and to his family, for not making the best decisions.

I don't know how he convinced that Shani girl to take the case, but she did and she is gone. I don't regret planting the drugs in the car, because everything turned out all right and I got her out of our lives for good.

I haven't heard her name mentioned anywhere. I checked her Twitter and Instagram pages and she's been quiet, like she fell off the earth. And as far as the other groupies of the world, I now realize they are everywhere and I will not go crazy trying to keep every single one away from Jabril. What I know now is that he loves me and that I am his everything. But if that ever changes, I will leave him and this life. I'm always prepared now for anything.

There are some things you have to take to your grave, and what I did is one of them. I don't regret my actions because they worked. I'm never going to be a little woman who lets her man do anything he wants. That's why I'm enrolled in school and I'm taking classes online. I changed my major from nursing to business and I am going to get my degree. And though I want a life with Jabril, if we ever part I'll still have my own.

Chapter 52

Shanice

"Shani, you up?" April's voice was muffled. I wasn't fully awake yet when I answered my cell.

"Yeah, I'm up. What time is it?"

"Ten. I hope you are ready to finally get back to business like you said you were, because I'm about to book you on a flight to North Carolina."

"What the hell is there?" I asked.

"I just got off the phone with Avion Massey's people. He is a new R&B singer, and he is turning twenty-five. They're having a huge birthday party for him, and they want some Eye Candy Queen girls to host. Catch a cab to the airport, and your ticket will be waiting for you at Delta."

"All right, I'll go. How much am I getting?"

"Fifteen hundred, and I'll have someone meet you at your hotel to do your hair and makeup."

"Okay, I'm getting up and ready now."

"Shani, you have less than two hours to get to the airport and you can't be late. They already sent the payment. I'm wiring it into your account and sending your full itinerary."

I jumped up and began to get pretty. I was glad I had some work coming in so I could afford to live. I'd kept my place even though I no longer had Jabril to pay my bills for me. I still had months of rent already paid for, and I didn't care what I had to do keep my place.

As far as my court case was concerned, Jabril's attorney got me off. I'm not on probation or anything—all the evidence just disappeared. I showed up at court expecting the worst and ten minutes later all my charges were dropped.

Then, a few days later, I mysteriously received an envelope with twenty thousand dollars in it. I knew where it was from.

I wasn't saying anything to anyone. I knew how to keep my mouth shut. That's why I'm a little hurt that Jabril couldn't contact me at least one time himself. I reached out to him a couple of times just to say what's up, but the last time I called, he had changed his number. It's cool. I mean, it was what it was. We had fun together. He showed me a new life and hopefully he'll be a good man to his girlfriend. I just say, people should be who they really are, and I don't see him as a family man with one chick because he likes too much freaky shit, but if that's what works for him, who am I to say anything?

For right now I'm going to let Raven stay with Ms. Valerie. I wanted to get her full time, but that's just not going to work out right now. I have to make money. When I settle down and get stable, I'm going to go get her. I have to do this modeling thing while I can. I may even try some acting or something, maybe even Hollywood. Who knows?

CHAPTER 53

Adrienne

Belize was closed, and I didn't have anything, all in the name of love. I trusted Ian, and he had me back to square one with nothing. At first I couldn't decide if I was going to give his recorded confessions to the agents. If I didn't cooperate, I might go down with Ian and Keldrick. And that wasn't going to happen. I wasn't sure if it was the best decision, but my back was against a hard, cold, steel wall and I couldn't sacrifice my life or be taken any further down.

I washed my hands, grabbed a towel, and walked out of the bathroom and down the hall to Courtroom 426, where Ian and Keldrick McKinley were on trial for extortion, distribution, and intent to sell narcotics, and a whole list of other charges.

I entered the noisy courtroom through the side door. I couldn't look into Ian's troubled eyes. Even though I know he did me wrong, I felt a little guilty. My guilt was only temporary, though, because I thought about him and Joi fucking behind my back. Then I thought about them taping and setting up my customers and keeping all the money. Maybe if he was who I thought he was, the good man who only wanted to be a filmmaker, I wouldn't testify against him. But he wasn't, and I'm not doing any time for him. We are not a team, and I'm not a ride-or-die chick. On that note, I stood up and raised my right hand. When the bailiff said, "Do you, Adrienne Sheppard, swear to tell the whole truth, nothing but the truth, so help you God?" I looked over at Keldrick and then over to Ian, who was slouched in his chair. I couldn't turn back now and so I said, "I do." And with those two words, their fate was sealed. They were going to jail and I had to start my life all over again.

CHAPTER 1

Tiffany Holcomb

"Don't answer the door," my husband Damien shouted. He ran into the living room as a loud, continuous knock became even louder.

"Why, what's wrong? What's going on? Who is it, Damien?" He snatched my arm and pulled me to the floor. I had no choice but to follow his lead and kneel next to him on our marble floor.

Moments passed, but the relentless pounding did not stop. Damien hadn't answered my question, so I asked him again, "Who is at the door? Who would have the audacity to drive onto our property and up our driveway?"

"It's the people from the bank. They're trying to serve me more court papers. "

"Why are they coming here, banging on our door? I thought you said your attorneys were handling everything."

"They are. He is. He said they may start coming around, but not to sign or accept anything. As long as they aren't able to personally serve me, it gives me more time."

"Okay." I took in a deep breath and tried to make sense of what was going on. Damien saw the defeated look in my eyes and comforted me with a kiss on the cheek. His kiss only made me sadder. I tried to hold the fear in, but a stream of tears flowed down my face.

He wiped my face with his thumb. "Babe, don't do this. Don't make me feel any worse than I already do. It will be okay. I'm in the process of getting this all under control. My lawyer put in all the paperwork. It's all going to work out. Trust me."

"I don't understand, Damien. One day you say we're okay, and the next day someone is at the door trying to serve us papers. What's going on? Tell me the truth. Can we afford to stay here, or do we have to move?"

"I told you already. We don't have to move. Once the bankruptcy filing goes through, everything will be back to normal. I'll get one payment to pay all the creditors, and they will leave us alone. I promise you. I told you I will take care of you, and I will. Do you believe in me?"

"Yes, I do."

He turned to face me. "Then know that I won't let anything happen to you."

"I understand, but my mom saw something on the news and people are sending my sister stories they've found on the Internet."

"I don't want to talk about this anymore. People owe me money and hopefully I will get a job covering sports somewhere. I don't know—maybe I'll get a scouting position. And in the meantime, I will be in the gym. I can have a comeback. Teams are still interested in me. I have a plan, Tiffany. Believe in me—I got us," he rambled on. "Believe. All right?"

I shook my head and told Damien that I believed in him, but I was lying. I didn't even like him at that moment.

After five long minutes, the knocking finally stopped. I got off the floor, walked to the window, and watched the man who'd been knocking as he got into a navy blue SUV. *How did we get here? What happened in our lives that led us to this awful place?* I thought to myself as the SUV pulled out of our looped driveway.

Since I was a teenager, my mother, Felicia, told me that I was never to be with a man who could not take care of me. She gave me detailed instructions on how to have a man provide for you. I followed them step-by-step, but now I needed a new set of plans.

The first half of my life, my mother was a hardworking single mom. She worked as a secretary and was struggling. Then, she met high-powered attorney Wilson Miller Jr. at a convention and everything changed.

My brother, Charles, and I knew our mother quit her job, but instead of having less money, she had more. She went on long trips for weeks at a time, and we moved in with our Nana. That lasted for about two years, from the time I was in fifth grade until the end of seventh grade.

Then out of nowhere, my mother came home

and said she was married and we would be moving to North Carolina. My brother and I were happy for our mom, but totally shocked when a tall, white man walked through our grandmother's door.

"*That's* Mr. Wilson?" I asked my Nana. She shook her head and instructed me not to say anything about him being white.

We moved into a house right outside of Charlotte, North Carolina, in a suburb called Huntersville. Our new home was four times the size of Nana's row house back in Baltimore—and that didn't even include the trees and grass that circled the gigantic house.

I remember how I walked into the house in amazement with my mouth wide open. All of the furniture was new, bright, and beautiful. I couldn't believe we were actually moving in to a house that nice. Then, my mother walked us into our rooms. I had a white canopy bed with pink sheets.

The next day, we went shopping for school clothes. Unlike other school years, there wasn't a limit to what we could get. If we liked a pair of jeans, my mom allowed us to buy them in every color, along with matching shirts and sweaters.

That night, as we unpacked all of our new clothes, my mom sat me down and said, "Look around Tiffany. This is how you live. A man is supposed to treat you like a queen. Like royalty. And if he can't, then he doesn't deserve you." That conversation stayed with me the rest of my life.

Life was great in North Carolina. However, Charles and I learned to stay out of Wilson's way. He was our stepfather, but not our dad. Our dad was the lazy black motherfucker that left us in

Maryland. Our mother reminded us of this all the time. Wilson didn't speak to us a whole lot, but he kept our bills paid. I always got the impression that he loved my mother, but tolerated us. He set up a small trust fund for my brother and me. He even made sure my tuition was paid in full and I didn't need any loans for school. My teenage years were great, but I was happy to go back up north for college.

My mother drove me up to Syracuse University. It was a long twelve hour drive up the east coast. The entire ride, she talked to me about planning and taking advantage of the opportunities that were being presented to me. She said that I only had four years to succeed. Initially, I thought she meant to complete college, but my mom was already thinking beyond college. She told me not to eat too much, to study hard to earn my degree, but, most importantly, to find a wealthy husband: a life partner that had the potential of making a six-figure income and also came from a good family. She warned me to stay away from future teachers and all art majors. My mother thought I should also date outside of my race because black men weren't any good. It was a lot to take in, but I took notes.

During my third week of school, I met Warren one day as I left the library. He was double majoring in both Political Science and Finance. Check. He was from a good family. Check. His father was a pastor at a mega church and his mother a city councilperson in Memphis, Tennessee. He was black, but I had checked off three out of four of my mother's requirements. The bonus was that he was also a football player. We dated freshman through junior year. He interned at Wilson's law firm in the summer. We planned to get engaged and married after we graduated, but then something changed during homecoming weekend of our junior year.

That something was his teammate Damien Holcomb. We met and connected instantly at a party one night. I remember it vividly. I arrived at the party early and Warren wasn't there yet. He didn't answer his phone, but Damien was there and wouldn't take no for an answer when he asked me to dance. Something was so ruggedly handsome about him. He had deep, fudge-colored skin, a chiseled athletic frame with a sexy, aggressive New York swagger and the talk to match. He was so confident. He didn't just simply ask me to dance, he took my hand and pulled me towards the dance floor. We danced and he held me for six songs straight. I left the party with Damien. A few days later, I broke up with Warren.

Warren didn't handle it well. He tried to win me back by sending flowers, crying, and begging me to come back to him. Everyone on campus knew that Damien stole his girlfriend, and he couldn't handle the embarrassment. I didn't know if he wanted to get back together because of his male ego or because he actually wanted me. When his pleading didn't work, he became depressed and transferred schools.

I felt bad, but Damien was everything that Warren wasn't. He was also everything I was supposed to stay away from. He was on scholarship, and his major was Physical Science. He was a football player who didn't come from a good family with money. Actually, he didn't have any family. He was brought up in the foster care system and only had cousins and an aunt and uncle in Brooklyn, all of whom he rarely spoke to. He said the only person that was there for him was his social worker. She was the one who told him he had a good head on his shoulders and should be in college.

She was right. He did well in college and excellent on the field. Everyone wanted a piece of Damien and they were all trying to put their bids in advance. He wasn't supposed to take any gifts from agents or teams according to NCAA rules, but they didn't know that his girlfriend was accepting things on his behalf.

Soon after we became an official couple, untraceable gifts would arrive at my parents' home from sport agencies and future sponsors. To my surprise, my mother was very accepting of Damien because even she knew he was destined for the NFL. And she was right. That next spring, Damien and I were married and he signed a contract with the Denver Broncos for thirty million dollars over five years and a five million dollar signing bonus.

Immediately, we were thrust into an entirely new world of privilege. The other side of a million dollars was something new for the both of us. While he was out on the field making the money, it was my responsibility to furnish the house and plan the vacations. We traveled to every continent in the world during the off season. We owned three homes. Our main house was in Alpine, New Jersey, but we also had a home in Denver, Colorado and a condo in Orlando, Florida.

We owned five cars: a Bentley, a Mercedes Benz AMG convertible, a BMW, a classic 1967 Chevy Camaro, and a custom Tahoe. Our life was great and money wasn't an issue. When I shopped, I didn't check tags or turn over a pair of shoes to check the price sticker before I charged them. We always picked up the tab at a restaurant when we went to dinner with our friends and we never had any financial worries.

Things changed when Damien had a career-ending injury. It happened right before his new contract was finalized. He was on the twelve about to go into the end zone, and the Saints linebacker charged him. His body fell backwards, but his leg went forward. From the stands, I could almost feel his leg as it cracked in half. I screamed as they led him off of the field. Damien went straight to the hospital and into surgery. I prayed and prayed, but I already knew he would never play again.

That was two years ago, and that's how our lives went from boarding private planes to creditors trying to knock down our front door. Our accountant wasn't paying the IRS or filing state or local taxes—he was too busy investing our money in various businesses that never turned a profit. He thought he was going to be able to put the money back before we noticed, but Damien's injury prevented that. Damien also liked to gamble, lend money out, and made horrible business decisions. Then Damien decided to get drunk and drive home. When a police officer tried to arrest him, he gave him a hard time. Not only did he get a DUI, but he also got a court date for resisting arrest.

All we had left was a measly eight thousand dollars in the safe in our guest room that I put to the side. I wasn't even sure if our car notes were even paid that month. He would tell me to keep the cars in the garage, so I had to assume they weren't. We voluntarily turned in the Bentley and the Mercedes, which only left us with my BMW, his truck, and the classic Chevy.

Things were rough right now, but Damien was a hustler. I knew that I could find a job if I had to.

On our wedding day, I vowed to love him in sickness and in health, for richer and for poorer . . . but what did they say about repossessions and foreclosures?